VAGUE IMAGES

Elaine Orr

ISBN-13: 978-1500193539
ISBN-10: 1500193534

VAGUE IMAGES

By Elaine Orr

Discover other books in the Jolie Gentil Series

Appraisal for Murder
Rekindling Motives
When the Carny Comes to Town
Any Port in a Storm
Trouble on the Doorstep
Behind the Walls

www.elaineorr.com
www.elainenorr.blogspot.com
@elaineorr55

ISBN-13: 978-1500193539
ISBN-10: 1500193534

DEDICATION

To my brother Dan, who always does the hard things well. And to Jim, Susan, and Michelle.

ACKNOWLEDGMENTS

Thanks to my good friend D. Lynn Gordon, who always offers astute critiques. Lorena Shute is a dedicated copy editor, always a reminder that words may be more (or less) than they seem. As always, thanks to my husband, Jim, for understanding the schedule I keep when I write.

CHAPTER ONE

If it hadn't been for the deer that ran in front of my car I wouldn't have hurt my foot jamming on the brakes. If I hadn't hurt my foot I wouldn't have gone to Ocean Alley's hospital. If I hadn't been in the hospital I wouldn't have seen him. Not that I could follow him. I was on my butt in the emergency room.

Doctor Birdbaum raised his voice. "Jolie, you need to lie still while I wrap your ankle."

"I need to…"

"You need to be still." His voice was firm.

I stared at the fluorescent light above me and winced. "Ow. Does it have to be that tight?"

"Only if you want it to do any good." Dr. Birdbaum is a short, round man who rarely exhibits any sense of humor. I didn't think he was kidding now.

I craned my head toward the door of my cubicle in the ER. I was certain that the face that peered in briefly had been Thomas Edward Finch. He had been ten when I last saw him twelve years ago, and it would be dangerous for him to be in Ocean Alley.

When I first babysat for him and his sister, Hannah, they were both a couple of real pills. By the end of my junior year, my only high school year living with Aunt Madge in Ocean Alley, the two kids and I had really liked each other.

And then they were gone. Aunt Madge, Scoobie, and I were warned never to speak of them again.

I stared at the ceiling more while Dr. Birdbaum finished wrapping my ankle. *Who knew you could do ligament or tendon damage by slamming your foot on the brake?* Apparently you can when you stomp on it so hard that you are almost standing up in the car. It hurt so much that I couldn't even get out of the car by myself. Oh well, I didn't hit the deer.

"How come there are more deer running around now than usual?"

"You think I'm a vet?" His tone was testy and I lifted my head a bit and he looked at me directly for a second. "It's fall. Mating season. Bucks are pretty stupid then."

I was tempted to make a comment about the aptitude of horny males, in general, but did not.

A familiar voice spoke from the doorway. "You left the best skid mark I've seen all year."

I looked at local reporter George Winters. "No doubt you took a picture."

"Of course. She okay, doc?"

Dr. Birdbaum looked at George. "You know those privacy forms? I only give information if the patient okays it." The doctor stood and winked at me as he walked into the hall. "You can tell him yourself."

Maybe he does have a sense of humor.

"So..." George asked.

"Nothing broken. They called it soft tissue damage, but it's a lump about half the size of a golf ball on the front of my foot, kind of between the two ankle bones."

"Scuttlebutt is you were trying to hit a deer?"

I didn't bother to ask why he thought this. George has spies all over town. *So much for privacy.* "Not hit, miss," I said, in a tone he likely recognized as barbed.

George sat and pulled a plastic chair closer to me. "Scoobie been in?"

My best bud Scoobie had not been to the ER, but he was in the hospital doing a practicum for his radiology technologist degree. "He was in the x-ray room."

"Ha! I bet he had something to say."

"Not so much. He was supposed to observe the woman operating the machine."

"I've heard of people trying to be transparent, but you didn't have to come to radiology to make the point." Scoobie grinned from the doorway. In his scrubs and hospital name badge and with more neatly trimmed dark blonde hair and beard than in the past, he could have been mistaken for a young physician doing his residency.

George stayed seated, but they gave each other a high five. Scoobie and George have been friends for years, and they sometimes outdo each other trying to rile me. Today I didn't care about any of that. I needed to talk to Scoobie. Alone.

"You want a ride home?" George asked. "You can't drive, can you?"

"It's my left foot, but they gave me some pain meds, plus it's swollen, so I need to get home and levitate it."

"Elevate," Scoobie laughed. "Have some more pain meds."

I had an idea. "Hey, George, I'd like a ride home, but I need crutches. Would you mind asking if they're giving me some soon?"

"Sure." He loped out. He was in his usual Hawaiian-style collared shirt and Khakis, both of which were rumpled, and the auburn in the shirt kind of matched his hair. There isn't exactly a dress code for reporters at a paper as small as the *Ocean Alley Press*.

Scoobie came closer, frowned at me, and lowered his voice. "I know you. Why did you want him out of here?"

"He was here, Scoobie. Thomas Edward looked in the door."

It took Scoobie a couple of seconds to get it, and then his eyes widened and he sat in the chair George had just vacated. "*The* Thomas Edward, the one the FBI guy said *never* to discuss?"

I nodded. "He looked right at me, and then pulled back into the hall."

Scoobie's expression was dubious. "He was ten, and that was more than ten years ago. It was probably someone who looked like..."

I shook my head. "It was him."

"It was who?" George asked.

George was a year ahead of Scoobie and me, and if I'd grown up in Ocean Alley I would have likely known him back then. But since I was with Aunt Madge only one year while my parents *worked things out* in their marriage, and I was mad at the world, I wasn't too social.

Back then, it was Scoobie who had been across the street from the house I was babysitting in and had called the police when he saw two men trying to get in the back door. Thanks to some quick thinking by Thomas Edward, he and his sister and I were locked in a closet upstairs when the men got in. It was just enough of a hiding place that the police were there before the men could find us.

And then the police took the kids, Scoobie, and me to Aunt Madge's B&B because they didn't want to call attention to what had happened. Eventually the FBI came and the kids were whisked away. The FBI told us not to discuss what had happened with anyone, even among ourselves, or the Finch family could be in danger. The Ocean Alley police chief came by the next morning to reiterate this.

So we kept mum. Even at age sixteen I'd watched enough television to figure the family was in some sort of witness protection program. They'd been in Ocean Alley less than one year, so they were barely missed.

When I didn't answer him, George looked from Scoobie to me. "Who are you talking about?"

"She thought she saw Lance Wilson in the hall." Scoobie did a circular motion with his forefinger, next to his head.

"Gotta love those drugs," George grinned.

Scoobie stood. "Break's over. Gotta get back to the world of funny film." He left.

"It might have been Lance," I said, continuing the ruse. "The person was really thin." Lance Wilson is on the Harvest for All food pantry committee, which I chair. He's in his early nineties and looks seventy-five.

George's expression said he thought I was ditzy. "I didn't see him. They're bringing you crutches. Where are Madge and Harry?"

"They went to one of those huge hardware stores near Lakewood. Aunt Madge wants a bunch of new handles for her kitchen cabinets." She and her fairly new husband, who is also my boss in his real estate appraisal business, are forever working on her B&B or the home he was fixing up before they met. Now they both live in the B&B, though Harry still has the appraisal office in his house.

"Did you call her?" he asked.

I closed my eyes for a second, seeing my sister's two-story colonial house in Lakewood. I grew up in that town thirty miles inland from Ocean Alley, and it's where I lived with my ex-husband until close to three years ago. I opened my eyes. "You were kidding, right? I don't know who called her, but she called my mobile and I told her I was fine. I think she cared more about the deer than me."

"You always land on your feet. Well, maybe not this time." George grinned. I ignored him by closing my eyes again. Whatever pain meds they gave me were literally mind-numbing.

There was a tap on the half-open door and a nurse peered in. "Ms. Gentil? We can let you go as soon as you have a ride." Since I'd been in this ER previously, she knew my name has the French pronunciation. Soft J and G, and a long e sound at the end of both words. Zho-lee Zhan-tee. This is thanks to my father, whose parents were French-Canadian. I have never thanked him for the name.

George raised a hand. "*Ocean Alley Press* taxi at her service." The woman giggled and left.

I frowned. "She didn't wait for me to answer."

"You are ready, right? It's only a couple of steps into your house, so once you're in there you can move around. Okay?"

"Yep."

"Here we go." A nursing assistant approached my gurney. She had a no-nonsense air and held a pair of crutches under one arm. "You've been on these before?"

"Yep." I sat up and swung the uninjured leg off the gurney.

George moved aside so the woman could stand in front of me, now with a crutch in each hand, ready for me to take them. "When you first get up it'll hurt more for just a bit while the blood rushes to your foot. Then it'll be okay."

Okay is relative. I swung the injured foot off the gurney and winced. But she was right. After a second or two it hurt less. I glanced at her name badge. "Thanks, Harriet."

I demonstrated that I could walk a couple of steps with the crutches. She left to get discharge papers for me to sign, and a wheelchair. I already knew that hospital rules meant they pushed me out.

"You wanna sit?" George asked.

"If she's coming right back I'll keep standing." I looked at my foot and its beige, tight wrap. My jeans were narrow and I'd been afraid I'd have to take them off so the doctor could wrap the foot and ankle. Fortunately, he'd been able to push them up enough.

"It's too bad it's not a cast we could sign." He snapped a picture of my foot.

"You wouldn't."

"It won't be in the paper." George grinned. "I have the skid mark for that. This is for my Jolie collection."

I did my best to glare at him. George and I dated for a while, but I ticked him off so he broke up with me. By the time he got over being mad, which he had every right to be, I was ready to move on. So, we've gone back to being sometimes friendly and sometimes at loggerheads. I'm mostly only mad at him when he publishes something inane about me in the newspaper. He's mostly only mad at me if I don't tell him about something he considers newsworthy.

Harriet came back with the wheelchair and looked me up and down. "How tall are you?"

This matters why? "Five-two."

She stared at my crutches. "They might need to be one notch longer."

"How about I take her home and if they need to be longer I can do it?"

She nodded at George and pulled the chair next to me. I handed George the crutches and hopped one step, turned, and sat. Hopping was not a good idea.

"Very good." Harriet's tone was kind of like how you'd talk to a toddler.

I looked at Harriet, and then George. "I won't do any wheelies on the way out. You can go get your car, George, if you don't mind."

He left and Nursing Assistant Harriet pushed me out of my cubicle and into the main part of the ER. Several staff were gathered at the nurse's station, some at the computer and a couple comparing notes on a clipboard. I said thank-you to the staff closest to me as we passed by. I thought for the umpteenth time that while the Ocean Alley Hospital is not large, we're lucky to have even a small one in a town of only a few thousand people. I didn't relish having a long ambulance ride any time I got hurt. *But you aren't going to get hurt again soon.*

Because the hospital is here, the local community college offers several two-year health science degrees. Scoobie is a mid-life student, as he puts it, having spent his college years majoring in marijuana. Now he's clean and sober, though there is nothing sober about his sense of humor.

George pulled into the portico and got out to help me into the car. It was warm for October at the shore, but after being in the warmth of the hospital, I rubbed goose bumps on my arms. I got settled and waved to Harriet as we pulled away. The sky was overcast and trees were a mix of bright fall colors and dingy browns. I remembered it was supposed to rain tonight and didn't relish walking on crutches on wet pavement.

"I'll try to get you home in one piece, assuming you don't...Nuts." George's phone was ringing and he glanced behind him before pulling into a parking space to answer it. "Yeah?"

I could hear his editor's clipped voice but could not tell what he was saying.

"I'll be right there." He pocketed his phone. "I gotta get to Markle's grocery store. Somebody just held it up." He pulled out of the parking space.

"What?! Is he okay?" The somewhat dour owner of the in-town grocery store is very good to the food pantry.

"Don't know. Editor probably would have said if he'd been hurt." George pulled into another part of the hospital parking lot and I could tell he was driving to the main entrance. "I can't take you with me. Could be some problems. I'm going to drop you at the main entrance."

I couldn't be truly irritated, but I wished the robber had waited until I was at home. "I'll sit in the lobby for a few minutes. I'll probably see someone I know, or I can call someone to pick me up."

"Your aunt's going to kill me." He pulled in front of the entrance and half jogged around his car to help me out. "I'm really sorry. Your car's already in the lot. I see it over there." He nodded and I followed his gaze to my taupe-colored Toyota, which was in a row close to the main entrance.

"How did…? Never mind. Don't worry about it. Call me to say how Mr. Markle is."

As he peeled away I was glad for automatic doors and made my way to the lobby. I scanned for Thomas Edward. I was sure that's who had looked in on me. No sign of him. Near the entrance was a wheelchair parking lot of sorts, and I decided to commandeer one.

HALF AN HOUR LATER, with my crutches stowed in the gift shop and my eyes sweeping the corridor near the physical therapy section, I was about to give up on finding Thomas Edward. My plan was to get to Scoobie and ask him to drive my car, and me, home after his shift ended. Preferably before my pain meds wore off.

I wheeled toward the gift shop at the other end of the first floor. Two men in surgical garb approached me. They had paper hairnets on and walked quickly, immersed in conversation. One man probably didn't even know they were passing, he was so absorbed in the sound of his own voice. The other man had his head cocked toward the speaker.

"She doesn't even want to have a stand-by team after eight P.M. Thinks anyone who needs more than a stitch should be driven or flown to Lakewood. I think…"

His voice trailed off as they kept moving. Less than a minute later I got to the gift shop and saw a Be Right Back sign taped to the door.

I started toward the physical therapy unit, which I had avoided searching because it was at the other end of a long hallway. It was not far from a side entrance, probably to provide easy access to outpatients. *Thomas Edward might be down there, getting ready to leave.*

No Thomas Edward, so I started for the elevator to go to Radiology. A cross corridor led to administrative offices, and I pulled next to a wide pillar and rested my head on the wheelchair's tall back for a minute. This wheeling business made for sore arms.

I was about to resume my journey to the elevator when subdued voices reached me. Subdued, but really angry.

"You can't just get rid of people. There are procedures," a man said.

The second voice was a woman's, and it had a condescending tone to it. "My job is to get this hospital in the black. Just five percent less in salary costs will do that."

"Layoffs are not as cheap as you think," the man said.

"We can get rid of some of them without paying unemployment or severance."

How does she do that?

"That's unethical. People have worked here for years, and you're going to manufacture reasons to fire them?"

I peered around the pillar and then quickly pulled back. The man looked familiar, maybe someone Aunt Madge had introduced me to, but the woman did not. The fast glance had shown she had short hair and dark-framed glasses, and she wore a deep purple cape over a dress of some sort. My guess was that she was about forty, but her hair made it hard to tell. Such a platinum blonde color came from a bottle.

"Leave it to me." The woman walked further toward the administrative offices, moving at a brisk pace.

A swinging door opened, I assumed to the nearby men's room. Before the man went in he said, "I could kill that bitch."

I sat there, angry at the mean-spirited woman but wanting to move away so the man didn't come back into the hall and realize I'd heard the conversation. As I wheeled myself toward the elevator, the door to the men's room swung open again and I could hear someone behind me, walking in my direction.

"Miss, do you need some help?"

Now that he was speaking in a normal tone of voice, I recognized him before I turned my head. Nelson Hornsby had agreed to participate in one of our food pantry fundraisers and been willing to go into the dunk tank at the Saint Anthony's carnival. I didn't talk to him too much, partly because he had a sort of hang-dog attitude and was likely to talk about whatever was bothering him at the time.

"You can push the up elevator button for me. I'm going to see Scoobie." I smiled at him.

Nelson's voice had a nasal tone and I suspected he had been crying. "Jolie. What did you do now?"

"I suppose I should get used to those words."

He flushed. "I should say how are you feeling?"

I grinned. "I'm good. I stomped on my brakes hard to avoid a deer. It's apparently a good way to sprain your foot, or ankle, or something."

"At least you didn't break it." He said this almost automatically as he pushed the elevator up button. He glanced at the discharge papers sticking out from a side pocket of my purse. "Do you want me to call someone for you?"

"I'm going to con Scoobie into driving me home. He's still staying at my house while his place in the rooming house is being repaired." Anyone in town would know I was referring to a fairly large fire a couple months ago.

Nelson was somber. "It was really fortunate no one was killed." The bell dinged and the doors slid open. Nelson gave me a push into the elevator, but backed out. "Call if you need help. My office is in Purchasing."

"Thanks. I'll be…good." I said the last word to the closed elevator door. I leaned over to push the number two button, and then stared at it for the brief time it took to get to the second floor.

The elevator dinged again and I wheeled into the corridor. It was not a patient floor, but the vinyl floor covering and the walls were the same beige color as the floors in patient areas. There was no sound from a nearby hallway, and no one was in the area where my chair and I sat. I realized it was after three-thirty, and fewer staff would be on the hospital's second shift than on the daytime shift. I was about to turn into the Radiology section when my phone chirped.

Sergeant Morehouse asked, "You don't wonder who the hell drove your car to the hospital?"

"I wondered. Where are the keys?" There was a two-second beat of silence. "Oh, thanks much."

He grunted. "Not me. Thank Corporal Johnson. And they're at the admissions window." As was his custom, he hung up without saying goodbye.

Sergeant Morehouse and I have crossed paths several times. He would say I poke into things he thinks I should stay out of, and I would maintain that I don't like loose ends. He's probably forty-one or two, which is about twelve years older than I am. I generally like him. He might not admit it, but he likes me, too. Most of the time. I smiled to myself. He was calling to be sure I was okay.

I wheeled into the Radiology waiting area and glanced further down that hallway. Thomas Edward had to be here somewhere.

"Hey, Jolie. You don't look like you're going to be able to appraise my mom's house."

I looked up to see one of the members of Aunt Madge's church, First Presbyterian or First Prez to people who go there. He was in his mid-thirties and his cherubic face looked concerned. *What is his name? His mom is Audrey.*

"No worries. Her house is one floor." I nodded at my foot. "Just a sprain. I'm waiting for Scoobie."

"Gotta pick my kids up from soccer." Looking less concerned, he gave a wave and walked off.

It's a good thing I don't have any secrets. Mostly I like the small-town atmosphere in the off-season. Summer at the Jersey shore is crazy with tourists. With Ocean Alley being only twelve blocks deep and a mile and a half along the shore, we're packed into the town when hordes of outsiders come to the beach. Now that it's early October, things are quieter.

Scoobie walked out of one of the x-ray rooms. "Yo, Jolie. The receptionist said you were out here. Where's George?"

"Mr. Markle's store got robbed."

"Damn. Anyone hurt?"

"George didn't think so. He's supposed to call me when he knows more. Can you take me home when you get off?"

"Did you bring a flying carpet or something?" Scoobie still doesn't have a car. He mostly takes the bus to school and the hospital. Except when it rains. Then George or I drive him.

"Sergeant Morehouse said Dana drove my car here. Keys are in the Admissions Office."

A plaintive voice came from behind me. "Did you say Mr. Markle's store got robbed?"

I should have been quieter. I wheeled my chair to face a woman who was apparently waiting for an x-ray. She was probably seventy-five or so and had on a cotton dress and knee-high stockings whose elastic had grown worn. They hung about her ankles. Older people like her live in Ocean Alley's small downtown and often can't drive to get to larger stores on the highway. "I said that, but I'm sure if anyone had been hurt my friend would have told me."

"Oh dear. I hope they left some stool softener." She bent over a magazine she had been reading. A younger woman next to her mouthed "my mom," and I gathered mom had a touch of dementia. I nodded at the daughter, who was probably in her fifties.

Scoobie's voice held controlled laughter. "Wheel to the snack machines, and I'll be out in about half-an-hour." He gave me a salute and walked away. I headed for the vending machines around the corner and down a few meters

I would have liked a Dr. Pepper, but the soft drink machine didn't have any, plus the only bill in my purse was a ten. After a minute of studying what was in all the machines – really, who would eat a white bread tuna sandwich that had been in a vending machine for maybe two days? – I decided to go to the restroom that was about ten meters further down the hall.

Midway to the ladies' room were two water fountains. The lower of the two was not solid all the way to the floor, so there was room for me to pull close to the fountain. I leaned over as I pushed the button to release the water, and was rewarded with a wet nose and cheeks.

"Damn!" I mopped my face with the back of my sleeve. I'd wait until I got home to drink something.

I had gotten pretty good at wheeling myself, but didn't know how I'd open the swinging door to the restroom. Fortunately, there was a button to push and the door swung open. It was a narrow entry area and the sinks and toilets were around a corner. I nudged the wall a couple of times as I turned the chair to get into the main part of the room.

That's when I saw the foot sticking out from under a stall. A shapely, high-heeled foot wearing nylons. It belonged to a woman who was not only lying on the floor, but appeared not to be moving. I was perfectly still for a moment, and then automatically tried to get out of the chair. I hadn't locked it, so I slid from the wheelchair onto the floor. Luckily, I didn't hurt any additional extremities. I crawled to her, grimacing all the way.

I wanted to help the woman, and peered under the stall. I had read an article about someone who got hit by a car and died because they aspirated on their own blood. I looked more closely. This woman was very still, but she wasn't lying with her face in a pool of blood. Or her head in the john.

When I saw her eyes staring at the commode she was lying next to, I knew it was hopeless. Then I noticed her dark purple cape and the cracked pair of glasses on the tile floor next to her. At least one person had thought about killing this woman.

CHAPTER TWO

THE HALLWAY WAS awash in police. I had kept my head and did not scream, but I attracted a fair bit of attention when I crawled out of the bathroom. I hadn't been able to figure out how to get back into the wheelchair. Even if I could have climbed back into it, I wasn't about to go further into the room so I could maneuver better to turn around.

I sat on the floor in the hall trying to stay out of the way as EMTs rushed into the restroom. They could do nothing, but they didn't know that. I had just asked one of them to bring my chair out when Sergeant Morehouse arrived and said the chair was part of the crime scene so I couldn't have it. He barked at one of the EMTs to find me another one.

An EMT brought a chair and helped me into it. I sat near the Radiology reception desk and looked toward the yellow crime scene tape just outside the entrance to the restroom. I had been told to expect a more thorough police interview. Other patients and all the staff had been moved to a nearby conference room, except for one woman who had a crying jag because she wanted to get her x-ray done and go home. I had no idea where they had taken her.

There was a thunk on the carpet next to me and I looked into the somber face of Corporal Dana Johnson, my favorite member of the Ocean Alley Police Department. She held both my crutches in one hand and had just set them on the floor, as if they were a single cane. "Looking for these?"

I kept my seat but reached for them. "Thanks for getting them."

She sat next to me. "How are you holding up?" Dana is not a lot older than I am, and she's very pretty, with soft brown hair and eyes that hint at her sense of humor. In her masculine-looking police uniform, it's possible to pass her off as plain.

I shrugged. "I'm okay, I guess. I think she works here."

"Yeah. Sergeant Morehouse or Lieutenant Tortino will talk to you more in a minute."

I nodded. "When can Scoobie come back here?" I'm a big girl, but between my foot throbbing and feeling queasy, unable to get the woman's staring eyes out of my mind, I wanted a friend nearby.

"Up to this guy," Dana said, nodding at Sergeant Morehouse as he walked up. She stood and he sat next to me.

"You look better." He scanned my face for a second and pulled out a thin notebook. "You said you went in there to use the facilities?"

I kept myself from saying *duh* and nodded. "Which I didn't get to do."

"In a second. Was anyone else in there?" Morehouse loosened his tie slightly. He wears solid-color ties, white or pastel colored shirts, and polyester pants. Between that and his closely cropped brown hair, he looks kind of like police detectives in a 1970s television show. His attire makes him look probably ten years older than he is.

"I didn't see anyone alive, and no one came out after me. Who is she? I know she works here because I saw her talking to..."

"To who?" Morehouse's tone was sharp, his Jersey accent more pronounced when he's irritated. Not with me this time, probably, but with the murderer.

"It was downstairs a few minutes ago. Nelson Hornsby. Near the elevator on the first floor." For some reason, I decided not to mention his remark about killing the woman. Although I rarely say it out loud, I often say I'd like to kill George. No way would I do it, most days anyway. I'd ask Aunt Madge if she thought Nelson capable of murder. If she did, I could always claim to have remembered what he said after the pain meds wore off.

"You talked to them?" he asked.

"Not exactly. I mean, no."

Morehouse gave an almost imperceptible sigh and looked directly at me.

"I was sitting near one of those wide pillars, and they were on the other side of it, talking."

"About what?"

"I'm not exactly sure, because I didn't know the context, but I think the woman wanted to lay off some hospital staff. Nelson didn't like the idea."

"A bad argument?"

I thought for a second. "Not yelling. I had the impression that this was the first time Nelson had heard what she wanted to do, and he was not happy about it."

"You don't know who she is?" When I shook my head, he continued, "Tanya Weiss. She was hired about three months ago as some kind of special advisor to the hospital's Board of Directors. Scuttlebutt was that she was supposed to help them reduce the hospital's budget."

I vaguely recalled a short *Ocean Alley Press* article about her hiring. "Popular job. How did she die?"

He gave me one of his I-wish-I-never-met-you-looks that I have seen before. "Don't know yet."

"So, not a heart attack?" I asked. "I didn't see any blood."

"What part of *don't know yet* don't you get? How long were you in there?"

"A few seconds. Well, a few seconds after I managed to get around that little corner. That probably took fifteen or twenty seconds."

He looked mildly amused. "I figured those were your wheelchair tire's black marks on the walls."

"So I'm not an expert wheeler. Anyway, once I got in, I saw her foot and slid off my chair to try to help her." I didn't mention that the sliding part was not intentional. "Didn't take long to figure out that I couldn't."

"Why'd you leave the chair in there?"

"It would have taken at least a minute to get it out of the room, assuming I could get back into the chair. I didn't feel like hanging around."

He stood. "Stay here a bit longer."

There was no point in asking how long. A sort of metal squeaking noise drew my attention to the hallway, and I craned to look toward the restroom. Two guys in scrubs had just brought a gurney to the entrance to the bathroom. *No way that thing can get in there.*

As if agreeing, they leaned against the opposite wall, talking in low voices.

A man and a woman wearing paper aprons and shoes and carrying tool boxes came out of the restroom. The woman had a camera on a strap around her neck. Based on TV shows, they were probably crime scene evidence technicians. One of them spoke in a low voice that I could barely hear. "You can go in now." This was apparently directed at the guys with the gurney, and they took a large black bag off of it and entered the ladies' room.

Yuck.

I glanced down the hallway away from the restrooms. I really wanted to see Scoobie walking toward me. I didn't, so I spent half a minute trying to position one of the waiting room chairs so that it was in front of me and I could rest my throbbing foot on it. Once that was done I leaned back in the chair I was sitting in and rested my head on the wall.

It wasn't the woman in the restroom who came to mind. There was nothing I could do for her. Instead, Thomas Edward lumbered into my thoughts. *It had to have been him in the ER.* If he were just someone who had moved away from Ocean Alley during my junior year, like the guy named Sean in my homeroom who loved to tease me, it would have been no big deal.

Seeing Thomas Edward *was* a big deal. It occurred to me that the Finch family probably had a new name these days. If it was not safe if people recognized them, surely Thomas Edward would have stayed away. Unless it was really important for him to be in Ocean Alley. If he had to be here, why not talk to me?

"You sleeping?" Sergeant Morehouse stood a couple feet away from me.

"Nope. Can I go? My foot is really throbbing."

"Corporal Johnson went to get Scoobie. You think of anything else? Something may not seem important to you, but it could matter."

I thought for a couple of seconds. "What I noticed most when I got off the elevator was how empty the hallways were. Maybe some of the people who were in Radiology before I got there saw something unusual."

Morehouse shook his head. "Doesn't sound like it. Two other hallways lead into the one with your restroom, so someone wouldn't have to walk by here to go to the john.

"So, how did she die?"

He gave me a cold stare. "You going to tell your reporter friend?"

"Not if you tell me not to." I grinned. "I love to keep stuff from… Hey, he was going to take me home, but he had to dump me because there was a robbery at Mr. Markle's place. Is he okay?"

"A little shaken, but okay. Same with his clerks." Before I could ask more questions, he stood. "Call me if you think of something."

He was about three feet from me when I remembered he had not said how Tanya Weiss died. "How? I won't tell George."

Morehouse turned back to look at me. "Lump on the side of her head, likely not from a fall." He pointed his index finger at me and turned to walk away.

"Jolie." Scoobie had stopped near me. He looked almost scared. "You were lucky whoever got to her didn't get you."

I nodded as he walked to me and sat in the chair next to mine. "Why do you think it was a murder?"

He shrugged. "Seems if they thought it was a fall they wouldn't have herded most of us to that conference room and then taken us to an office next to it to ask us questions. Separately ask us questions."

My stomach was cramping, and I knew why. "Can you take me home so I can tinkle there? I'm not up for wandering into any more public restrooms today."

He stood and grinned. "Tinkle, tinkle, little star…"

CHAPTER THREE

ON TUESDAY, the air had a clean smell, thanks to rain the night before. I sniffed from a window, as I had no plans to leave my house today.

My foot hurt somewhat less, but enough that it was on my mind anytime I moved. My bungalow is small. From my position lying on the couch, I could see the arched doorway that led into the kitchen, which is at the end of the very short entry hallway.

If you turned right just before entering the kitchen, you'd be facing the bathroom. On either side of it were the bedrooms. I had done some roof patching and replaced a lot of drywall before I moved in, but there was much left to do before the house would be the way I wanted it. I'm not picky, I'm just not fond of scuffed hardwood floors and chipped bathroom tile. But, no complaints. I'm happy to have a place of my own.

The murder had taken up nearly all of the news space in the *Ocean Alley Press* that morning. There was a brief article on the robbery at Mr. Markle's store—short and ski-masked person in grey sweats, no suspect, little money taken. The robber had kept one hand in a pocket, and Mr. Markle assumed the person had a gun.

George had stayed at the robbery scene for half an hour, then he got a call from his editor about the murder. He was royally irritated that neither Scoobie nor I had called him, but calling a reporter is not the first thought in your head when you find a body. He had talked to me on the phone last night for ten minutes, and finally gave up trying to learn more than what was in the police statement. There just wasn't much to tell. I kept my word to Sergeant Morehouse and did not say he thought she died from being hit on the head.

Anyway, thanks to the murder and the need to meet the paper's evening deadline, there was no mention of me avoiding the deer or a photo of any skid marks I made in not hitting the animal. I gave myself a mental head slap for thinking about this when a woman had lost her life.

George now has a daily column called "Around Town." He usually only has one or two items in it. Some are mildly humorous, some announce a Lions Pancake Breakfast, or something like that. When the paper's editor created the column a few months ago, he said it was so that all the non-essential stuff was in one place. I doubt George was supposed to repeat that term. Some days I think George spends more time on that column than he does writing news stories. Today, the column was absent.

I read the article on the murder for the third time. It mentioned that Ms. Weiss had recently moved to Ocean Alley from Perth Amboy, and that she was known as an efficiency expert in health care. The Ocean Alley Hospital's CEO and Board of Directors issued a joint statement that spent more time stressing the hospital was a safe place for patients and staff than on the death of a woman who reported directly to its Board of Directors.

Because there was little time to write the article before the paper went to press last night, there was only one quote from someone she had worked with previously. A man at Trenton General Hospital had said that Weiss was, "Renowned for putting hospitals in the black, no matter what it took."

It sounds like he's saying she didn't give a tinker's damn who she hurt.

The statement from Ocean Alley Police said only that they had no suspects and were exploring all leads. They could have been talking about a fight at the Sand Piper, a local bar.

It was almost five o'clock. Scoobie was observing x-rays on the evening shift at the hospital. He likes the shift, which goes at slow speed except when there are car wrecks. Not that Scoobie is lazy. He just is not fond of hordes of people. That's why he's studying radiology instead of nursing or something.

I had a turkey sandwich on a table near my couch, courtesy of Aunt Madge who had stopped in last night and this afternoon to check on me. She had also put a casserole in the fridge, and I was trying not to drool in anticipation. There was a clink of plates from the kitchen. "Don't do the dishes, Aunt Madge, I can stand in front of the sink for a minute with no problem."

"You can practice that when Scoobie's home. I don't want you falling on my watch."

I rolled my eyes.

The paper and my little cat, Jazz, were on my stomach. As was her custom when anyone was in the house besides me or Scoobie, my recently acquired pet skunk, Pebbles, was under my bed. Jazz raised her head and sniffed in the direction of the turkey sandwich. She looked at me and I shook my head no. She curled into a tighter ball.

Aunt Madge called from the kitchen. "You said yesterday you wanted to ask me something, and then you fell asleep. What was it you wanted to know?"

"Probably about Nelson Hornsby from First Prez."

I heard the water shut off and she walked into my living room as she wiped her hands on a dish towel. "What about him?"

"You first."

"Don't be a twit." This is one of Aunt Madge's regular names for me. I consider it a term of endearment. She sat in the rocker, which faced the couch on which my foot and I were propped.

"I heard him talking to Tanya Weiss just before, before she was…killed." I still saw her eyes every time I thought of her. Green eyes wearing false eyelashes, and broken eyeglasses on the tile floor next to her. It was unnerving.

"Nelson works in purchasing, doesn't he? I know Tanya was fairly new."

I nodded. "Sergeant Morehouse said she was brought in to cut the budget, and I heard her tell Nelson she was going to try to get rid of some people without actually laying them off. He figured she meant some sort of trumped-up stuff so she could fire them. He was mad. It sounded like she didn't want to talk to him, and she walked away."

Aunt Madge pursed her lips, something she rarely does. "Ever since the hospital merged with that for-profit health care group from New York it seems all you hear are words like efficiency, cost effectiveness, and maximizing resources. Never anything about a new MRI machine or reduced waiting time in the Emergency Room."

"I remember the merger, guess I didn't pay a lot of attention."

"The hospital is the biggest employer in town, after the schools. And even if it weren't, at my age you pay attention to health care. Of course, if you get yourself in trouble a lot you should probably pay attention when you're younger."

"Hey, I don't ask for…"

She waved a hand. "No matter right this minute. Are you asking me if I talked to Nelson about the new owners, or whatever they are?"

"Um, more like if you think he's a violent person."

Aunt Madge laughed. "That's like asking if your friend Lester Argrow is quiet. Nelson Hornsby and violence are impossible."

Lester Argrow, my friend Ramona's uncle and a local real estate agent, is loud and nosy. I felt relieved to hear Aunt Madge's comparison. It was no big deal that I hadn't repeated Nelson's muttered statement.

"What?" she asked, apparently seeing something in my expression. Then she shook a finger at me for a couple of seconds. "Don't bother him. His wife just finished a round of radiation for breast cancer. Successful, from what I hear, but still stressful."

"That's too bad. I don't think I know her."

We spent a minute talking about Nelson's forty-something wife asking for aggressive treatment because she wanted to be sure she lived to see their kids graduate from high school. Then Aunt Madge got back to my business. "Why are you asking about him?"

"After that woman talked to him, she walked back toward the main part of the administrative office area and he walked into a men's room. Just as he walked in he said something in a low voice. He said he could kill that bitch."

She frowned, nodding her light brown hair. Aunt Madge changes hair color every month or so. I have no idea why, and it's seems to be her only frivolous habit. "Not something I would expect him to say, but it sounds more like an expression, like 'if you don't quit butting into other peoples' business I'll cut you out of my will.'"

I gave her a look that showed I got her point. "I thought so, too. That it was an expression. So I didn't tell Sergeant Morehouse about…"

"Oh, you need to do that."

Aunt Madge rarely tells people what they should do. She says things like 'you might want to consider' something.

"You think?"

She nodded, very firmly. "And I'd love to be a fly on the wall when Sergeant Morehouse finds out you kept something from him."

WHEN I TOLD HIM ON WEDNESDAY, Sergeant Morehouse definitely wasn't happy, and he didn't seem to believe the pain medicine excuse.

"I guess it was kind of sub-conscious. Nelson's a mild-mannered person, so it didn't occur to me to think he meant it." I was trying to maintain an expression of innocence, and apparently failing.

It was two days after my near-collision with the deer and my first day driving. We were sitting in Morehouse's very tiny office in the police station. His desk is wedged between two four-drawer file cabinets, giving the impression that I shouldn't bother him because there really isn't room for me in his office.

"That's a crock. If you remembered that he was annoyed with the deceased about getting rid of some staff, you remembered that he said he could kill her." He drummed the eraser end of his pencil on his desk. "Why didn't you tell me?"

The real reason is that I have a hard time being a tattle tale in general, but in the few moments I had listened to her, I thought the woman *was* a bitch, and anyone around her *would* want to kill her. I saw no point in saying this.

"I really did forget. Like I said, it was probably sub-conscious. He volunteered to help Harvest for All at the fundraiser we did at the carnival. Food pantry volunteers don't murder people."

Morehouse snorted. "Get someone mad enough, anyone can kill. Anything else you *forgot*?"

"No." I reached for my crutches, and hesitated. I settled back into my chair. "I know you weren't here twelve years ago, but did

Lieutenant Tortino ever mention some people I used to babysit for?"

He flipped a page in the notebook where he writes down what people like me say. "Oh yeah, we always talk about how you made money in high school."

"Okay, it was more than that. Could you ask him if he's seen any of the people from, um, my babysitting job?"

Morehouse had an odd expression. "You didn't hit your head when you got out of that wheelchair, did you?"

"No."

"Leave him a note."

"I can't."

Morehouse picked up a folder on his desk and opened it, not looking at me. "Your fingers work, you can write a note."

"It's not something I can put on paper. Could you just ask him? That secretary who sits by the captain and Tortino will give me the fifth degree. I *can't* say it to anyone but Lieutenant Tortino."

Morehouse looked at me for at least five seconds, which is a long time when you're the one being eyeballed. He stood. "C'mon." He walked out of his office and started down the narrow hallway.

I followed, concentrating on keeping up with him without crutching too fast. I didn't want to land on my derriere. Going by the so-called bullpen where the junior officers sit made me feel as if I was on display.

"Jolie and me need to see Tortino." Morehouse was a few feet in front of me, talking to the secretary.

"Do you have an appointment?"

"Gladys, you know I don't. He'll see us."

While Gladys, who is in her mid-fifties and dresses like she buys her clothes in the thrift store, made a big deal of looking at the lieutenant's appointment calendar, I heard the squeak of a chair and Tortino walked to the door of his office and gestured to us. I thunked in behind Morehouse."

Tortino has a long face and usually wears an impassive expression. Just now he looked half amused. "To what do I owe the honor, Jolie?"

I hadn't sat down yet, so I pushed the office door shut with my crutch. That wiped the smile off Tortino's face.

"You remember that night, when I was babysitting at the Finch house?"

Tortino's tone was sharp. "That night we are not to discuss? Ever."

I was seating myself as he spoke, and looked at him as I put my injured foot on top of the other one. "I know we aren't…"

"Then don't." Tortino was not impassive now.

Morehouse was moving his head slightly to look at Tortino and me in turn as we spoke.

"I think I saw…the boy."

"What boy?" Morehouse asked. He was ten or twelve years younger than Lieutenant Tortino. He probably hadn't even heard scuttlebutt.

Tortino was silent for several seconds, then he asked, "Where? Where did you see him?"

"He stuck his head in my room at the ER, after the deer ran in front of me."

Morehouse gave a small groan, and stood. "Everything's different on narcotics. Sorry, Lieutenant. We'll just…"

"We should talk a bit more. Sergeant, I'm sorry, but I have to ask you to step out. Jolie can meet you in your office."

Morehouse didn't even look annoyed. Just surprised. He said nothing as he left. When he had shut the door to the office, Tortino looked at me. "How sure are you?"

"I know it was a long time ago, but I spent a lot of time with those kids. And that night, that night is hard to forget. But I've never talked about it." I said the last sentence very quickly.

"Not even with Scoobie?"

"Only in the ER, after I did this." I nodded at my throbbing foot. "He didn't see the guy, he figured I was mistaken."

"Bottom line is, the kid would be in his early twenties, I think. He doesn't have to stay with his parents." Tortino thought for a moment. "My understanding is that when kids in protected families get to be about eighteen, they get briefed again on how important it is to maintain their new identity. One of the things they are told is never to go back to a town they lived in under a previous identity."

I nodded, slowly. "That makes sense, but I know what I saw."

"I'm not saying you didn't." He looked at me for several seconds. "Has anything else in the last ten or twelve years made you think you saw him or the others?"

I shook my head.

"I don't think I'd be able to learn where his family is. In fact, it's better that I not say anything, even to someone at the U.S. Marshal's Service. If the kid is here, you don't want anyone asking questions, even the good guys. "

"Sure. I just…figured if he was here it must be important." I bent over and lifted my sore left foot up and placed it on my right knee.

"If you see him again, don't approach him. If he shows up at your house, you don't need to let him in. If you feel at all unsafe, call us. Call me." He took a business card out of the top drawer of his desk and wrote a phone number on it. He stood and walked around his desk and handed the card to me. "My mobile. Don't leave it where George can see it."

I made polite exit conversation, all the time wondering if people would ever forget that I dated George for a brief time.

I crutched to the door to Sergeant Morehouse's office and looked in. He was on the phone and pointed to an empty chair. I nodded toward my foot and he gave half of a wave as he reached for a pencil to take notes. If I'd been him, I'd have wanted to know what Tortino and I had talked about, but Morehouse didn't look especially interested. That was good, since I couldn't talk to him about Thomas Edward.

Since it was early October, Ocean Alley was not too crowded and the weather was still kind of warm. This was good because I was not moving too quickly as I crutched to my car. I had been lucky to get a spot in the visitor parking area by the police station.

"Nuts." My car keys were in my purse, which was on my shoulder. It was quite the balancing act to keep it there rather than have it constantly slide down my arm to where my hand gripped a crutch. I got to the car and placed one crutch against it and kept the other under one arm as I slid my purse down my arm and wrestled with its zipper. I had just grasped the keys when I heard footsteps and looked up.

A man was getting into the car a few cars away from mine, but just a few feet beyond him someone was quickly walking away. I was pretty sure the back of that head was Thomas Edward.

"Hey, T...you! Come on over."

He didn't look back, but he hesitated for barely a second and then kept walking. His head was ducked and a hoodie kept me from seeing his face. The man at the nearby car gave me a funny look but didn't say anything.

I couldn't tackle Thomas Edward even on a day when I wasn't on crutches, so I didn't try to follow him on foot. Or feet with crutches. Instead, I opened my car door and threw my crutches into the back seat and purse on the passenger seat. I climbed in awkwardly and then drove around for several minutes trying to find him.

All of the Ocean Alley streets that are parallel to the ocean have letters as names. They start with B Street because a hurricane in the mid-1940s wiped out the boardwalk and A Street. It's why Aunt Madge wouldn't buy a B&B closer to the ocean than D Street. Hurricane Sandy came ashore eighty miles south of Ocean Alley, so we still had B Street, though the boardwalk and its shops had sustained a lot of damage.

I sat at the stop sign at the intersection of G and Conch and looked around for about ten seconds, taking in the bungalows and two-story apartment buildings that comprise most of Ocean Alley. "It's no good. He isn't going to let you find him." The car behind me gave a light honk. I waved into the rear view mirror and drove through the intersection.

After another fruitless two or three minutes of driving around, I pulled into the In-Town Market parking lot. I had called Mr. Markle yesterday to say I was sorry he was robbed, but he said he was too busy to talk to me. *Typical.*

I was crutching into the store as Nelson Hornsby came out. We stared at each other for a second before he spoke.

"If you're here to ask me to sit above the dunk tank this year, I'm not dried out from the last time." His smile seemed forced.

"No, not that. Just checking on Mr. Markle."

Nelson gave me a blank look.

"His store was robbed the same day the woman was killed at the hospital. Tanya Weiss." *He knows her name, you dolt.*

He stared at me for a couple of seconds. "I guess we were all so stunned at her death that it was hard to pay attention to much else that day. It must have been a shock to you, finding her."

"I'll say. Guess no one there knew her really well," I said, wondering how he would respond.

"True. She was just getting to understand what all of us did." He made to continue to his car.

"Have you heard anything about who might have done it?" I watched his face as I said this. "I heard she wasn't too popular."

He flushed. "People seem to think she was simply in the wrong place at the wrong time. Maybe walked in on someone selling drugs or something like that."

"Ah, do you…" I began.

"Have to get home and fix dinner." He gave his shopping bag a shake, apparently to emphasize that he had bought food to cook.

I crutched into the store, and was surprised to see Mr. Markle at the cash register, which was unusual. My gaze swept what I could see of the store. There were almost no customers. *Because of the robbery? That's not good.*

I crutched to the part of the store whose sign proclaimed 'Health and Beauty' and scanned for some nonprescription pain reliever. The price was annoyingly high, much more than the chain drug store down the street, but I wanted to buy something, and I needed pain reliever. The prescription stuff made me too woozy to drive.

Mr. Markle was still at the cash register, but since there was no one waiting to check out, he was ticking items off on his clipboard. He looked up at me as I neared the register and then back at his clipboard. "Hello Jolie. Need any dented cans?"

"No, Harvest for All is in good shape at the moment. I just came by to say I'm sorry you got robbed. It must have been scary." I put the bottle of pills on the counter.

Pen in hand, he gestured around the store. "Obviously other people thought so, too. Two of my staff quit." He picked up the bottle and scanned it while I dug in my purse.

"Gee, what about Clark?" The senior in high school dated Alicia, daughter of the best volunteer at the food pantry.

"Didn't want to. Parents made him. Four-forty-nine."

"And, um, customers?"

"Still get the older ones, but they come in the morning, in a group." He handed me change for my five. "Quite the social hour here around ten o'clock."

"I'm sorry."

"You said that." He was back to his abrupt self.

I felt almost panicked. If Ocean Alley's small downtown lost its grocery store, it would be bad for Harvest for All and there would be little reason for anyone except tourists to come downtown. Unless you counted people going to the courthouse, but most of them had their minds on traffic tickets or divorce proceedings. "I'll, um, think of something to help."

He had a bemused expression as he handed me the plastic grocery bag with my medicine. "Planning to move Harvest for All here? Save you some travel time."

The food pantry that First Prez houses is about three blocks away, and Mr. Markle gives us a steep discount if we have an urgent need for baby food or something that can't wait. I ignored his jibe. Mr. Markle sometimes makes it hard to like him. "Not this week. Give me time to think."

As I crutched away, he said, "Don't take too long."

I kept my head down, trying not to step in a hole in the patched parking lot. A light honk startled me, and I looked into a car with Harriet, the nursing assistant from the ER, smiling from the driver's seat. I stepped back a foot or two and she motioned that I should cross in front of her. She pulled into a parking space next to my car.

She was laughing as she got out of her car. "Are you trying to come back to the ER?"

Ah. More hospital news. "Hey Harriet. Thanks."

She walked around a small pothole and passed even closer to me as she walked into the store.

"Harriet. Have you got a sec?"

She glanced at a watch on her wrist. "A couple. What's up?"

"I wondered if you had heard any more about the death of the woman from the hospital?"

She gave me an intense look. "What are you up to?"

I was mildly annoyed. People seem to assume I'm *up to something* if I ask questions. I'm not. I just like answers better than questions. Mostly I asked her because I knew that Sergeant Morehouse wouldn't tell me anything he didn't tell reporters. I was the one who came face-to-face, well almost face-to-face, with Tanya Weiss. Okay, the former Tanya Weiss.

"Nothing. It was just...upsetting to find her like that."

She grew somber. "Of course it was." She paused. "No one has really *heard* anything about her death. Lots of speculation. I guess that's normal."

That's what I want, speculation. "Oh, sure. I heard her job was to cut the budget. Guess that wasn't too popular."

"It was more the way she went about it. She acted like all the decisions were hers, and she wasn't a health care professional. All she was supposed to do was give ideas to the Board of Directors, but I heard she was on real friendly terms with some of the Board members."

I was leaning against my car, probably getting my capri pants dirty. "You mean you knew the cuts already?"

"No, but I heard it was all going to be announced soon. She came to the ER a couple of times to be *briefed on our activities.*" Harriet's tone was derisive. "I think that was her favorite phrase."

"Hmm. Gee, I hope your job's safe."

She kept her elbow at her side, raised her fore finger, and drew a couple of circles in the air with it. "I like working there, but the thing about being a nursing assistant? Everybody wants to hire you. Especially the nursing homes. Pay's better at the hospital, so I hope I get to stay."

She asked about Aunt Madge, as do most people in town, and then walked into the store.

I hadn't learned much, but Harriet had confirmed that Tanya Weiss would not win any popularity contests at the hospital. Then something else dinged in my brain. Could Tanya Weiss' so-called friendly terms with a Board of Directors' member have gotten unfriendly?

CHAPTER FOUR

I WAS DOING my sixth Goggle search for words such as Thomas Edward Finch, Finch and witness protection, and new identities in the witness protection program. Nada that related to the Finch family.

Tortino's comments confirmed that it might not be a good thing if Thomas Edward showed up, but if he was in Ocean Alley I really wanted to see him. There had to be a good reason. If it was just nostalgia, why not visit the beach and leave?

My fingers slowed on the keyboard and I thought back to that night in early spring of my junior year of high school. Thomas Edward and Hannah and I had been getting along really well since Christmas. In the fall they were kind of whiney, but I had not wanted to spend my junior year in Ocean Alley, so I wasn't in such a good mood either.

I smiled, seeing an image of the six-year old Hannah earnestly reading me the list she had prepared for Santa. It was a long list. *Thomas Edward wanted one thing. What was that?*

A board creaked on or near the back porch. When I first moved into the two-bedroom frame house a few months ago, every unusual noise sent me to the window, mobile phone in hand as I checked for burglars. Now, I'm an old hand at tree branches that brush the side of the house when it's windy and various other explainable sounds.

At night I knew it could be a raccoon creeping onto the porch. I could usually tell if one did because I'd hear Jazz growling at it from her perch on a kitchen window sill. Her partner in hijinks, Pebbles, would paw at the back door when Jazz issued alerts from the window.

Jazz jumped from her spot next to me on the couch and Pebbles sauntered after her, toward the kitchen. Neither of them appeared to be in a particular snit. I pulled my crutches toward me and stood, wincing slightly, and clumped into the kitchen. The light was off, and I decided to leave it off until I could look out the window.

I slid the curtain to one side and peered out. "Holy crap!"

Thomas Edward Finch looked at me. "Can I come in?"

Even Aunt Madge would have to say that the shock of finding Thomas Edward at my window would make all but the rudest words understandable. I forgot Lieutenant Tortino's instructions. With fingers that shook slightly I pulled back the swing bar lock that was supposed to make it impossible for an unwanted person to get through the door.

Thomas Edward walked in without speaking, and while I locked the door again he looked around the kitchen. He started and backed up a step. "What the…?"

I nodded at the skunk, which was sniffing Thomas Edward's shoe. "She doesn't have scent glands." His eyes met mine. "What are you doing here? Is it safe?"

"I, um, I'm not sure." His eyes followed Pebbles as she made a quick exit from the kitchen. At about six feet, he dwarfed me. His hazel eyes looked as if he hadn't slept for a couple of days and his expression was strained. His brown hair was cut neatly but looked as if it hadn't been washed lately, and his navy blue hooded sweatshirt had what looked like a smeared ketchup stain on the front.

"Are you hungry?" I asked.

He grinned and for a moment I saw the face of the fun-loving ten-year old. "Yep. Can you make me a grilled cheese?"

"I'll make it and sit. You can flip it." I clumped the couple of steps to the refrigerator.

"I'm sorry you broke your foot because of that deer." He shrugged out of the hooded jersey jacket and hung it on the back of a kitchen chair.

So, it was him outside of my ER cubicle. "Just a bad sprain or something. How did you know to look for me in the ER?"

"I was sitting in that little roadside park and saw you screech and sorta spin because of the deer. I was coming to help after you skidded onto the shoulder, but that car pulled up right behind you and a lady got out. I didn't want to talk to anyone but you. And I hadn't really decided about you."

I finished buttering two pieces of bread, slapped a piece of cheese between them, and took a frying pan from the cupboard. "Am I allowed to say I know you now?"

He sighed and sat at the very small kitchen table. "Not by my old name. And I didn't think anyone would recognize me now, so I figured I could check here."

I put the sandwich in the pan and crutched to the little table. As I sat I swung my foot onto the table. Thomas Edward stared at the foot. "It needs to be elevated," I said, "or it swells. It's nice to see you, but you didn't come from wherever to sit in my kitchen."

"No, no I didn't." He studied my face for several seconds. "I need your help. Hannah is missing."

That was not at all what I expected him to say. "Good heavens! She's how old now?"

"She just turned eighteen, but she doesn't look that old. She left home a week ago, and she texted me every day. But the last time was three days ago."

I pointed to the stove. "Flip it." As he got up I asked, "Why do you think she's missing? Maybe she has a new boyfriend or some…"

"No!" He stood there, spatula in hand, with an expression that begged me to understand.

"Why don't you start at the beginning?"

He nodded but didn't say anything right away. Instead, he studied the sandwich as if willing it to cook faster. Without asking, he opened one of the kitchen cupboards, took out a plate, and put it on the counter. He then flipped the sandwich in its pan. *Same responsible Thomas Edward.*

The kitchen in my little house is painted bright yellow, which is a big step up from the muddy color it was when I bought the little hurricane-damaged house. However, not even light-colored paint could expand the size. It's barely big enough for the two-person table and chairs. When one of the people in the kitchen is six feet tall, the place feels a lot smaller.

Thomas Edward slid the cooked sandwich on the plate and then sat across from me.

I studied him as he almost inhaled the sandwich. Thomas Edward had a slim build, and I could imagine him on a high school basketball team. Not college, too little muscle. He could run track, I thought. *Why are you thinking about this? Get to the point!*

"I can fix you some soup or another sandwich in a minute, but how about you tell me why you think Hannah is missing."

"Okay." He took a deep breath. "You didn't know where we went, did you?"

I shook my head. "The police said we couldn't even discuss your family among ourselves. Scoobie and Aunt Madge and me."

"Atlanta. Can you hear my southern accent?" He grinned and then grew serious again. "My mom, she didn't like big cities. But the Marshal's Service--you know who they are?"

I nodded. I knew witness protection was one of the many jobs of the Department of Justice. "They're the ones who actually relocate you, right?"

"Yeah. Anyway, the marshal who was our main guy said the reason the bad guys found us was because we were in a small town. So they said we had to go to a big city, where we'd just be one family in a huge town."

"I'm surprised they didn't pick New York or LA," I said.

He shrugged. "It wouldn't have mattered where we were, my mom was going to hate it. She missed my aunts, her sisters. It wasn't so bad for me. I did sports some, and I was on the debate team for a while in high school, but the marshal said it was too much visibility, so I quit."

"I'm sorry."

He shrugged again. It seemed to be almost like a tic with him. "It was harder for Hannah. She was never anywhere she could feel content. I mean, she was when we were little, but she doesn't really remember it. We were in temporary places while my dad…did some stuff for the government. Then we came to Ocean Alley. Hannah really liked it here. She loved the beach."

"So, you were in Atlanta the whole time after you left here?"

"Yeah. It wouldn't have been so bad, but my mom was scared, well maybe more like worried, all the time. She put black construction paper over the window in our wood front door, and she peeked out of the curtains all the time."

"Plus, she wanted to be able to call her sisters, and she wanted to live in a place that had more snow. And maybe not ice storms." The shrug again. "And Hannah was with mom all the time. Hannah just got more and more sad, and pretty soon *she* thought people would find us if we weren't careful every minute."

I felt tears welling. I remembered the sweet little girl who looked up to her brother so much. She had seemed totally at home in Ocean Alley. "Why do you think she ran away? And would she really come here?"

"We weren't supposed to talk about anyplace we used to live, about any part of our old lives. But sometimes I'd let Hannah talk about the beach. And you. You used to play Go Fish with her."

I smiled. "She loved card games."

He leaned back in his chair. "Yeah. And she loved the beach, and looking for shells. I figured this is where she'd gone, and she didn't call me because she knew I'd be mad that she came here. I kept telling her it was too risky. Last year I even said I'd take her to another beach, like Myrtle Beach. But she said it wouldn't be Ocean Alley."

"You were always so good to her," I said, softly.

He smiled briefly, and then teared up a bit.

I passed him a napkin from the holder on the table and he blew his nose.

"I guess it doesn't relate to where Hannah is, but why did your family have to go into witness protection?"

"Wit-sec, they call it." He said this in an absent-minded tone as he apparently thought about what he would say next. "Witness security. And I know it was something my dad did. Before we moved the first time, I heard him and my mom arguing about laundry. I was maybe eight, and I thought she was mad because he always left his clothes on the floor. When I was older, I realized they were probably talking about money laundering. I looked up exactly what that meant." The shrug again. "My dad had a used car lot, and he kept his own books. He had a lot of cash transactions. My guess would be someone who sold drugs to wealthy people had him somehow disguise illegal money as car income. Or something like that."

That made me curious. "Why do you say wealthy people?"

"I never saw anyone in there who looked like a street thug."

"Ah. What do your parents think about Hannah being gone?"

"My dad won't talk about it. And my mom committed suicide ten days ago. That's mostly why Hannah left." He said this in a very matter-of-fact tone.

I'd known the ten-year old Thomas Edward. He was hurting a lot. "I'm sorry, Thomas Edward, I wish…"

"It's Lucas Householder now." He flashed a smile. "I like to hear you say Thomas Edward, but you probably should make sure you don't."

A key turned in the front door. Lucas stood and looked toward the kitchen door, panic on his face.

"Don't worry, it's Scoobie."

From the front hall came, "Is my favorite gimp home?" Scoobie shut the front door.

"In the kitchen, as long as you aren't carrying anything that might spill." I smiled at Lucas as Scoobie walked toward the kitchen.

"What do you…? Holy crap! Thomas Edward."

Thomas Edward…Lucas, relaxed. "That's exactly what Jolie said."

Scoobie regained his normal expression and looked at me. "I guess you really did see him in the ER."

"I saw her almost hit the deer, and I wanted to see if she was okay."

"I didn't almost *hit* it. It just ran in front of me."

Scoobie gave a sort of grunt, and he and Lucas exchanged a look that said they were putting up with me. "Come on, let's go into the living room."

"Can you be sure the shades are down?" Lucas asked.

"Sure." Scoobie walked ahead of us and lowered by a few inches the one shade that was still raised. He knows that if I don't leave one up a bit Jazz will fight with the blinds to see outside, but that was hardly the biggest concern now.

Scoobie took my crutches as I sat on the couch and propped my foot on a pillow. Thomas Edward - Lucas! - pulled over a chair from my dinette set and sat in it, leaving the rocker for Scoobie.

"I'm looking for Hannah. Only she's Kim now. I like calling her Hannah, but I shouldn't. I'm Lucas Householder, by the way."

Scoobie nodded and sat. "You don't know where she is?"

Lucas recounted what he had told me, and I studied Scoobie's face as Lucas spoke. Scoobie is doing okay now, but he had years of depression and sometimes still struggles with what he calls his demons. I know I'm not responsible for his mood or feelings, but I do worry about him. I couldn't help but wonder if Lucas' secretive presence and a perhaps futile search for Hannah, no Kim, would be hard on Scoobie.

Lucas was so intent on his story that he leaned forward in his chair and occasionally gestured to emphasize a point. As he began to talk about arriving in Ocean Alley two days ago, Scoobie and I glanced at each other and then back at Lucas.

Lucas finished and his expression was expectant, as if Scoobie or I should say we'd seen Kim at Mr. Markle's store.

"Where have you been sleeping?" I asked.

Scoobie gave me a look that conveyed, "Do NOT let him stay here."

"It's still warm, at least during the day. You know that park I was sitting in when I saw, um, saw the deer run in front of you?"

I knew that park better than I would like to. It's not even two acres, surrounded by light woods. A main road in and out of town goes past it. It's not too far outside of Ocean Alley proper, and there was a murder there a couple of years ago.

"Sure," I said, and Scoobie nodded.

"I have a back pack, not a big one, and a dark blanket. I leave my pack there during the day."

"Leaves will be gone soon," Scoobie said. "Listen, Lucas, last I knew there weren't showers hanging from the trees out there. You want a chance to get cleaned up?"

"Boy do I. I stuck my head in the sink at a gas station, but it's not the same."

I sat, thinking, while Scoobie showed him where towels were and said T…Lucas could borrow a shirt and unmentionables. I can interpret Scoobie's expressions pretty well, and right now he was being very guarded. He's usually the first to help someone down on their luck, as Aunt Madge would say. Why wouldn't Scoobie want Lucas to stay with us?

Scoobie came back to sit near me. "Jolie. Did you read the paper today?" He took it off the end table next to the couch and tossed it to me.

"Yes. What do you...?"

"Look on page three at the very end of the follow-up article on that woman's murder." He leaned back in the rocker and looked at me intently as I read.

"Okay," I murmured. "They're looking at all the security tapes, no real suspects..."

"Keep reading," he said.

"Oh." I had come to the end where it reiterated there were no suspects, but the police would like to talk to anyone who had been in the hospital just before and after the murder. They would especially like to talk to "a white man in his late teens or early twenties, about six feet tall, who was wearing a dark-color hoodie."

"It's probably him," Scoobie said.

"I can't imagine he would have killed that woman."

Scoobie looked at me with a skeptical expression. "Doesn't seem likely, but we don't know him. At the very least he needs to talk to Morehouse or someone."

The shower went off and I leaned all the way back on a bedroom pillow that I had plopped on the couch. "That might not be...good for him."

"I care about whether he can find his sister, but if he stays here when we know the police are looking for him you could get in a lot of trouble."

I registered that he said *you* instead of *we*. Scoobie moved into my spare bedroom after the fire at his rooming house. Most of the building could be occupied after a few days, but three rooms were badly damaged. The fire hadn't gotten to his room, but it had been soaked and smoke-damaged, plus the wall his room shared with the next unit had almost burned through when that unit got toasted, as Scoobie said. George, our friend Ramona, and I had helped him clean and dry his stuff. Some of it is now at George's and some in Aunt Madge's cellar. The only really good thing was that he kept most of his books in plastic tubs, so they were saved.

Sometimes I wondered if we might get to be more than friends, or whatever euphemism could be used. For some reason I think most about this when we're cooking a meal together. Cooking is a very intimate process. Even though I think I know Scoobie really well, I can't tell how he feels about me. More specifically us, if there is an *us* in our futures.

I sighed. "Maybe we can get him to write a note to the police."

Scoobie almost growled. "You're talking as if staying here is definite."

"But the park, Scoobie."

"Aunt Madge can keep him."

I laughed and clapped my hands once. "The headline would be 'respected local businesswoman arrested for obstructing a murder investigation.'"

"I'm going back to the park." Neither of us had heard the bathroom door open. His hair was tousled, and in bare feet and a t-shirt that read "We Feed Your Needs," Lucas looked like a teenager. A scared teenager.

Scoobie surprised me. "It's not safe. You aren't the only person who crashes there. You might not get hurt, but you could get your stuff stolen."

"I don't want you to get in trouble." Lucas hesitated. "Why would letting me stay here, or someplace, be obstructing whatever?" He came into the living room and sat on a dinette chair.

"It's about that murder at the hospital." I said this as Scoobie took the newspaper from my lap and handed it to Lucas. As Lucas glanced at it, Scoobie pointed to the end of the article on the murder.

"I guess I don't know about that. I don't...damn! I should have been reading the paper every day. If Kim got hurt it would be in there." He looked anguished.

"I didn't see anything like that in the last week or so," I said, and Scoobie nodded. "The same day I hurt my foot, one of the senior staff at the hospital was murdered. You were on some of the security tapes, so they want to ask if you saw anyone, I don't know, suspicious, I guess."

Lucas' eyes widened and his eyebrows went up. "I didn't see…I don't really want to talk to the police." He gave yet another shrug. "I mean, if I didn't see anything, being quiet can't keep them from finding the killer."

Scoobie's tone was patient. "You might not know if something you saw was important."

I thought for a second. "Like maybe they saw someone on a tape and they're really interested in them, but they don't know when the person left the building. Maybe you saw them leave."

"Good one, Sherlock," Scoobie said, amusement in his tone.

Lucas' shoulders sagged.

"If Han…Kim were in trouble, you'd want someone to help," I said, in a gentle tone.

He nodded, but looked at the floor.

"Did you eat?" Scoobie asked, standing. "I make a mean omelet. Always easier to talk about tough stuff on a full stomach."

"Just a grilled cheese. I am real hungry."

I used my foot as an excuse to stay on the couch while Scoobie fixed Lucas an omelet and, from what I could hear, two more grilled cheese sandwiches. I hoped for a little male bonding. Scoobie had not really known Thomas Edward and Hannah. Other than probably saving their lives, of course.

The kids were my charges, and one of the few rules I never broke in high school was the no-friends-while-babysitting rule. Scoobie had met them a couple of times when I picked them up at the elementary school when it dismissed early. I hadn't thought about where Mrs. Finch was, but I knew she didn't work. What I liked was augmenting my allowance. At the moment, my guess was that Scoobie wanted a chance to assess what kind of person Lucas was.

"Jazz!" It was Lucas' voice.

"What did she do?" I called.

"She jumped on the table and grabbed the last bite of my sandwich and jumped off." Lucas sounded gleeful. "Where did she go?"

"She's not thieving for herself," Scoobie said.

"Did you see her go into the hall? She took it to Pebbles," I said.

Lucas peered out of the kitchen. "Where is the skunk?"

"She goes under my bed when strangers are in the house."

"And," Scoobie threw in, "she might need her litter box soon, so we need to finish the dishes and get out of here."

"It's not in the kitchen," I called. "It's in the coat closet by the back door. But she goes through the kitchen."

"Yeah, when we don't like someone, we hang their coat in there."

Lucas laughed at Scoobie and then they turned the water on to wash dishes.

Since I didn't want to get up more than I had to, I kept a notebook on the coffee table by the couch. I pulled it toward me and started a list. A couple of lists, each with a new page.

I almost wrote Thomas on the first page, but managed to make the T into an L. The other pages were Hospital Murder and Kim.

Lucas
HS or college grad?
Source of $$ --job?
Can we do a background check on him?
Lucas--talk to Tortino

Hospital Murder
Lists of jobs to cut?
Who benefits?
Enemies before she came?
Who hired Tanya?

Kim
Where to look?
Who to tell to look?
Need a photo.

I would add items to each list as I thought of them. I closed the notebook as Scoobie and Lucas walked back into the living room. The look on Scoobie's face told me that Lucas had passed some sort of test.

Lucas looked from Scoobie to me.

Scoobie cleared his throat. "You can't sleep in the park. Probably the best thing about spending a couple of days here is that you can work with Jolie to find your sister. Me too, but I'm in class a lot."

I felt a surge of relief at Scoobie's change of heart and looked at Lucas. "I could do some of the running around for you, so you aren't so obvious."

"*Running* around," Scoobie said, quietly. Lucas grinned.

I frowned at the two of them. "You know what I mean. I'm out and about town a lot. If I'm poking around, no one will suspect something."

"Unless they know her," Scoobie said. Lucas kept staring at me.

"It's less crowded in the off-season," I continued. "You're not known here, and you'd get noticed."

"But I haven't done anything," Lucas said.

"I know, but if you walk in and out of every store or public building, look around, and leave, you might get stopped. How will you explain what you're doing? Do you want a lot of people to know Kim is here?"

"That might help," Scoobie added.

Lucas shook his head. "I dunno. I figure if she hasn't been in touch, she's maybe...doing something she shouldn't be doing. I don't want her arrested or something."

"Drugs?" Scoobie and I asked this together.

He shrugged again. "She likes to smoke pot. Dad hates that. I don't think she'd do more, but maybe she's, I dunno, stealing to eat...or something."

I nodded, slowly. "The bottom line is if you're with Scoobie or me occasionally, no one will think much of it."

We talked for a couple more minutes, and only stopped as Lucas' yawns grew wider. I gave him an air mattress to blow up and we decided not to get his back pack until morning. It would be odd to drive into the park at such a late hour.

I could hear Scoobie and Lucas talking as Scoobie gave him sheets and a blanket. I was suddenly exhausted and began getting ready for bed. As I switched out the light, it occurred to me that I should get contact information for Lucas' father. It never hurts to know how to get in touch with someone's relatives. As long as you don't need to.

CHAPTER FIVE

I SCANNED GEORGE'S follow-up article in Thursday morning's *Ocean Alley Press.* It sounded as if Tanya Weiss would have ticked off anyone she came in contact with. There could be forty suspects.

Hospital Staffer Led Effort to Cut Jobs

Ocean Alley Hospital hired Tanya Weiss six months ago for one reason. Cut costs. Since the most flexible item in the budget was people, this translated to cutting jobs. And since nurses and certified nursing assistants comprise the largest proportion of employees, Weiss focused her recommendations on the nursing staff.

Two weeks before her death, Weiss offered options to the hospital's Board of Directors. Since Board meetings are closed, her ideas were not well known. Rumors flourished.

The Ocean Alley Press has learned that Weiss proposed, for medical and surgical patient units, to reduce the ratio of nurses to patients from one nurse to every four patients to one nurse for every five. Her rationale was that skilled rehabilitation units and nursing homes used the 1:5 ratio. Nursing-to-patient ratios in units such as cardiac care and ICU were recommended to stay the same, at 1:2.

The hospital's director of nursing had no comment on the recommendations.

Weiss' other recommendations are said to have dealt with postponing or denying purchase of several pieces of equipment, and automating some routine functions so that staff who oversaw them could be paid at a lower rate.

The hospital's administrator, Quentin Wharton, declined to comment on any of the recommendations.

Board President Jason Logan issued a statement through the hospital's attorney. "Ms. Weiss' death is a tragedy for her family and friends and her work family at Ocean Alley Hospital. Her role was to help the Board initiate changes that would make the hospital the preeminent community hospital in the region. As technology changes and medical knowledge advances, the Board will likely realign some resources. As always, Ocean Alley Hospital is committed to providing excellent care in a pleasing environment."

No hospital employees were willing to comment on the Board's statement.

The medical examiner released Weiss's body yesterday, and funeral arrangements have been finalized. The service will be private. (See page B-4).

"Rats." You can learn a lot at funerals. Even if it wasn't private, I supposed it would be odd for me to attend.

I shifted my position on the couch and flipped to page four in the second section of the paper. Prior editions had a death notice and said arrangements were pending. This one had a full obit. It said that Tanya Weiss was forty-two and had garnered a reputation in the health care field as someone to help hospitals improve operations.

That's a bland way of saying cutting to the bone.

She was raised in Connecticut and was an only child. Her father died a few years ago and her mother was in an Alzheimer's care unit at a hospital in New Hampshire. *You'd think that would make her see the importance of having the right number of nurses.*

The only other survivor was a cousin. He lived in the assisted living area of the complex where Weiss' mother lived. That likely explained why the mother was in New Hampshire, and it meant that no one in Weiss' personal life could shed information on her background, sense of compassion (or lack of it) , likelihood to accumulate enemies, or anything else.

I lowered the paper to the table and thought about the article. What it made clear was that Weiss' recommendations would gore oxen throughout the hospital. Lots of motives to get rid of her, though not necessarily in a restroom with a blow to the head.

I thought about other reasons someone might want to hurt her. There was always the personal angle. Maybe she was having an affair with someone's spouse. But it seemed more likely that a scorned partner would find a way to let the Board of Directors know about Weiss' spouse-stealing efforts. Would the Board even care? Likely only if the stolen spouse was the husband or wife of one of its members.

Professionally discrediting her made more sense. The Board might still implement some of her recommendations to reduce staff, but at least she would be one of the people in the unemployment line. I frowned. She hadn't been at the hospital long, and unless her work-related boo-boos were especially obvious, they would take time to uncover.

A motive for murder didn't seem likely in any situation I could come up with, especially premeditated killing. It was more likely that someone acted in a fit of rage. Maybe they tried to talk to her about some of the budget cuts. Weiss wouldn't listen and they struck. But what would they have had to hit her with? It would take a lot of force to hit someone hard enough to render them unconscious. And dead. It wasn't likely someone's fist could do it without injuring the murderer's hand.

There was also the issue of a woman committing a murder. I didn't know any exact statistics, but I'd read several times that murderers were more often men, and by a large margin. A man could have entered the women's restroom, but guys I knew would not do that unless not using it would be really embarrassing. Of course, guys I knew didn't murder people.

Jazz hopped on my chest and put her nose on mine. She knows this annoys me. "I take it you're hungry." She apparently heard something she liked because she jumped to the floor and sauntered to the kitchen, black tail in the air.

I winced as I stood and tried to put weight on my foot. Still not a good idea, and it seemed even stiffer than yesterday.

With Jazz and Pebbles sated, I planned my day. I needed to appraise a house not far from Aunt Madge's B&B, and wanted Lucas with me. He had gotten up when I did, but he looked so exhausted I suggested he get some more sleep. I delayed my work by a couple of hours. The house was vacant, so no one would care when I got there.

I decided to do at least one constructive thing while I waited, and called Aunt Madge.

"Good morning Jolie. I heard you felt good enough to drop in on Sergeant Morehouse yesterday."

"You have more sources than George does."

"I'm older. Did you tell him what you heard Nelson say?"

"Yes. I thought I was pretty convincing about pain meds making me forgetful, but he didn't believe me. No surprise to you, I'm sure."

She chuckled. "True. What are you up to today?"

"Not what I expected. Remember that night in eleventh grade when my babysitting job got, um, interrupted?"

"That night we were never supposed to discuss?"

"You sound like Lieutenant Tortino when I told him. Anyway, I have a reason for bringing it up."

Her sarcasm came through. "Of course, if you have a *reason*."

"One of those kids came to Ocean Alley. Both, maybe."

She didn't say anything for several seconds. "And they got in touch with you?"

"The elder one stayed here last night."

"But not the girl?"

"The brother is looking for her." We were avoiding the names. I felt kind of silly, as if I was playing spy.

"And Lieutenant Tortino knows." She said this as a statement, but I knew she wanted to be sure I wasn't fudging on that point.

"Yes, ma'am."

"When you call me ma'am, I know you're up to something. How long is he staying, and why doesn't he know where his sister is?"

I told her Lucas and Kim's names and explained their mom's suicide and Kim's apparent distress. When I said that Lucas had taken off work, she stopped me.

"So, they've had structure in their lives?"

I smiled at her precise question. "It sounds as if they went from here to Atlanta and stayed there. Lucas went to college, I don't know what Kim's plans are."

She sighed, something Aunt Madge rarely does. "Are you and Scoobie going to help him look?"

"Maybe a bit. Mostly I told him he could bunk here for a few days. He'd been sleeping at that park just outside of town."

"Hardly a safe place. Your house must be cozy."

I thought she might offer to have Lucas stay with her, but she didn't. "A bit, but it's fine."

"Be careful for a change." She hung up.

I debated telling Lucas that Aunt Madge would be a good resource in his search, and decided to wait a day or so. A glance at the clock told me it was time to wake him.

Although he was anxious to keep looking for Kim, I planned to get him to help me this morning. I had an ulterior motive. He could come to the vacant house and hold one end of the tape measure as I crutched around with the other end. And then I'd talk him into going to the police station with me.

It seemed like a no brainer. No one there needed to know his or Hannah's...Kim's former names. The police might even publicize Kim as a missing person. Ocean Alley police are good about keeping an eye out for someone. They get calls from worried parents every summer. A high school or college student whose parent is worried about them has usually just forgotten to call, or is hung over. If the police see the kids, they tell them to get in touch with whoever's looking for them. End of story.

Scoobie had left for class at about eight, so at ten-thirty I was the one to awaken Lucas again. "Come on, lazy bones. We have stuff to do."

He was quickly wide awake. "I thought of another place to look..."

"First you're going to help me with an appraisal. Then we can both look." I lifted a crutch from the floor to stress that it was hard to work alone.

Lucas' sense of responsibility won over his worry. "Sure, I can help. But can we go fast?"

HALF-AN-HOUR later, I unlocked the door to a large ranch-style house on the edge of Ocean Alley. "Lock it for me, will you? It's a safety thing with me."

"Sure."

We both took in the large living room with its huge stone fireplace at one end and a hallway leading to other rooms at the far end. The house looked like an everyday brick and frame ranch from the outside, but the interior had been thoroughly remodeled at some point.

"So what do we do here?" Lucas asked.

I dumped my purse on the fireplace hearth, took a cloth tape measure from my pocket, and handed it to him. "What Harry Steele, my boss, and I do is establish a value for the houses we appraise. Walk to the fireplace, please." When he was in place, I continued, "If a bank is going to lend money to someone, they want to make sure the house is worth at least what they plan to lend."

Lucas stood by the fireplace. "Now what?"

"Put one end of the tape measure on the floor. I'll walk over there and put a crutch on it, and then you unfurl it to the other end of the room so I can take measurements."

Some appraisers use really long metal tape measures to do this. One day when I was complaining about how the large measure had ripped the edge of my pocket, Aunt Madge had suggested sewing a couple of plastic tape measures together, the kind she uses for sewing. It was a great idea. Less weight in my purse and I could easily sling it around my neck while I wrote. Leave it to Aunt Madge.

When he saw I was going to take pictures in each room, Lucas' face lit up. "I took a couple of photography classes in college."

Aha. You went to college. "Great. Take a few and I'll look at them before you take more."

He walked into the kitchen and shot a couple, and then the dining room.

I scrolled through them. "These are really good. You picked good spots for the centers."

"I'm an excellent photographer." He said this in the same tone Dustin Hoffman used in the movie *Rainman*. We both laughed.

Given my throbbing foot, I would have taken well more than an hour to measure and photograph all the rooms. We were done in half that time.

"Now what?"

I could tell from how he asked the question that Lucas wanted to continue his search. "In a bit I'll go to Harry's and my office, which is in his house, and enter all this information into a computer. It'll spit out nice-looking floor plans. But before that, I'd like you to come to the police station with me."

For the first time I understood what the saying *mulish expression* meant.

"I can't..." he began.

"You can. They won't know who you are. And if you tell them about Kim, they won't consider her a criminal. They'll just keep an eye out for her."

I could almost see his brain working. "Lucas, you aren't going to find her by walking around town for another week."

"What about the hospital hoodie thing?"

"They probably wouldn't have a clue it was you, but you have to tell them what you saw. Then they can stop trying to figure out who was on those security tapes and spend more time on other clues."

"Jolie, I can't..."

"What are you so afraid of? If someone saw something that would help you find Kim, you'd want them to come forward." I sat my purse on the kitchen counter and leaned against it as I stuffed my camera and notepad into it my bag. When I glanced at Lucas he had tears in his eyes.

"It might get her hurt." He said this in almost a whisper.

"What do you mean?"

From a pocket, Lucas took a paper towel he had brought from my kitchen and blew his nose. "I think maybe the people my father ticked off figured out who we were. Because of my mom's funeral. So someone might *really* be looking for us."

I stared at him for a couple of seconds. "Sit next to me by the hearth. I'm tired of standing."

We sat. "My dad put an obituary in the paper in Atlanta. The kind you pay for, so he put in a picture. He said maybe my mom's sisters would see it and they'd know what happened to us."

"Couldn't he send them a note? Like from another town?"

Lucas gave a brief smile. "You watch cop shows on TV. The Marshal Service guys told us a hundred times not to do something like that. They said any kind of what they called direct communication could be dangerous for us, and for my aunts."

"So he did an obituary."

"Yeah. Well, my mom was really good looking." When I nodded, he continued. "I guess these guys my dad did…stuff for read a lot of obituaries. I think they recognized her."

"Wow. Why do you think that?"

"Because the day after the funeral, a man came to the door. I answered. He had flowers, and said one of his kids went to school with Kim. He said he couldn't make the funeral, so he wanted to drop off flowers. I said my dad was out, but I'd have him call. The man just grinned and said that would be good."

"But he didn't have kids in school with Kim?"

"I don't think so. My dad was sitting down when he read the card or I think he would have sat on the floor. All it said was 'thinking of you.' It was signed by someone named Benny."

"Did your dad say who it was?"

Lucas shook his head. "No, but I could tell he knew, and he asked a lot of questions about what the guy had said, especially the part about Kim. I think that's why she left."

"I don't get it."

Lucas gave his trademark shrug. "She would probably have left anyway. Mom's suicide really shook her up. All of us. But Kim was with her all the time. I could tell she thought she should have seen it coming. So she could have prevented it."

"If someone is determined to kill themselves, they'll do it."

He nodded. "Probably. Mom had been on meds. I guess Kim knew she stopped taking them. Mom told Kim she was cured." He put the word in air quotes. "She said she didn't need pills. If Mom had told Dad, he would have made her start again. Kim didn't know there's no cure for bipolar disorder. That's what Mom had. So, Kim didn't tell Dad that Mom stopped the pills. Mom said it would be a surprise for him."

I winced. "There's a need for a boatload of therapy."

"Mom had a lot."

"I meant for Kim. So she knows it's not her fault."

Another shrug.

"So, this is all horrible, but how does it translate into not getting help from the police?"

He thought for a moment. "Whoever is mad at Dad now knows her name. We were listed as survivors. If they're paying attention, they can see Kim's gone. Maybe the people Dad ticked off are looking for her. Now she's not where anyone can protect her."

"But why would they care? You really think they'd hurt someone who was five or six when your Dad did whatever he did?"

"Leverage," he said, in a flat tone. "I've always figured they want Dad to tell them something."

"You said he laundered books at his car dealership. He helped the FBI put someone in jail?"

"I suppose. My guess is that he either took some money or somebody helped him do it, and they want to know if he had a partner."

I groaned. Near the end of our marriage, my husband embezzled money from the bank he worked for. He *spent* it at New Jersey casinos. "I can't believe this," I said, more to myself than Lucas.

"Maybe he didn't, but I'm pretty…"

"I didn't mean that. My former husband went to jail for embezzling money from the place he worked. I never thought I'd know someone else who did something like that."

Lucas' tone was bitter. "It's easier than you'd think. If you take a lot at once, somebody notices. But if you set up a command to transfer a little at a time you might not get found out for years."

"How do you know that?" My tone was kind of sharp. I hoped he hadn't inherited any of his father's bad habits.

"Did I tell you I have a double degree in math and computer system design?

"We hadn't gotten to that tidbit yet."

He laughed for several seconds. "That felt good."

"I remember you wanted a computer video game the year you lived here."

"Yeah. That *Game Boy* was the first electronic gadget I took apart to see how it worked."

Only a boy.

He grew somber again. "I don't do it, of course, but I could hack into almost any system. Even ones with all kinds of security."

"And do you?" What have I gotten myself into?

"Only for fun, and nothing like stealing money. I made a Burger King ad show a Big Mac once."

"How could you even do that?"

Shrug. "It's just a digital feed from their advertising firm. It only showed a couple of times, and then the ad was down."

"So you hack into a lot of systems?"

"Of course not. I just meant that if someone could get into a company's computer and they knew a lot about accounting systems and stuff..."

His voice trailed off, partially in response to my look, which was intense. "I already knew you were smart. But you're being really dumb about not getting help looking for Kim. We're going to the police station right now." I think my babysitter voice persuaded him.

WE HAD COMPROMISED. I phoned Lieutenant Tortino's mobile phone and said I had someone he would want to meet, but there was no way I could get the person to go to the station. Tortino suggested the food pantry, and we settled on the diner. A few of our food pantry customers have been arrested for vagrancy or shoplifting. They would not be happy to see a police officer in the place where they get food.

Lucas wolfed down a cheeseburger while we waited. I had my favorite item on Arnie's Diner's menu, a chocolate milkshake. The diner draws the tourist crowd, but it's especially popular with locals in the off-season. It's not just Arnie's reasonably priced blue-plate specials. It's the dozens of framed pictures that hang on the walls. They have local people or autographs from celebrities who have eaten at the diner. Most are from long ago. One even has Aunt Madge's long-dead first husband, Uncle Gordon, who died when I was five.

There's a newer bulletin board for Hurricane Sandy photos. Arnie told me he'll take most of those pictures down at some point, but for now it's important for people to see them.

The door opened, letting in a cool breeze and Lieutenant Tortino. Arnie asked if he wanted his usual, and Tortino gave him a sort of salute and walked to our booth. The lieutenant marched me off the boardwalk once during my junior year, for smoking a cigarette. Took me straight to Aunt Madge. He was on foot patrol–and trim. Now that he's in is mid-fifties, he has a slight paunch and his hair has a lot of grey. I've met him many times since I moved back to Ocean Alley two years ago, but Sergeant Morehouse usually handles investigations, so I deal with him.

Tortino sat without saying anything. I had told Lucas that Tortino had heard my suspicion that I'd seen Thomas Edward, so Lucas stretched his hand across the table. "I'm Lucas Householder. I lived in Ocean Alley for a year when I was ten."

Lucas took twenty minutes to quietly tell his story. Even then, he didn't mention why he thought his family was in witness protection. He only said his mother had committed suicide and he was really worried about his sister. It would have taken less time but a couple of people stopped at the table to say hello to the lieutenant. I probably should have picked a different place, but Tortino created a good reason for being there. He said the police union was going to help do a fundraiser for Harvest for All. And then he'd look at his watch and the person would walk away.

Tortino was thoughtful as he put sugar into his second cup of coffee. "It's no problem to ask the officers to look for her. We don't have to put up signs with her name. I can ask them to call me when they see her rather than approach her. We'll say she has emotional issues or something."

"Not far off, probably," Lucas said. "And then you'll call me?"

"Yes. It would be better if they approached her and asked her to come with them. She could be long gone before you get to where they saw her. But if you think she'd panic…"

"She would," Lucas leaned forward. "I know she'd try to leave, and if they made her come it would just attract attention."

"She's not a criminal. We can't make her do anything unless we think she's a danger to herself or someone else. You have a photo, right?"

Lucas took one from his wallet and Tortino promised to return it.

"There's something else," I said, quietly.

Lucas' expression conveyed a great deal of stubbornness. "It's not important."

"Yes, it is."

With reluctance, he looked back at Tortino. "I might be the person in the hoodie who was at the hospital when the lady was killed."

TO SAY THAT one sentence changed the tenor of the conversation would be an understatement of some magnitude. It also changed the location.

I was on an uncomfortable plastic chair in the small waiting room of the police station, my foot propped on one of the other chairs. Lucas was in the locked area where officers sit. The only time the waiting area is remotely cheerful is around Christmas season, when local elementary children provide drawings of snow people, decorated trees, Menorahs, and Santa Claus.

My mobile phone chirped and I looked at the caller ID and sighed. "Hello, George." My mind cursed all of his informants around town.

"What are you doing at the police station?"

"Waiting for one of the teen volunteers from Harvest for All. He said he needed to talk to the police about something but didn't want to go alone." *Let him believe my lie.*

"Scoobie's the one who works with them. How come he didn't ask him?"

"Scoobie's at school or the hospital most of the time." So far the only true thing I'd said had to do with Scoobie's whereabouts.

"What's up with the kid?" George asked.

"Don't know. Family stuff, probably." The door to the inner office opened and Lucas walked out with Sergeant Morehouse. "Gotta go, George."

"Whaddya talkin' to him about?" Morehouse asked. He let Lucas follow him to where I sat.

"He called me. Someone in here spies for him."

"Humph." Morehouse looked at the young officer at the front counter, who raised her arms in mock surrender. He turned back to me. "Your young friend going to keep in touch with you?"

I looked at Lucas. "For now. Right, Lucas?"

He nodded without saying anything.

Morehouse nodded. "Good. We might need more help on the hospital thing." He turned and walked back into the secure area.

"You okay?" I asked Lucas.

"Yeah. We can go, right?"

The temperature had dropped at least five degrees while we were in the station, and the sky was getting cloudy. Lucas opened the car door for me and took the crutches to place in the back seat. "Guess it's good I won't be sleeping outside tonight."

I started the car. "You want to talk about it?"

He shrugged. "Not a lot to say. They showed me a couple of the security photos and I said it was definitely me. They have cameras at some of the places where hallways cross, but not covering every inch of the halls."

"So not one of you near the restroom?"

"No, but I was walking toward it in one of the photos. Or so they say. I can't tell one hallway from another."

"Were you able to help them?"

He shook his head. "I don't think so. I remembered seeing her near the cafeteria a few minutes before the time they think she died, but I only remember because of her purple cape. They kept asking if I had seen anyone *suspicious*, but they didn't say what that meant."

We drove the rest of the way to my house in silence. I'd been a bit nervous about Lucas talking to the police about his time at the hospital. It didn't sound as if they had any real leads, and I worried they might focus on him simply because he was in some security camera's field of vision. That didn't seem to be an issue.

We just made it onto my front porch as huge raindrops started plopping onto the sidewalk. And everything else.

Jazz bounded to the front door as I unlocked it. Pebbles waddled behind her until she saw Lucas. Then she turned and made for my bedroom.

Lucas stooped to pick up Jazz. "What's with that skunk?"

"Who knows? She was the former owner's pet and I inherited her."

Lucas placed Jazz on the floor as I sat on the couch and stretched my injured foot in front of me.

"Jolie, do you have an umbrella I can borrow?"

"You're going out in this?"

He stared at me very directly. "If she's out there, I should be too."

"Sure. It's in the closet with Pebbles' litter box."

"I'll let the rain wash off the smell." He grinned.

We exchanged mobile phone numbers and he left, refusing my offer to use my car.

Now what? I needed to stop thinking about Tanya Weiss' murder. I had found her and it rattled me, but she had nothing to do with my life, so I needed to let go of my temptation to look into her death. *As if.*

CHAPTER SIX

ON FRIDAY MORNING, Scoobie and I were careful not to clang pots or drop silverware as we fixed breakfast. Now that Lucas had been to the police, Scoobie seemed okay about Lucas continuing to stay with us.

I glanced at Scoobie, who was expertly flipping pancakes as he stood at the stove. When he moved in a few months ago, we'd been kind of awkward around each other. I wondered if we'd get closer than best buds. I'm pretty sure he thought about this, too. After a week we achieved an undemanding coexistence. I still wonder, but I'm glad we didn't rush into anything. George and I were able to get back to a friendship footing because we hadn't been together, heck known each other, all that long. With Scoobie, I figured I had to be sure. Nothing would be the same if we broke up.

I did an involuntary sigh.

Scoobie looked at me as he slid a couple pancakes from a spatula to my plate. "What?"

"I was just, uh, thinking that it's not fair that Lucas is in your bedroom."

He wiggled his eyebrows at me. "I didn't know you went for younger men."

"Jerk. I meant we should probably set him up in part of the living room. You need to study."

"Yeah, I don't mind if he keeps his stuff in there, but it would be easier if he slept out here." He thought for a moment. "Why don't you go see Ramona? I bet the Purple Cow has portable partitions like they use in offices."

"Cubicle walls. Good idea." Ramona and I didn't hang out in high school, but we had geometry together. She once said that I did better than she did, and I reminded her that I had to battle to get a C for a final average. Since she said nothing, I guess my C was better.

A rumpled Lucas appeared in the kitchen doorway. "Morning."

"You're drier." Scoobie nodded to a plate sitting on the stove. "I left you a couple pancakes."

"Thanks. I should maybe pay you for…"

"Get real," I said.

"You don't have a secret trust fund, do you?" Scoobie asked.

That got a full grin. "No secret fund." He grew serious as he leaned against the counter to eat. "I saved a lot of money from my job, and I'm searching on the cheap. Ditched my rental car when I figured I could walk most places here. My company said I could take a couple of weeks of leave without pay to look for Kim."

My guess was that *a lot* was a very different, probably lesser, amount for a twenty-two year old than someone who'd been working for a while.

"That was good of them," Scoobie said. "Jolie may know what you do, but I don't."

"I guess we only talked about Kim and stuff like that. I'm a computer programmer. For a hospital, actually. In Atlanta."

No wonder he can hack into a business. "Gee. My buddy is all grown up."

Lucas gave his trademark shrug. "It was kind of weird picking a major. Our Marshal kept saying I shouldn't pick something that would *put me in the public eye.*" Lucas said the last few words with a heavy degree of disdain.

"Because someone might see you and find your parents?" I asked.

He nodded. "They said Kim was only six when we left here, and no one would recognize her now. I was ten, and they say my face is a lot the same. I don't think it is."

"When your dad dies, it won't matter?" I winced as Scoobie asked this.

"Supposedly. I guess he really made some people angry. My parents never talked about it, and I asked a lot of questions they wouldn't answer. The Marshal thinks if whoever my dad ticked off knows who I am, they could take me to get back at him." He shrugged again.

I thought for a second. "Or convince him to give them something they want."

"On that unhappy note," Scoobie stood, "I've got to do a couple things before I head over to campus." He pointed a finger at Lucas. "I'll help you look for her this weekend."

Lucas stared at me when Scoobie had gone into his bedroom.

"Scoobie thinks I sometimes...get interested in things that are none of my business. I consider you my business."

His look was impassive. "Thanks. You have ideas for where I should look?"

"I'm going to the food pantry this morning. Without saying who you are, I'll see if some of the volunteers know where a young woman with little money would stay. Come by about ten this morning."

BEFORE HARVEST FOR ALL I stopped at Ocean Alley's office supply store, the Purple Cow. Ramona has worked there since before we graduated from high school. She went to college, but she worked at the store during holidays and went full-time afterwards. Art is her passion, and she doesn't want a job that keeps her mind so busy that she thinks about it too much. She loves to know what's going on in town. Aunt Madge knows a lot, but she won't pass on gossip. Ramona isn't mean about it, but she'll let me know who's doing what to whom.

I parked in front of the store, noting the white board on its easel on the sidewalk just outside. Ramona writes sayings on the board every day that she's working, and she now suspects that Scoobie is the one who rewrites them sometimes. She isn't sure, though, and I'm not about to play tattle tale. She told me a few weeks ago she's ignoring the graffitist, as she has begun calling the person. She figures if she ignores them they'll stop.

Today the sign said:
To be or not to be, that is the question.
Shakespeare, in Hamlet
Below it someone had written:

If you know the answer, get on Jeopardy.

Ramona saw me coming and opened the door. Her long blonde hair was piled on the crown of her head with a clip, and she was in her normal garb, which is a mid-calf skirt in what I think of as a gauzy material. She loves the fashions of the 1970s, and wears them well. She should look good; she makes almost all of her clothes. Sometimes I think she should be a fashion designer.

Ramona glanced at the sign, ignored its change, and said, "Jolie, you're looking better than Scoobie said you would."

I almost groaned. "You must have learned never to believe him."

She smiled. "There's usually a kernel of truth, you just have to figure out which part it is."

"What did he say?"

"Something about a large cast and you swinging about in some kind of traction."

"Great." I looked around the store. "What's different?"

The Purple Cow has hardwood floors and a few wood bookshelves that display decorative items that are not for sale. In December there are things like engines from old train sets, or an antique manger scene. The vintage look also includes leather-bound books (also not for sale) on some of the shelves. Other shelves have things that are for sale.

"I thought it would be good to have some of the greeting cards and personal stationary items near the front. If they're in the back we miss impulse buying opportunities. Roland liked the idea."

Ramona's boss appreciates her design skills. It's probably one reason she is content to keep working in the store.

"You didn't come here to see if I'd rearranged some items." A smile played on her lips.

Like Aunt Madge and her husband Harry, Ramona thinks I should leave well enough alone. I tell them I will when whatever I'm interested in moves from bad enough to well enough.

"Thanks for the card, by the way." Ramona nodded and I continued. "I've been thinking a lot about that woman who was killed."

"Jolie! She was nothing to you. Let the police handle it."

"I am."

Ramona gave a sort of ladylike snort.

"It just…" I stopped. Ramona didn't know Lucas, much less that he'd been questioned, and she didn't know how rude Tanya Weiss had been to Nelson Hornsby.

"It just what?"

"I did have an encounter with her not long before she died. Well, not exactly an encounter." I explained my accidental eavesdropping without relaying Nelson's probably metaphorical death wish for Tanya.

"That's too bad. Nelson is a good person. He…"

The bells above the door jingled as two men, one older and one younger, walked in. Roland doesn't mind Ramona chatting, in fact he says it brings people into the store. However, at the first sign of a customer, she is supposed to wrap up a conversation.

I half-listened as she made note of the dimensions of a wall in their office. They wanted a desk that was a good size, but would not be longer than the wall. I gave myself a mental head slap. I was supposed to be here looking at screens or maybe cubicle walls that would give Lucas some privacy in the living room.

I crutched to a display of miniature cubicles, next to which was a price list. *Yikes.* If I had that kind of money lying around I'd get a garbage disposal.

Ramona suggested that the men look in one of the furniture catalogs because none of the display desks would be big enough. "I won't bug you while you look for a couple of minutes, but call me if you need me."

She strolled over to me. "Getting cubicles for Steele Appraisals?"

"No, but I was thinking of one for my living room. These are a bit pricey for me."

"Your living room is tiny. Why would you need a screen?"

"Some brands are cheaper." Roland had walked out of his office at the back of the store. Ramona walked back to the two men.

"I'm afraid even half the cost would be a bit much for what I want it for." I was now envisioning using Aunt Madge's sewing machine to rig up some kind of a curtain. Preferably without running the needle through a finger.

Roland stared at me. "Does it have to look good?"

"Nope. A kid I used to babysit for needs a place to stay for a couple of weeks." I have always found it better to have a bit of truth in every fabrication or omission. Makes it easier to keep track of, as Mark Twain would say.

"Come back here."

I crutched behind him as he walked toward his office, which was in the storage area.

"Sorry you had to find that woman," he said. "Terrible situation up there."

My ears perked up. "Besides her murder?"

"My wife works part-time as a medical coder." He saw my blank look. "Every bit of treatment has a separate code, for billing purposes."

"And she doesn't like some of the changes?"

"No one knows what they will be. Everybody's on edge."

We had entered the storage area and he pointed. "If you only need it for a short while, you can borrow that. The customer didn't like the color and kept it so long I can't send it back. The scuff marks wouldn't have let me return it anyway."

"Ouch. They can return it damaged?"

"Not at a bigger store."

I focused more on the wall, which had large plastic feet at the bottom so it didn't tip over. It was maybe five feet tall and six feet wide, in mauve. "It's perfect."

"Good." He smiled. "George has an SUV. Make him pick it up for you."

"I'll give him a call. And thank you." I decided not to push him on his wife's thoughts. Roland is not a gossip. More to the point, he would talk to Ramona about my questions and she'd warn me about minding someone else's business. *As if a lot of what she hears in here isn't someone else's business.*

The two men were leaving with a catalog under the arm of the older one. Ramona turned to me. "Is Roland giving you that piece in the back?"

"Lending. It's perfect."

"Why do you need it?"

This would be a trickier explanation than the one I had given to Roland. Ramona probably hadn't known the Finch family, but their abrupt departure during our junior year had been a topic of conversation in the cafeteria.

"The mom of a kid I used to sit for…"

"Ten years ago?"

"More like twelve years ago. They moved away, and his mom just died. I guess he was feeling kind of melancholy and came back here for a few days. When I ran into him and he told me the story, I told him he could bunk at my place for a few days."

"That was nice. Scoobie okay with it?"

"After he got to know him. Anyway, you talk to everybody. What do you hear about the hospital?"

"Before she died, two women in my yoga class regularly castigated the Weiss woman. They thought she was going to recommend letting a lot of people go, and she hadn't really gotten to know what people did. Plus they said she was bitchy to women and not to men."

"Now what do they say?"

"I think they're a little embarrassed about how virulent they were in describing her. A woman who works at Fries Place on the boardwalk kind of kidded them about whether they had a contract out on her, and they said it wasn't them."

"That's kind of callous," I said.

Ramona shrugged. "No one knew her well, and what they knew they didn't like."

"So that's all you've heard?"

Ramona pushed her glasses further up on her nose. "Are you snooping? Why?"

"Not really. It was just…unpleasant finding her."

"If you won't be deterred, at least be careful this time."

I'm always careful. Sometimes people around me aren't.

I HADN'T BEEN TOTALLY honest with Lucas. I planned to tell Megan, our most regular volunteer, that a young man was looking for his sister, who was probably stressed out because of their mother's death.

I lucked into a parking space at the side entrance to First Prez. It's a traditional Protestant church made of brick, with white trim and steeple. Aunt Madge said they've been offered what she called substantial sums to sell the land and rebuild the church on the edge of town. I doubt that will happen. My commercial real estate background tells me the lot isn't large enough to make housing a worthwhile investment, and there probably would not be enough space for parking for an office building. Even if someone could figure out how to make the parcel profitable, Ocean Alley's zoning laws have kept the town from becoming a condo community, and they probably always will.

Behind the church itself is an attached flat-roofed building that houses Sunday School classrooms, plus a large community room and the food pantry. One door of the pantry opens to the street and another to the hallway by the community room. The pantry looks like a dry cleaner's shop except with shelves of food behind the counter instead of racks of clothes.

I was sitting in a tall swivel chair with a back, my injured foot propped on the food pantry counter. I had a clipboard with our monthly food order form for the food bank in Lakewood, and Megan was unpacking a box of donated canned goods.

"You know," Megan said, "this girl he's looking for is close to my Alicia's age."

"I can't believe I didn't think of that."

Megan pointed at my foot. "You have other things on your mind."

"The swelling's down. I'm going to try putting weight on it for real this evening."

Megan nodded, thinking. "There are a couple of places, non-alcohol places, that the high school kids hang out."

"Besides the diner?"

"They wouldn't be caught dead in there. Teachers and parents go there. No, there's a place on the far north end of Ocean Alley that's set up like a bar, but it sells food, coffee, soft drinks. You have to be under twenty-one. They'll let people a bit older in if they're dating someone younger."

"Why didn't I know about that place?"

"You don't have kids. It's called Step 'n Go. They do some dance lessons, too, I think."

"How do they get enough money to stay in business?"

"Technically it's a club and costs $30 a year. The kids can pay in small amounts."

"Scoobie probably knows," I said.

"Alicia's talked to him about it. That's why I figured you might know." She looked at me intently for a second, and then went back to her work.

Megan is a very private person. She's a single mom, and I've dropped her and Alicia at their apartment, which is not far from First Prez. While Alicia is tall and appears to have some Latin features, Megan is fair. And much more no-nonsense. I could tell Megan was trying to gauge how close Scoobie and I had gotten, but was too polite to ask.

"What about other places? I know there's a women's shelter in Lakewood, but we don't have one. Or don't I know about that?"

"We need one, but no, no shelter here. A lot of the homeless or runaways go south for the winter."

I nodded. "Some must stay, it's…"

The door that led to the street opened and Sergeant Morehouse walked in. "Mornin' ladies."

We greeted him with a bit of question in our voices. He's donated money to Harvest for All, but I couldn't remember him stopping by.

Morehouse nodded at Megan and turned to me. "I need to talk to Lucas again. Stopped by your place, but no one home."

"He's out," I said. Then I remembered I'd never told Morehouse Lucas was staying with me, and I doubted Lucas had told him. "Nuts."

Morehouse actually smiled. "No secrets in Ocean Alley. He one of the teens Scoobie's worked with in that volunteer stuff Reverend Jamison and Father Teehan talked Scoobie into leading?"

This called for quick thinking. I doubted Tortino had told Morehouse who Lucas really was, but Tortino had said that he'd ask officers to watch for Kim. I opted for partial truth. "Did Lieutenant Tortino ask you guys to keep your eyes open for a girl who's eighteen but looks sixteen or seventeen?"

He was surprised. "Yeah. What's she to him?"

"Sister. They live in Atlanta and I guess she ran away or something."

"Or something," Morehouse almost snorted. "How'd you end up with him?"

I hesitated. I wished Scoobie and I had rehearsed a story. Morehouse stared at me and I saw his expression change. *He figured out this is what I talked to Tortino about the day Tortino asked him to leave the office.*

"Never mind. You know where he is?" Morehouse asked.

I glanced at the clock exactly as Lucas walked in the door. He paused for a second and then shut the door.

"Hey, Jolie."

"Hey, Lucas. Sergeant Morehouse wants to talk to you again."

Morehouse was all business. "Let's go into one of the church's conference rooms back there." He nodded at the interior door.

"Sure." Lucas' tone was cold and I realized he thought I'd asked him to come here at ten to talk to Morehouse.

The door shut and Megan looked at me. "The guy with the sister?"

"Yes, but he was also on hospital cameras at about the time that woman was killed. They don't think he had anything to do with it," I said, hurrying the last sentence.

As if to contradict me, the interior door opened and Lucas walked the short distance through the pantry, yanked open the door to the street, and left. Megan and I looked to Morehouse as he walked toward us, shaking his head slightly.

"What did you do to him?" My frown was accusatory.

"Nuthin.' He's the only person who was near her in the cafeteria and close to where she was killed."

"He's not from here," I said this as if that should make it clear he had no reason to kill her.

Morehouse adopted the patient tone he sometimes uses with me. I hate it. "No one's saying he…did anything. It's just damn odd that a stranger with no reason to be in the hospital was where she was, twice, right before she got killed. He needs to explain better."

"I was near her in two places."

"Yeah, but you ain't walking and she was dead the second time."

Megan winced.

"Wait. Am I on your tapes?"

"About twenty times. Good thing you don't pick your nose."

Megan laughed as she opened another box to unpack.

I frowned. "I was looking for something."

"I'm guessing someone and it was that kid."

I said nothing.

Morehouse put his hand on the doorknob. "He needs to calm down. Tell him to call me or stop by again." He looked at me. "You sure know how to pick 'em."

He shut the door, not banging it as Lucas had done, before I could think of a smart comment.

Megan looked at me. "He doesn't really think Lucas killed her. He'd be a lot more persistent about talking to him."

I nodded. The problem was that a lot of people were now very aware of the former Thomas Edward Finch, even if they didn't know him by that name.

I SAT IN THE hospital parking lot staring at the building in between periodic swishes of the windshield wipers. With Scoobie doing a twenty-hour per week observation this semester, I'd been there more than a few times during the last month. If I was picking him up, I might chat with the Radiology receptionist or grab a drink from the cafeteria and sit in the lobby while I waited. Even so, I didn't walk through the halls every day, and I certainly didn't crutch through them.

But I wanted to talk to Nelson Hornsby, and since his wife was maybe still recovering from her treatment, I didn't want to call him at home. I'd left Harvest for All about eleven-thirty and hoped to catch him in the hospital cafeteria.

Megan had offered to help me practice walking with one crutch, but it still hurt too much to put much weight on my injured foot. I crutched to the front entrance.

The gift shop was near the cafeteria entrance so I thanked the woman who had stored my crutches the other day and browsed the greeting cards. When Nelson got off the elevator and headed for lunch, I quickly paid for a sympathy card—which I never have when I want one—and stuck it in my purse.

He was a couple of people ahead of me in line and had the *Ocean Alley Press* under his arm. The poor guy probably thought he'd get a minute of peace while he ate. To keep my tray light, I bought only a carton of milk and a pre-made vegetarian sandwich with some sort with limp lettuce at the edges. After I paid, I stuck both in my purse so I could refuse any offer to carry the tray.

"May I join you?" As Nelson started to stand, probably to pull out a chair for me, I added, "Don't get up. I've gotten to be quite independent with these things."

"Sure, have a seat." His smile was perfunctory.

I put my sandwich on the table and shook the milk. I had forgotten a straw, so I opened the wax container and took a swig.

"Can I get you a cup? Or a straw?"

I shook my head. "I rarely mind my manners."

Nelson simply nodded, and took a bite of his lasagna. For a moment I wondered why he was behaving so coolly, then I remembered Sergeant Morehouse. "Did Sergeant Morehouse tell you who heard you talking to Tanya Weiss?"

His look was appraising. "No, but you were close when I walked out of the men's room. I figured it was you."

"Did he tell you I waited a day?"

He looked surprised. "No. Why did you do that?"

"I wanted to ask Aunt Madge if she thought you could murder someone."

Nelson raised his eyebrows. "So, what was the verdict?"

"That you wouldn't hurt anyone, but Aunt Madge said I had to tell Sergeant Morehouse anyway." Nelson raised an eyebrow at me, and I added, "She just meant I couldn't withhold what I knew."

"I get that." He went back to his lasagna.

"Um. How do you think she got up to that restroom so quickly?"

He stared at me. "You should probably leave this to the police."

"I am. It's just when you find someone like that..." I let my words trail off, more for effect than because I couldn't figure out what to say.

"Of course." He seemed to consider that for a moment. "The police have been asking everyone that. There's a stairway not far from the entrance to the admin offices. She always made a big deal about how we'd all be in better shape if we took the stairs."

"Was she obsessed with health stuff?" I flushed, thinking of Nelson's somewhat pudgy physique. "I guess everyone here is."

"Oh, somewhat." His tone was bitter. "One of her cost-cutting suggestions was to decrease the hospital's contribution to our health insurance if we smoked or were overweight. Or whatever else wasn't like her."

I had taken the limp lettuce off my sandwich, but it had made much of the bread damp, so I was trying to eat only dry parts. "She didn't seem to be well liked."

He looked at me, curious. "What did you hear?"

"Someone, a friend, said when she made recommendations about cuts that she didn't ask for a lot of input from staff." Okay, Harriet's not really a friend. But there has to be some kind of bond when someone pushes you out of the ER in a wheelchair.

Nelson nodded. "Her focus was definitely on cutting costs."

I said nothing while he ate his last couple of bites of lasagna.

He stood. "I have a pile of work on my desk. Can I get you something before I go back to my office?"

I declined and sat nibbling at dry portions of my sandwich for a couple of minutes, trying to think of whom I could talk to without getting Morehouse or Aunt Madge to accuse me of meddling.

Two women in surgical scrubs walked by. "Guess you don't believe in not speaking ill of the dead." The woman who said this was very tall, maybe five ten or so, and her flaming red hair was tied back with a scrunchie.

The other woman was shorter and African American, and sounded kind of grouchy. "It's not like I hit her over the…"

I glanced to my right to see whose presence had stopped their conversation. Two very well dressed men had walked into the room. Both had on three-piece suits. The older of the two looked as if he was made to wear silk ties. The younger man, who was about forty, kind of looked like a kid imitating an older sibling. His vest was wrinkled, probably because he had gained a few pounds since he bought it, and his shirt looked like a cheaper brand than what the other man wore.

I looked for the two women in scrubs. They had seated themselves on the far side of the cafeteria.

"You see, that's the wall I meant," better-dressed man said. He pointed to the far wall, near where the women were. "That could be moved in a couple more feet and we'd have space for a conference room."

People studiously ate their food as the younger man, who spoke too low for me to understand him, nodded. They left the cafeteria without exchanging greetings with anyone.

A man two tables away said to his lunch mate, "Figures. We get a smaller cafeteria and they probably get a glass-topped conference table."

I had finished eating and sat for a couple more minutes. People sat in two's and three's, but there wasn't the kind of cross-table friendly conversation that I would expect from people who probably at least knew one anothers' names.

Is anybody happy to work here?

"May I take your trash, Miss?" The man was about forty and very thin. He wore a white cotton apron over white slacks and a white work shirt.

"That's nice of you." I rolled the remains of my sandwich in its plastic wrapper and handed it and the empty milk carton to him. "Quiet place for a cafeteria."

"Lately." He nodded as he took my trash and moved away.

I quickly stood and grabbed my crutches and hobbled after him. He was about to move a metal cart of empty trays when I came to a stop next to him. "I wondered who those two men were. The ones in the suits. Would you happen to know?"

He nodded, and looked over his shoulder as he spoke. "The younger guy was the hospital CEO, Quentin Wharton. I think the other guy is his boss or something."

"Thanks." My eyes followed the worker's progress toward the kitchen. I had thought it kind of odd that no one from the hospital had called to see how I was. After all, I had found a dead employee, and it was just after I'd been in the ER. When I had mentioned this to Scoobie yesterday, he just rolled his eyes and made one of his observations about the center of the universe not being wherever I was standing.

I wanted to meet the hospital chief executive. *No time like the present.*

CHAPTER SEVEN

THE HALLWAY NEAR the administrative offices was carpeted, and it was plush stuff. My crutches and I made no noise, and I felt like a kid sneaking out of the house after dark to go to the boardwalk.

I paused at the closed wooden door that led into the executive suite. It had a vertical pane of glass about four inches wide and twelve inches tall, and I looked through it. Two women in their mid-thirties were preoccupied with their separate tasks. One was working on a desktop computer while the other was inserting folded papers into envelopes.

There was no button to open the door, so I moved my left crutch to stand with its right mate and opened the door with a whoosh. I let it swing back toward my derriere as I quickly put the left crutch under my left arm and kind of sidled into the room.

"Oh, next time do knock and one of us will open the door for you." The brunette who said this had perfectly made-up eyes, manicured nails, and what looked to be an expensive blouse.

"Thanks. I'm getting better about his." I moved closer to the two desks, which sat near each other. "I wondered if I could talk to Mr. Wharton. My name is Jolie Gentil."

The second woman did not look as if she had just left a make-up artist, but she had an intelligent face and a friendly smile. "Do I know you?"

"I don't think we've met." I nodded at my crutches. "I've been in the building before."

Before either of them could say anything else, Quentin Wharton appeared at a door to my right. "Please come in Ms. Gentil."

"Thanks."

He stood to one side to let me into his office and closed the door. With him in the office was the man the cafeteria worker said was Wharton's boss. That man was seated on a sofa and ignored me by looking at his fingernails.

"How is your foot?" Wharton asked.

Clearly he knew who I was and had been briefed on my injury. If not he would have asked what I had done to my foot. Or been super polite and not referenced it. "It's much better. I'm going to try to put some weight on it soon."

"Have you met the chair of our Board of Directors?"

Perfect. Two birds with one stone. "I don't think so."

The impeccably dressed man stood and held out a hand. I leaned my armpit on a crutch and held out my right hand.

"Jason Logan. How do you do, Ms. Gentil?"

"Very well, thank you." Not really. Did you hear I found a dead body in the restroom a few days ago?

I sensed I had interrupted them, and was surprised that Quentin Wharton had invited me in. There were about five seconds of the kind of awkward pauses you read about in novels.

Logan spoke as he looked at Wharton. "I have a late lunch appointment in Ocean Grove." He looked at me. "I certainly hope you heal quickly." He gave a wide smile, kind of like a politician who sees a camera, and walked out.

"Please, Ms. Gentil. Have a seat." Wharton went to a chair behind a large maple desk and I sat opposite him and stowed my crutches on the floor next to me.

"Please call me Jolie."

He nodded. "I was going to call you the night…that awful night, but the police asked me to wait a day. Then I simply had so much to do, what with Tanya's death, that I didn't make the call. I apologize."

I'm not sure what I expected, but it wasn't an almost contrite CEO. "I'm sure it was a difficult time."

"Still is." He folded his hands in front of him and waited for me to speak.

"I thought I should stop by, let you know I'm okay and see if you had any questions for me."

Wharton stared at me for several seconds. His skin was almost pallid and it looked to me as if his clasped hands were gripping each other. *Maybe he thinks I'll sue him or something.*

"I'm sorry that you had that experience. I understand you were on the second floor waiting for a friend."

He knows I was waiting for someone working in Radiology, probably knows it was Scoobie. I nodded. "I was looking for a ride home. It's funny, I had just seen Ms. Weiss, Tanya, downstairs a few minutes before I found her."

Wharton's eyes widened for a second and he unclasped his hands and reached for a pen and a memo pad. "I didn't realize that. You spoke to her?"

"No, I was passing at the other end of this hallway, going to the elevator. I doubt I would have remembered her, except for her purple cape."

He wrote down a few words and then looked back at me. "The police are handling the investigation, of course, but our security team is working closely with them." Wharton hesitated for a second and then asked, "Would you be willing to talk to Todd Everly? He's our head of security. You may be able to tell him something he doesn't know."

"Sure." While Wharton spoke on the phone I gave myself a mental high five. Maybe I'd get a look at those security tapes Morehouse had talked about.

I HAD EXPECTED EVERLY to be a tall man with a weight builder's figure and perhaps Nordic blonde hair. Instead, I met an average-size man with curly brown hair. He was probably in his early thirties. Hospital security guards wore uniforms, but Everly did not. However, his navy blue blazer, dark blue and grey striped tie, and grey slacks had a regulation-style look to them.

Everly sat in a chair next to mine and we both faced Quentin Wharton. I felt as if I was in the principal's office.

"Todd, I thought you might want to talk to Ms. Gentil. You've probably recognized her name as the person who found Ms. Weiss' body."

Todd alternated his gaze between Wharton and me. "You probably didn't notice me, but I saw you sitting in the Radiology waiting area, talking to the police."

I didn't remember, but Todd struck me as someone who would easily blend with the paint on the walls. Probably a good talent for a security officer. "I was more or less in shock."

"No doubt." He cleared his throat. "The police have the lead, of course, but maybe you would be willing to walk me through what you saw."

I started to recite the evening's events, but he interrupted me. "I was being literal. Can you make it to the second floor?"

I agreed, and refused his offer of a wheelchair. Wharton escorted us to the door that led to the hallway. The two women in the outer office gave Everly friendly good-byes, but they basically ignored Wharton when he turned to walk back to his desk.

"SO YOU WERE in Radiology and the vending area just before you went to the restroom." Everly said this as we got off the elevator at the second floor.

"Yes, and I was in a wheelchair, so it took me an extra minute or so to get to Radiology." I glanced sideways at Everly as we walked, him matching my crutch pace. He was very tense, unless he usually walks around staring straight ahead, with his spine as straight as a telephone pole. He probably worked out, because his shoulders and upper arms had more bulk than I would have expected for his height. His curls were even, suggesting that he used hair spray.

The Radiology waiting area was at the intersection of two hallways, with only a breakfront separating it from the corridor Everly and I were in. There was a check-in counter for people coming for x-rays. I nodded at the receptionist, whom I knew because of Scoobie. She didn't smile, but did do a finger-wave before answering her ringing phone.

"How long did you remain here?" Everly asked.

I went over how I'd waited for Scoobie, and that after he told me he had to work for a while longer I'd gone to get a drink. Instead, I decided duty called. When Everly looked puzzled, I added, "Duty called, bladder mentioned it needed attention."

He flushed and asked me to take about the same amount of time going from one place to another as I had on the day I'd found Tanya Weiss. We'd been to the vending machines and were walking by Radiology again, en route to the restroom, when a tall man in tan scrubs walked into the hallway from a door marked private.

Though I would not have thought it possible, Everly stiffened more and said, "Afternoon Sam."

I thought Sam was Scoobie's boss, maybe even the head of Radiology. He ignored Everly and looked at me. "You found Tanya's body, didn't you?"

"Sam," Everly appeared exasperated. "Ms. Gentil is here at Quentin's request."

"I didn't say she shouldn't be here." He faced me. "We've all wondered about what happened." He continued talking to me but looked at Everly. "The hospital administration isn't providing any information."

I shifted my weight a bit. Crutches helped me balance, but they made my shoulders sore. "I don't think I can add to what I told the police. Pretty much all of that was in the paper."

"So you didn't see anyone else near the ladies' room?"

There's no reason to be as rude as he is. "As I told the police, no. If you don't mind, I don't like to stand too much."

Sam put his hand on door he had just come out of and turned slightly so he could push numbers on the security lock pad. "I simply want my staff to know as much as they can. Knowledge can reduce fear."

He walked through the door and it swung shut behind him. I looked at Everly, whose jaw was clenched. "I suppose you could say he's being a thoughtful manager."

"Sam Dent is not someone I would call thoughtful," Everly said, and began to walk again. I kept pace. "I understand it's disconcerting, but all the staff have been asked not to discuss the murder, unless it's to provide information or ask questions of someone on the hospital's security team. Loyal employees have abided by that."

So now I know what he thinks of Sam Dent. "Human nature, I guess."

We had arrived at the restroom, and Everly knocked on the door and said, "Security. May I come in?"

There was no response, and as he began to push the door I realized that I had no desire to go into the room. "Um, Todd. Maybe we could talk out here."

His expression was puzzled, and then cleared. "I'm sorry. Thoughtless of me. I'll look inside to remind myself of the layout. Then we can go down to the vending area and sit at the tables to talk."

I crutched back to the vending alcove and was already seated when Everly sat across from me. He pulled out a notebook and asked me more questions than Morehouse had. Were the lights on when I went in? I said yes, and he told me that they were the kind that went off after a period of no motion in the room. The fact that they were on said that someone had left the room within three minutes. Otherwise, the lights would have been off and come on when I entered.

"Gee, you make it sound as if I just missed the murderer." I gave a nervous laugh.

Everly did not smile. "That's quite likely." He asked more questions—was her foot pointing to the right or left? (right), did I notice a purse? (no), were her eyes open or shut? (ugh, open).

"Didn't you go into the room before the uh, Ms. Weiss, was, uh, taken away?" I asked.

"No. I was out of the building and returned as the staff were taking her downstairs. I've seen all the police photos, of course. However, nothing replaces direct observation."

I stared at him for a couple of seconds. My first impression of Todd Everly had been that he was kind of passive, but I had revised my view. He asked good questions. "May I ask you a favor?"

He looked wary. "You can ask, and I'll respond as appropriate."

"May I see some of your security tapes?" When he looked almost startled, I added, "I don't know if the police have told you, but the young man in the hoodie is someone I know."

He was taken aback, and irritated. "How do you know this?"

"It's an odd coincidence, really." Without giving his name, I implied that Lucas was at the hospital to visit me in the ER and then walked up to see someone he knew on the second floor. "When I read that the police were looking for someone in a hoodie, I suggested that my friend contact the police to see if he could be the person."

"So, the young man was not connected with Ms. Weiss?" Everly appeared to be holding his irritation in check. Sort of.

"He just happened to be on a couple of the tapes. He didn't know her and," I smiled, "doesn't make a habit of wandering into women's bathrooms."

Everly shook his head. "I shouldn't have to learn this from you."

"I'm sorry." It's not my fault if the Ocean Alley Police keep you in the dark.

"Not your problem." He stood. "Our security tapes are digital. I made the police copies, but I have the original files. You've earned a look."

THE DIGITAL IMAGES were organized by hospital location. Everly explained that he had done some editing, because a lot of the time there was no one in a hallway for a minute or two. "I have the full tapes, but you'd have to watch a couple of hours of nothing."

I told him that would not be my preference. "You really had to spend a lot of time to organize all these."

"The police were pleased. I want to figure this out. It's not just my job, this place is almost a second home. I want to keep it safe."

Everly did some paperwork as I studied the screen. As Lucas had indicated, there was no camera at the entrance to the women's restroom. The camera caught me wheeling away from the Radiology reception area.

There was no sound on the tapes, but Nelson Hornsby's irritation with Tanya came through on the camera that pointed down the hall toward the administrative offices. I was glad no one could read his lips as he walked into the men's room.

There were cameras at every exit, even the loading dock. One camera was about thirty or forty meters from the restroom where Weiss was killed, and Lucas was on that one. Unfortunately, his actions could be called shifty. He glanced swiftly from side to side, as if he were uncertain of his destination. Then he stuck his hands in his pockets. As he was leaving the camera's range he looked back over his shoulder.

In another segment, Quentin Wharton and Jason Logan walked swiftly by the Radiology receptionist without so much as a nod of greeting. Wharton was doing all the listening.

The cafeteria images made it clear why Morehouse wanted to talk to Lucas again. With his hoodie and youthful face he stood out in a cafeteria of health care workers. Lucas scanned the cafeteria's occupants. I knew he was looking for Kim, but if I hadn't known that I would assume that the extra second or two that he looked in Weiss' direction meant something important relative to the murder. My guess was that the vivid purple of her cape caught his eye, even if he wasn't aware of it.

I broke the silence. "I could be staring at the person who killed Tanya Weiss, but since no one is carrying a club or other weapon, I wouldn't know."

"You're right," Everly said. "These images are the equivalent of an inventory of occupants. After several days of checking, everyone has been identified as having a reason to be at the hospital."

"I've seen my fill. I'm no investigator, but beyond your inventory, I can't see how these help."

"If, as you say, the police have ruled out your young friend, then I agree with you."

I frowned. "I saw myself in the ER waiting area as I was leaving. Sergeant Morehouse made it sound as if I was on a bunch of the tapes."

"You were." Everly seemed to be suppressing a smile. "The police must know you well. They made several comments about you appearing so often. Sergeant Morehouse asked me not to include you in the edited tapes unless it directly tied to the crime."

Thank heavens for small favors.

CHAPTER EIGHT

I PULLED INTO MY driveway, which is really just a bit of gravel on one side of the house, in time to see Lucas walking down the front steps. He wore his backpack and, when he saw me, a scowl.

He was well mannered enough to walk toward my car. "I left you a note."

I adjusted my purse on my shoulder and arranged my crutches. "And it says you thought I arranged to have Sergeant Morehouse at Harvest for All at ten o'clock."

Lucas just stared at me.

"I did not. He came by because he had stopped by the house to see if he could find you. When he didn't, he came to Harvest for All."

"What did he want?"

"Gee, if you had actually talked to him, you could have found out." I watched Lucas have a debate with himself. "Come in. If you still want to leave later, I certainly won't stop you."

Lucas nodded curtly and walked up the two steps onto my front porch. "Oh, I turned the lock on the handle and left the key inside."

I joined him and handed him my keys so he could unlock the door. "Where'd you get the key?" I hadn't thought to give him one, or arrange to meet him to let him in.

"I stopped at the hospital to get one from Scoobie."

Great. "Did you tell him you were ticked with me?"

"He said there's a lot of that going around, but I should tell you what I think rather than just leave."

Pretty soon Scoobie will have Lucas at an All-Anon meeting. Lucas pushed the door open so I could walk in ahead of him.

"Why don't you pour us some iced tea while I get settled?"

Lucas picked up his note from the dinette table and walked into the kitchen. While he fumbled with ice cubes I thought about what to say to him. I wanted to tell him not to be such a hothead, but that probably wasn't a good way to start the conversation.

Instead, I mentally replayed the security tapes. The most exciting thing was someone I judged to be a physician stepping on a piece of ice on the cafeteria floor and almost landing on his buns. Lucas had looked out of place, but it wasn't as if he looked thin in one sequence and appeared to be hiding a murder weapon under his jacket in another.

"So, what did he want?" Lucas sat my glass on the dinette table and sat across from me.

"Sergeant Morehouse does not exactly confide in me, but when he left Harvest for All he said you should more or less calm down. Since you're the only person on two tapes with her and they basically seem to know nothing, he just wants to pick your brain."

"You sure?"

"If you tell him someone paid you to kill her, he'll probably have more questions."

Lucas took a drink and looked at me as he put the glass down. "I'm sorry I walked out on you."

"Apology accepted." Not fully, since I've helped you a lot, but you are kind of stressed. "Did you have any luck today?"

He shook his head. "I went to the Chamber of Commerce and got a list of hotels and B&Bs, and I went to almost all of them. No one recognized her."

"Megan, the woman you saw with me at Harvest for All, has a daughter who's fifteen. She said there's a place high school kids, anybody under twenty-one, hang out a lot." I described Step 'n Go. "Teenagers have radar. Maybe Kim heard about it."

Lucas looked almost excited. "What time does it open?"

"I'm not sure. I can call..."

We both looked toward the front door. It sounded as if it was being attacked by its key. There was lots of scraping and I heard Scoobie swear. Since he doesn't usually do that, my look to him was questioning as he walked into the living room.

"Jolie, did you...?" He saw Lucas and stopped.

"Maybe that's my cue to go out," Lucas said.

"Not at all. I just had the day from hell." Scoobie's smile was forced.

Lucas stood. "Jolie's friend just told me a place I can look for Kim. I'll be back in an hour or so."

"Take Jolie's car," Scoobie said.

Lucas gave me a questioning look and I nodded. I took keys from my purse and tossed them to him.

After tense goodbyes, I looked at Scoobie. "What?"

"You were in Radiology today."

"I walked by it with Todd Everly. Why?"

"Who is Todd Everly?"

"Head of Security. Would it matter if I was in Radiology?"

Scoobie looked at me directly and then looked away for a second.

"Sit." I pointed to the dinette chair Lucas had just vacated.

Scoobie took off his brown windbreaker and tossed it on the sofa, then walked to the table and sat. "Sam was in a bad mood this afternoon. When one of the x-ray techs asked him if he felt okay, he said that you and some guy were nosing around about the murder."

"First, we weren't nosing around."

"And second?" Scoobie asked.

"The hospital administrator, somebody named Wharton, asked me to talk to their Security guy. He said police had the lead, but the hospital also wanted to look into Tanya Weiss' murder." I implied that Wharton had called me, and Scoobie seemed to accept what I said.

"So you were *supposed* to be there?"

I started to give a smart-aleck answer, but stopped myself. "Todd..."

"Oh, it's Todd now."

"You want to know or not?"

Scoobie gave me a look that was almost a glare.

"*Mr. Everly* was out of the building until about the time Tanya was, um, removed. He wanted me to go over every step I took that day. Except I wouldn't go into the bathroom with him."

Apparently hearing that reliving finding Tanya Weiss' body bothered me, Scoobie relaxed. "So how did you see Sam?"

"Someone must have said Security people were around, because Mr. Personality came out of a door marked private near Radiology. He said that the hospital administration people weren't telling them much, and his staff was concerned." I paused. "I think he just wanted to know more than the official line. I said I didn't know more than I read in the paper."

Scoobie looked mollified, so I smirked and added. "You'd be a lot more relaxed if you didn't worry about stuff outside your control."

"I'd be a lot more relaxed if people didn't expect me to know what you're up to."

THE PHONE WOKE ME Saturday morning. I groped for my mobile and found it on the floor next to my bedroom slippers.

"Jolie? You were up right?" Morehouse's voice sounded as if he didn't really care how I answered his question.

"I had to get up to answer the phone. Did you find who killed Tanya Weiss?"

"I wish. I just got told I'm supposed to work with you on some kinda Harvest for All fund thing?"

"Huh?"

He sounded delighted. "Oh, if you don't know about it, then it must be a…"

"I remember. Lieutenant Tortino told some people the police were doing a fundraiser for us. I didn't think he really meant it."

"He didn't. But your buddy Councilman Cambridge heard about it and stopped by to say what a great idea it was."

It took me a few seconds to remember who that was. Stuart Cambridge had pulled over to help me one time when my car ran off the road. It wasn't my fault.

"Okay…I guess we need to plan something anyway. We haven't had a big one since the liquid string contest in the spring."

Morehouse snorted. "This one can't ruin anyone's clothes. They'll sue us, not you."

"You have any ideas?"

"That's your job. I already coordinate raising money for Shop with a Cop at Christmas."

Some of the kids whose parents come to Harvest for All also did that every year. It meant a lot to a kid with no money to buy presents for others. "Okay, what about…hey, why don't we make it something that benefits Harvest for All and the shopping stuff?"

Even as I said it, I remembered that I might chair the food pantry committee, but I had to clear big decisions with the others. I'd have to line up some votes before the next meeting.

"This'll mean you can call me without minding someone else's business." He hung up.

I groaned and swung both legs out of bed and onto the floor. At least my foot didn't throb any more. Last night I had walked on one crutch all around the house, but no way would I try that outside. What was most annoying was that my ankle was still stiff, and it hurt more after I put even a little weight on my foot.

After a moment I dialed First Prez and asked Reverend Jamison's secretary if we could use the church's community room for a committee meeting two evenings from now. Ever charming, she said it was not free that day, but we could use it the day after that.

That settled, I called Monica, our most timid committee member. I like to divide work among the members, and not solely because I don't want to do it. People feel good when they help. Monica organizes bake sales for us, usually with help from Aunt Madge because Monica gets flustered. However, Monica has also volunteered to call people when we schedule a meeting. I can't just do an email, because Monica and Sylvia Parrett don't use email, and Dr. Welby never checks his.

CHAPTER NINE

I MOSTLY RESTED ON Sunday. It's tiring to walk on crutches. I did drive Lucas through town so he could look at sidewalks without running off the road. We saw no sign of Kim.

Lucas had been in town for a week, with no success. I saw no point in mentioning that she may have left—if she ever was here.

ON MONDAY, I headed to Harvest for All. I knew at least a couple of volunteers would be there because it was one of our thrice-weekly giveaway days. Recipients can come twice a month for a box of food about the size of a copy paper box. They give us a list of what they hope to get and we load the box.

I wanted to pick the brains of volunteers for ideas for a fundraiser. Usually Scoobie suggests something crazy for an event and other committee members and volunteers figure out how to do it. Volunteers would likely suggest something saner than anything Scoobie would come up with.

After a breakfast of straight-from-the-freezer scrambled eggs and sausage I headed to Harvest for All. I hadn't gotten all the way in the door when Megan said, "Thank goodness. I didn't want to call you because of your leg."

"What's up?" I crutched toward the gate that leads behind the counter.

"The daughter of one of our regulars has bronchitis. Ramona was going to help but she just called to say some delivery truck came earlier than planned and Roland was out, so she didn't want to leave one of their newer employees alone in the store."

I could imagine my fit friend helping delivery drivers throw boxes off a truck.

"Okay. Good I stopped by." I placed one crutch against the wall where we hang aprons for workers and grabbed an apron.

Megan frowned. "You can't be filling orders. Just stand at the counter to take orders."

"I can fill boxes until my foot cusses at me." She gave me one of those looks only a mom can give. Or Aunt Madge. "Honest, it's a lot better. Let's see how it goes."

On days that we distribute food, Harvest for All is open from ten until noon and three until six. That way we can get people after school and work as well as people who don't work. We tend to get older people in the morning and families in the afternoon.

I had arrived at the pantry just before ten, and by ten-fifteen realized I could not roam the shelves filling boxes. I was slowing down the operation and about ready to call Reverend Jamison to see if he could help when Megan had one of her good ideas. She put a table in the aisle that has most-requested kinds of food (cereal, flour, pasta, and canned fruit and veggies), and said she'd set a box on it for me to fill an order. When I was done with my part, she'd switch out the box with another one to fill. I would have to do very little crutching.

I was searching for another box of corn flakes when I hear Megan saying, "I can give you a small box today, and after you register with Salvation Army or human services I can give you a larger one."

A meek female voice said, "Okay."

I was going to have to move to the counter to see who it was when Megan walked to me with an empty box and whispered, "I think it's her. She's really out of it." Out loud she said, "No list, so give her a mix of goods."

I packed the box with canned vegetables, fruit, and dry cereal. Then I took a piece of paper from a pad in my purse and wrote, "Kim. It's Jolie. Lucas is staying with me. Come to my house at 346 Bay Street. Or come with me now. PLEASE." I tucked it in the box where she couldn't see it right away. I wanted her to take the food rather than see a note, or me, and run away empty-handed.

Megan came toward me and brought some Vienna sausages and tuna and placed them in the box with some juice. It was all I could do not to run to the counter and grab Kim, but I knew I would scare her and she'd run. I cursed in silence that I would not be able to follow her.

Megan told Kim where the Salvation Army office was, and the quiet voice said, "Thank you."

When she brought me another empty box, Megan had a questioning look.

"I was afraid she'd run. I put a note in the box."

"She's really thin, and her color's not good."

She better not get so sick she crawls off somewhere to sleep and gets hurt.

IT WAS ONE o'clock and my foot was propped on a pillow on my couch with an ice pack doing its job to make the swelling go down. I was frustrated that Kim hadn't made contact, and determined to stay home until Lucas got back.

I left a message on Lucas' mobile to let him know about the likely Kim sighting, and when he called back he was excited. "Megan said Kim looked out of it, and I didn't want to frighten her into running. So I put a note with my address in her box of food. I told her you were staying with me."

Frustration dripped from Lucas' words. "She wouldn't have run from you, Jolie."

"You can't *know* that. I'm sorry, Lucas. It was a judgment call. She knows you're with me now. She'll come tonight."

"Okay. Sure." He seemed to have to force his tone to be polite. "I'm going to look in all the shops and on the boardwalk near First Prez."

I stared at the ceiling, hoping I hadn't made a mistake about Kim.

INCESSANT KNOCKING WOKE me. I stumbled off the couch and balanced on one foot. I shouted, "Who is it?"

"It's George. Open up."

I wonder how many women have former boyfriends who pound on their door? At least I knew George wasn't a stalker. I glanced at the clock. It was after six. I'd napped for hours. I crutched to the door and unlocked it. "What's up?"

"I'm writing...I thought you'd be off crutches by now."

"Hello to you, too. You can sit on the rocker and talk to me while I prop my foot. I was on my feet a lot at Harvest for All."

"On one foot, you mean," he said. I was tempted to flip him the bird, except that I needed both hands for the crutches.

As I settled back onto the couch George took his thin reporter's notebook from a pocket of his Hawaiian shirt. "I've never had so many anonymous sources on a story."

"People who know who the murderer might be?"

"Nah. People who want to let me know how horrible Weiss was. It's almost as if they're building a case for her murderer to get off. Assuming he's ever caught. Somebody mailed me a memo she's supposed to have presented to the Board of Directors."

"About…?"

"About the cost reductions." He began reading from a list. "As many as fifty jobs, some new diagnostic equipment for cardiology and some kind of portable x-ray thing for Radiology, recumbent bikes for Physical Therapy…"

"What was the radiology stuff? She was killed near there, you know."

George gave me a *duh* look. "There were two things. One looks like something you could make in a carpentry class. Supposed to help with foot x-ray positioning. Nine hundred dollars! The other was a portable ultra sound machine."

"What kind of jobs are they cutting?"

"Mostly in nursing, but they're all over the hospital. I hear there's a second memo, but I haven't seen that yet."

"How can you tell if what someone sent you is fake?"

"I've thought a lot about that. I came over now because Scoobie should be home soon. I want to see what more he knows."

As if on cue, a key turned in the lock on the front door. "Is it safe to come in?"

"Yeah, Scoob. Got some questions for you," George called.

Scoobie stood at the entrance to the living room. "You two are up to something. That's never good."

"I didn't ask George to come over." I made that clear because I knew Scoobie wouldn't like answering George's questions.

As Scoobie took off his coat, George summarized what he had told me. "So, what I really need to know is whether your Radiology guys actually asked for new equipment and got turned down."

Scoobie pulled a dinette chair close to the couch so he could face George and me. "Are you going to use me as a source?"

"Of course not."

"The thing is," Scoobie spoke slowly, "even if you don't quote me, people know we're friends. If you have more details on Radiology cuts than others, it'll be clear it came from me. I had to sign all kinds of privacy documents before I started my internship."

"I'll be careful." George looked like a kid about to win a prize for most points in a video game.

"I have no idea if it was cut, but my boss wanted this portable ultrasound equipment that..."

"Yeah, I know," George said.

"So why are you asking?" Scoobie was irritated.

"I mean, I heard that. Is it true?"

"They want to be able to use the portable equipment in the ER. A kind of triage. If it shows somebody has an appendix that looks like it's about to rupture, that's more important than a simple head wound that needs stitches."

"And...?" George asked.

"And what?" Scoobie answered.

"Did the Board decide to cut that out of the budget?"

"No idea. Way above my pay grade."

"Nuts. I was thinking that would be a helluva motive for murder." George closed his notebook.

"Sounds like a motive to look for a job somewhere else," I said.

"Is that someone on the porch?" Scoobie asked.

Kim! "Oh, that could be...one of the volunteers from Harvest for All," I said. My eyes met Scoobie's. He had no idea what I was talking about, but he's a quick study.

Before I could say anything George pulled up the blinds for the living room window that overlooked the front porch. There was the immediate sound of someone running off the porch and down the short front walk to the street.

"Looked like a girl, maybe fifteen or so. Hard to tell anymore."

"Probably the wrong house," Scoobie said. "Hey George, I'm kinda tired. Do you mind?"

"Sure." He began stuffing pen and notebook into pockets. "Read the article tomorrow and tell me what you think."

Scoobie walked George to the door, and I stayed on the couch but put my head in my hands.

"Was that Lucas' sister, you think?" Scoobie asked. He sat in the rocker.

"For sure. She came to Harvest for All today." I told him about putting the note in the box. "When she saw a strange face and no sign of Lucas, she took off."

"Damn," Scoobie said, softly. "Where's Lucas?"

"Out looking for her. Probably be back here any minute."

Another set of footsteps on the porch proved me right. When he got into the living room, Lucas looked from Scoobie to me. "You guys have a bad day or something?"

"As of now," I said. "I think Kim might have come on the porch. George looked out the window and she took off."

Lucas leaned against the wall and hung his head.

"Come on, Jolie. You and I are going into the kitchen. Lucas, pull up the shades and keep the lights on so she can see you."

When we got to the kitchen, I sat and put my foot on the table.

Scoobie looked at me. "Nice. I'll make a batch of grilled cheese. I bet she'll be back." Scoobie called the last few words to Lucas as he pulled the frying pan out of a cupboard. Then he looked at me. "You didn't talk to her?"

"Megan said she seemed kind of out of it. I didn't want to scare her away." I explained what was on the note I put in the box.

"Hmm. She must trust you at some level. She did come to Ocean Alley."

I didn't say anything. From what Lucas had said, she came for the beach.

CHAPTER TEN

I WOKE UP at about six-fifteen Tuesday morning to the sound of raised voices in my living room.

Lucas was the loudest. "It's not to put you in a hospital. It's just to see if different meds will..."

"I'm fine without medicine! I got myself here, didn't I?"

"Yeah, and you got all your stuff stolen."

I reached for the crutches next to my bed. I heard Scoobie's door open, but he didn't seem to come out. Probably didn't want to scare Kim.

The argument continued as I crutched into the living room. They were trying to talk over each other and both stopped mid-sentence. Kim's face was thinner than in the photo Lucas had, and she had deep circles under her eyes. Her hair was also different, now a brassy blonde color. *She'd get along with Aunt Madge.*

"I'm glad you're here, Kim."

"My name is Hannah." She managed to scowl and looked almost cowed at the same time.

"In here you can be Hannah." Lucas started to say something, and I stopped him with a babysitter look. "Outside it's safer to be Kim."

"Are you guys hungry?" Scoobie asked. He spoke from the doorway of his room.

"I am," Lucas said.

Kim frowned at Scoobie. "Are you the person who told the police to look for me?"

"I told you he..." Lucas began.

"I asked *him.*"

Scoobie walked into the doorway to the living room and stood next to me. "You're almost never taller than anyone, but you've got Kim beat by an inch."

Kim actually smiled for a couple of seconds. "You have some grey in your beard."

"You can lend me some of your hair color."

I laughed, and stopped when Kim stared at me stonily. "It's not the right color."

"Okay, now that we've all had our introductions," Scoobie said, "I'm up in time to make pancakes and scrambled eggs. Lucas, you're doing the toast. Kim, if your clothes were stolen, Jolie can lend you some. I have first dibs on the bathroom."

Lucas looked at Kim. "I told you they were okay."

"Stop saying I-told-you-so."

"Come look in my closet." I glanced around the living room, which was strewn with pillows, sheets, and blankets. I had no idea when Kim had arrived, having gone to bed about midnight. I looked at Lucas. "You pick up the living room."

"What did you do to your foot?" Kim asked. She was studying the clothes in my closet, but not taking anything out to look.

"Slammed hard on the brakes to avoid hitting a deer. Kind of sprained it."

She gave me the look most people do when I say this. Who sprains an ankle stepping on the brakes?

While she looked, I went over what had been said in the last few minutes. I still had no idea where Kim had been staying, but she definitely knew that the police were aware of her. I wondered if she had talked to one of them.

Kim pulled out my Harvest for All tee-shirt. "I went to this place."

"You saw the note, so you know I was there."

She nodded. "Do you have a belt I could use when I wear your pants?"

I nodded to a hook at the back of a closet. I could hear Scoobie and Lucas working together in the kitchen. "I'm not about to lecture you."

"Good."

"And I can see why you don't want to listen to Lucas."

She looked at me, surprised.

"He's probably made his points before," I said, dryly.

This earned me a weak smile and she flipped through more clothes.

"But Scoobie had a really crappy childhood. Talk to him sometime."

"As long as he doesn't talk about medicine."

I shrugged, or as much as you can when standing on crutches. "You can ask him what he takes. He won't bring it up."

She didn't turn from where she was flipping through my hangers, but she did pause for a second. "Okay if I borrow these jeans?"

Borrow. She said borrow! "Sure. You'll probably have to roll up the cuffs once."

She came out of the closet and I pointed to the top drawer of my chest with a crutch. She opened it and pulled out a pair of underwear and a bra. She took the bra by each strap and looked at it. "I don't think so."

I am not that well-endowed, but I did beat her rail-thin figure. "Rinse yours in the sink and stick it in my drier. I can give you a few dollars to get underwear."

"I was in the Salvation Army thrift store yesterday. If you lend me ten dollars I can buy a lot."

"Sure." I was relieved to hear her talk about practical things. She sounded much calmer than ten minutes ago.

"Yo. Jolie. Lucas is finishing the eggs. I'm grabbing the shower."

The three of us ate in silence for almost a minute. Then Lucas said, "There's a good community mental health center…"

"No."

"Lucas," I tried to speak gently. Not always my forte. "She needs to make her own choices about that."

"You don't know how our mom was." He was wearing his mulish expression.

"I'm not crazy. I'm not mom." Kim's tone was fierce.

"Yes, but…"

"Enough!" I spoke louder than I intended, but it had the effect I wanted. Lucas' fork paused near his mouth and Kim sat very still. I looked at Lucas and gestured to the stove. "Pour some pancake batter into the pan so they're ready for Scoobie."

"Yes, ma'am."

For some reason, his exasperated tone made Kim giggle, and I saw his shoulders relax.

I looked at Kim. "On Lucas' first day here, I made him go with me when I appraised a house. You want to come?"

At her blank look, I explained what I did, and said she would help me with the measuring tape, since I was, obviously, still on crutches.

"I promise I will tomorrow. I'd really like to sleep for a while. Unless you want us outside during the day."

"Of course not," I said.

Scoobie, towel drying his hair, stuck his head in the kitchen. "It's not a hostel. Your turn, Lucas. Hey, thanks for the cakes. Be right back."

As he left the kitchen, Lucas looked at Kim. "Remember what I said."

Kim scowled just as Scoobie walked back into the kitchen with bare feet, jeans and a tee-shirt. He looked at me and I shook my head. "Not at you and me."

"I just get tired of him trying to boss me around." Kim's tone was petulant.

Scoobie sat next to Kim and began pouring syrup on his pancakes. "You should live with her." He jerked his head in my direction.

"Hey. I don't boss you around."

"Yeah, but you try." He winked at Kim, and she smiled briefly.

The shower went off.

"I'm not in a big hurry today. Only one house to appraise. You can go next." Kim stood, and I added, "There's a pack of cheap toothbrushes under the sink."

"Unused," Scoobie added.

I couldn't hear what Lucas said to Kim in the hall, but she gave a short reply in a grouchy tone. The bathroom door shut and Lucas walked into Scoobie's room to get dressed.

"I might have to take him to a meeting," Scoobie said, in a low voice.

"Can't make him go," I said, knowing he was referring to the twelve-step meetings at St. Anthony's.

"Duh. A couple of people in the All-Anon group have had family members commit suicide. I found it helpful."

"Getting over your mom?" I asked, though I knew her death was not a suicide.

He nodded. "Some people think suicide is the ultimate form of selfishness and, as you met her a couple of years ago, you know my mother thought what she wanted was all that mattered."

It was my turn to nod. "Hey. Whatever happened to your dad?"

"No clue. Thought he might hear about her death and contact me, but no dice."

I was about to ask him if he really wanted to see his father when Lucas walked back into the kitchen.

"Still ticked off?" Scoobie asked, in a casual tone.

"I'm not ticked off," he responded in an angry tone.

"Sure you're not," I said, but I smiled at him and he gave a grudging smile back.

"I can't tell you what to do," Scoobie said, "but if I were you, I'd give the mental health stuff a break for a while. Take her to a movie, or to buy some new clothes. You have a little money, right?"

Lucas nodded. "She'll need an outfit for prunes."

"She has been in there awhile," I said.

I crutched the short distance to the bathroom door. The shower was running full tilt. "You getting super clean in there?"

No response. It suddenly occurred to me that, given the size of my hot water tank, the shower water would be ice cold by now. Without knocking I pushed open the door.

Kim was gone and the window curtains danced merrily in the light breeze.

HALF AN HOUR later, after running through the neighborhood, Lucas sat at my kitchen table with his head resting on his folded arms. "Why? Why would she do that?"

Scoobie was in the doorway in his scrubs, and I knew he had to leave. "It's okay," I said to him.

"No, it's not!" Lucas started to sob.

I touched his shoulder. "I meant Scoobie could go to work. You and I can figure out what to do next."

Scoobie walked to Lucas and gave him a guy kind of pat on the shoulder, winked at me, and left.

I kept a hand on Lucas's shaking shoulder, and after a few more seconds his sobs began to subside. "I'm sorry we're so much trouble," he said, choking back more sobs.

I pushed the napkin holder to him. "We'll figure it out. She knows good places to hide, so she won't let us find her quickly. When I get out of the shower we'll talk about what to do."

Lucas sat up and blew his nose, careful to turn so I wouldn't see his red eyes.

As I shampooed my hair in the tepid shower water, I thought about places Kim could hide. It was only in the upper forties or low fifties at night, so it would have to either have heat or she had to have a warm sleeping bag. Since her stuff was all stolen at some point, that pointed to the former.

But where she is isn't really the issue. I'd learned enough from Scoobie over the last three years to know that it was the why that mattered when it came to how people acted. Nothing could be changed without addressing what was really wrong. Why wouldn't Kim get medication or counseling? Had she tried an anti-depressant that made her feel worse? I knew that could happen, usually only briefly, and then the medicine had its intended effect. But if she was the one feeling worse, she wouldn't want to stay on medicine long enough to see whether she would feel better in a week.

I finished blow-drying my hair and getting dressed in the bathroom. When I was finally done, I was alone in the house. I went to the kitchen and mentally thanked Lucas for doing the dishes. *Always Mr. Responsibility.*

There was a note on the kitchen table. "I know you're right. When I find her the first thing out of my mouth will be *no meds,* and then I'll ask her what movie she wants to see. I'll be back tonight, with or without Kim."

I sighed, with a sense of relief. I knew it was selfish, but I didn't really know how to help Lucas or Kim, in the emotional sense, anyway.

As I swung my foot away from the spot where I'd stood to read the note, my foot collided with a kitchen chair and I cursed. Jazz meowed from the kitchen doorway. I wiped away the kind of instinctive tears that come from sudden pain and regarded her. "Where have you been? Usually it's only Pebbles who hides." She meowed in seeming agreement and walked to the fridge.

"Okay." I opened the door and pulled out a half-eaten can of cat food for her and raw veggies for Pebbles. "Pebbles. I'm not crawling under the bed with your food." I could hear her gently walking across my bedroom floor, and she came into the kitchen as nonchalantly as if she had planned her visit. She ignored me and went straight for her food.

When I had been surprised by Pebbles' sudden appearance last spring, I had no idea what to feed her. It turns out there is pet food for skunks, and she can also eat certain raw vegetables. More important, she and Jazz get along well. Jazz had been lonely without her two playmates, Aunt Madge's retrievers, Mister Rogers and Miss Piggy.

I took the Ocean Alley phone book from a kitchen drawer, tossed it on the table, and crutched over to sit with my foot on the table. I was tired of crutches, whether one or two. Annoyed that my ankle still would not bend, I put in a call to Dr. Birdbaum's office.

CHAPTER ELEVEN

AFTER A LECTURE from Dr. Birdbaum's nurse about waiting a week before I called with questions, she relayed his opinion that there was enough pain that I could not force myself to wiggle the almost-immobile ankle, and a physical therapist could massage and move it for me. The therapist could also teach me some exercises to do at home. While I generally like a massage, having someone force my ankle to move did not sound like fun.

Since crutches are less fun, I discussed the matter with my health insurance company, a process that required me to be on hold three times during a ten-minute conversation. I got an appointment quickly because someone cancelled. *Imagine that? I'm having good luck for something medical.*

I SAT WITH MY FOOT resting on the arm of the chair next to me as I filled out forms in the PT waiting area. Most dealt with my injury, but some were designed to find out if there would be insurance companies or lawyers arguing about who would pay. "Were any other individuals involved in your accident? If yes, please provide contact information, including an email address."

Oh yeah. That would be Jane Doe of Woodland Gardens.

When I passed her the papers, the receptionist said it would be another fifteen minutes before I was seen. I tried to hide my irritation in a smile. They were seeing me on short notice. I crutched to the water fountain and did not lean over until I was certain I wouldn't get splashed in the face.

The clunk of a can hitting the metal bottom of a soda vending machine drew my attention to an alcove about three meters away. I started for it, intending to get a Dr. Pepper, but voices stopped me.

"No one will say anything. How are we supposed to feel safe?" The speaker was a woman, and she sounded fairly young.

An older woman's voice continued the conversation. "I went to the HR office to see if they were hiring more security. They said they were installing more cameras."

The first woman's tone was exasperated. "We're supposed to work a thirty-six hour week instead of forty and see the same number of patients, but they can't hire a couple more security guards?"

"Ms. um, Gentle?" The voice was behind me, and I turned so quickly that I almost toppled into the wall.

I crutched a couple of paces toward him so the women would not realize I'd been standing right outside the alcove listening to them. "It's pronounced Zhan-tee, it's French. But please call me Zho-lee."

The therapist was older than I expected, perhaps fifty-five or sixty. I was anticipating someone who looked more like a fitness trainer at a club that advertised on television. "Thanks. I've seen your name, but I don't think we've met. I'm Bob Ellis, and I'll do your assessment."

He led me to a tiny room that had only two chairs and a massage-type table. "You told the receptionist something about a deer and stomping on the brakes?"

I told my story again, and he smiled as I finished. "Did the deer send flowers?"

"If it did they went to the wrong address."

"Hop on the table and take off your shoe and sock and lets have a look." He made a couple of notes on a computer tablet as he spoke.

Even though the table was low, hopping did not seem a good option. I set the crutches against a wall, leaned against the table, and pulled myself onto it. Then I took off my shoe and sock and stretched my leg out, placing the swollen foot at one edge of the table.

Bob sat on a small, round stool with wheels and touched my foot lightly. "Hmm. Okay, I'm going to gently feel around your ankle. It might not feel good, but it shouldn't be really painful." He started gently poking me. "You still have a lot of swelling. How does that feel?"

"I don't like it, but it's not…yikes!" He had pushed on the lump at the joint where my leg merged with the foot.

"Yes. That anterior talo-fibular ligament can be touchy."

You don't have to tell me that. "Can you fix it?"

"I think we can help you out. It's kind of hard to inflict pain on yourself. I'll help you get it more limber and then teach you some exercises. I'll put some moist heat on it for a few minutes, then I'll massage a bit, then follow with a cold pad. Just lie back."

While he went to get his hot pack or whatever it was, I stared at the ceiling and wondered if he knew anything about the murder or any suspects. *Why would he? You never know. If you don't ask you could be missing an opportunity.*

Bob came back before I could decide which part of the mental argument won. As he carefully put the moist heated pad around my ankle, my natural curiosity won out. "That was a shame about Tanya Weiss."

His expression grew guarded. "I read that you found her. When I saw your name on the chart, I wondered if this was maybe an injury from that night."

"It was, but I did it before I came to the hospital. Did you know her?"

"Oh, she spent some time down here." His tone was noncommittal.

"It sounded as if she had a tough job, cutting costs and all."

"She was some kind of workforce efficiency expert. I think she actually liked it." This time there was a slight edge to his voice.

"I have a few friends who work here." *That should give Scoobie enough cover.* "Their departments were getting some equipment cuts."

"I'll be back in a couple of minutes." He gave a tight smile as he left.

I had probably gone too far and it made him uncomfortable. Or maybe he left because there was no reason for him to stay in the room while the moist heat did its job. I spent the next ten minutes thinking about how to be more tactful, and not succeeding.

Bob came back in and pulled the rolling stool to the bottom of the table. "Ready for a work out?"

"If you say so."

He began to gently massage around my ankle and then the top and bottom of my foot. "You have an injury to the top of your foot, but you haven't been using any of your foot muscles for days, so you're going to have some strengthening exercises to do."

"Listen, I'm sorry I asked you questions about…"

"It's no problem. I can definitely see why it would be on your mind." He worked for another few seconds, and added, "We were about to order three recumbent bikes. Had the budget approved. Supposedly that's on hold because of her recommendations."

"Can't you make a case that they're for, what would you call it, direct patient care?"

He smiled as he worked the bottom of my foot. It tickled.

"In theory, almost everything relates to that. It wouldn't be so bad if there was a clear reason for the cutbacks. It's," he paused, "it's like changing the rules in the middle of the ball game."

"I can see where that would make people angry, but it's hard to see it as a motive for murder."

I don't think the extra hard rub was because I said that.

I SAT ON MY couch with an ice pack. This time it was to reduce inflammation from my workout, as Bob had put it. I glanced through the several pages of exercise that he had printed for me.

Ankle rotation. I took the cold wrap off and started to do it, then remembered I was supposed to wrap a warm towel around my foot for a couple of minutes before I started. *How complicated can toe wiggling be?*

I didn't feel like getting the couch wet or sitting on the edge of the tub, so I began rubbing my ankle and foot sort of like Bob did. I could already bend my ankle some, and the swelling had gone down a bit since he had worked on it. Something about dispersing fluid build-up.

The key in the door announced either Scoobie or Lucas. "Hi, guy."

A dejected Lucas came in, collapsed on the rocker, and put his head in his hands. "She's gone. Just gone."

I wanted to jump up and cradle his head, but that was out of the question, so I let him cry for almost a minute. As his sobs subsided, I said, "She may not want to listen to you, but she'll only get as far as ten dollars will take her, Lucas. She'll be back." When he looked at me, I smiled slightly and added, "Maybe this time we should have Scoobie and me in the living room with the shades up and you in the kitchen."

He stared at me for a second, and then acknowledged me with a shrug. "What should I do?"

"You have to understand. You may love her and want to protect her, but she's going to make her own choices. Some of them may be bad."

"I didn't know you listened in the meetings." Scoobie had come in through the unlocked door, so I hadn't heard him. He stood next to Lucas, and stared at me for several seconds.

"I was channeling you."

Lucas looked between us. "What *are* you talking about? This doesn't help find Kim!"

Scoobie squatted in front of Lucas. "Actually, it might make her more willing to find us." He stood. "Come on. We're going out."

I looked at the clock on the wall. It was almost time for the evening Twelve Step meetings at Saint Anthony's. Scoobie goes at least weekly and alternates mostly between AA, NA, and Codependents Anonymous. I go, much less often to the All-Anon meeting, which is for anyone who has a family member or friend with any kind of addiction or compulsion. Scoobie and George consider my ex-husband's gambling to be what Scoobie calls a starting point for me, though he says they should create one called Controllers Anonymous just for me.

"Where are we going?" Lucas asked, standing. He pulled a paper towel from the pocket of his jacket and blew his nose.

"I'll tell you on the way," Scoobie said, and pointed at me. "Your car okay?"

"Of course."

Scoobie picked up the keys from a small table by the front door, and I listened to them going toward my car. Lucas would either begin to learn to let go of what he couldn't control, or he'd rage at Scoobie. I'd find out soon enough.

Still, someone should look for Kim. "Crud." I didn't have my car. Maybe Megan would take me to Step 'n Go.

Megan's tone reminded me of the one I've heard her use when Scoobie wants to play a prank at Harvest for All. "They won't let you in."

"Not even to look for Kim?"

"Especially not to look for Kim. It's for the kids."

"Yes, but…"

"No buts, Jolie. Besides, Alicia has one of the photos. Sergeant Morehouse brought it to Harvest for All and asked me to give it to her. If Kim is there, Alicia will see her."

"Will she call me?"

"Only if she thinks the girl is in immediate trouble. And maybe not even then if she thinks it'll make Kim run. You need to put some faith in Alicia and let go of what you can't control, Jolie."

What an overused concept. I just wanted to help.

CHAPTER TWELVE

A HARD KNOCK ON the front door woke me on Wednesday. As I swung my feet to the floor of my bedroom I heard someone else open the door enough to peer out through the chain, then heard the chain being released.

"Lucas up?"

Sergeant Morehouse? Uh oh.

"He will be now," Scoobie said. "Come on in."

I put on my bathrobe, thankful that I could put at least a little weight on my injured foot, and crutched to my bedroom door.

"Did you find Kim?" Lucas asked.

"Kim? Your sister? You ain't found her yet?" Morehouse asked.

"Have a seat," Scoobie said, and I heard Morehouse walk into the living room.

"I kinda did, but she left again." Lucas had been sleeping on an air mattress on the floor, behind the screen Roland of the Purple Cow had provided. I could tell Lucas had moved closer to the couch.

I crutched through the hallway toward the kitchen. "I'll start coffee."

"We'll keep keepin' an eye out for her. I need to talk to you about the hospital."

I could envision Lucas with his mulish expression.

"I told you all I remember," Lucas said.

"Yeah, but I want you to walk through there with me. Somethin' might come to you." Morehouse was being a lot more polite than he sometimes was with me. He must really want the help.

"I have to look for my sister."

There was a brief pause, then Scoobie said, "They can't release health info, but if she's been in the cafeteria or something she might be on tapes there. They wouldn't show you, but they might show the sergeant."

The coffee had started to perk, and I thought I would contribute more by staying out of the way. I took down four mugs from the cabinet over the sink.

"Okay, sure." Lucas' tone sounded anything but compliant. "Let me pull on some clothes and brush my teeth."

The bathroom door shut, and I peered out of the kitchen, toward the living room, so I could hear better.

Scoobie spoke in a low voice. "She was here briefly yesterday, but her judgment may not be the best now. She left out the bathroom window."

"Suicidal?" Morehouse asked this in an even quieter voice.

"Hard to know." Scoobie looked toward the bathroom. "Do you have Lucas' mobile number, in case you see her?"

The bathroom door opened, and Lucas met my gaze as he started to walk back into the living room. I blew him a kiss, and he ignored me.

"I'll get it," Morehouse said.

Lucas looked as if he could bite a shark, so I chimed in. "Coffee's ready. Anyone for toast with PB to eat on the road?"

"Got paper cups?" Morehouse asked. He was staying in the living room, probably so he didn't have to talk to me when I was in PJs.

"Sure, I save Burger King coffee cups," I said.

"Used paper cups?" Morehouse muttered.

"I wouldn't go there," Scoobie said, and I could hear the humor in his voice.

I popped two pieces of bread in the toaster and smelled it cook as I poured two cups of coffee and fastened the lids. I got the idea of saving the cups from Ramona's Uncle Lester, who is nothing if not cheap. I don't keep them if they have coffee rings in them.

Lester would have taken me to the teen hangout last night. Why didn't I think of that?

Lucas walked in, took down the peanut butter jar, and spread it on the two pieces of toast. He put the pieces together, like a sandwich, and wrapped them in a paper towel.

"You can carry in the coffee, too," I said. I knew Morehouse took his black, and Lucas could do whatever he wanted with his.

"I'll catch you later," he said, without looking at me.

A minute later Sergeant Morehouse and Lucas were pulling away and Scoobie walked into the kitchen. He had on an old pair of sweats and a Harvest for All tee shirt that was maybe a size too small. I glanced at him for a second, and then looked back at the coffee I was pouring. *When did he get such broad shoulders?*

"Have you been working out?"

He picked up an empty mug, added water, and stuck it in the microwave for his decaf coffee. "The hospital has an employee gym and I can use it when I'm interning there. Trying to build up the old back muscles."

Scoobie injured his back a couple of years ago. Rather, someone injured it for him. "I keep forgetting about that."

"I try to. I'll get my coffee in a sec."

He headed for his room and I high-tailed it to the bathroom, aware that my cheeks were flushed. *What is that about?*

I DIDN'T HAVE a house to appraise and I could not walk around to look for Kim. I kept wondering whether their father's long-ago enemies really would hurt Lucas and Kim.

I wanted to check out their father, assuming I could find anything. I fired up my laptop and started with a search for their mother's obituary. I knew her first name when it was Finch, but Lucas had never mentioned either parent's first name as Householders. My guess was that this was not deliberate. To him they were simply Mom and Dad.

It was not hard to find an Atlanta area obituary for someone with their last name. Annette Householder had been fifty-two, and there was no cause of death noted. Though it was more common to note a cause than it was years ago, the obit had one of the codes for suicide, noting that she had died "suddenly, at home."

There was not a lot to learn. Her fictitious parents were said to be Martin and Maureen Boyle, who predeceased her. While she had sisters in real life, the obit said she had had only a brother who died in infancy. I studied her photo. It was not large, but her face was easily identifiable as the Elizabeth Finch I had known, and I suppose whoever she was before then. I hoped the sisters she missed so much had seen her.

It was the survivor information that interested me. Husband Douglas and daughter Kim - of the home - lived in Atlanta, while son Lucas lived in Sandy Springs, one of the city's suburbs. The only personal information about Annette was that "after high school she worked as a receptionist before her children were born," and she enjoyed flower arranging.

How sad. Elizabeth Finch had seemed to be a good-humored woman. She could have graduated from a prestigious university and been a noted economist, or gone to Julliard and had stage roles on Broadway. Instead, life for the Finches and Householders was about keeping low profiles.

A Google search for Douglas Householder and Atlanta turned up only his mention in his wife's obituary. No Facebook page, not even a telephone directory listing. I conjured his face. When he was Nicholas Finch he had been a good-looking man, with jet-black hair, though he had always seemed kind of nervous. That had made sense once I learned he had been in the Witness Security Program. I hadn't thought much about any of the Finches after I returned to Lakewood for my senior year of high school.

I decided to visit my favorite haunt for digging up information, the Ocean Alley Library. I cleaned Jazz's litter box, which was under the sink in the bathroom, and tackled Pebbles', which beckoned from its spot in the coat closet.

I had just dumped both plastic bags in the trash can next to my back porch when the sound of Pebbles' nails on the floor reached me. She waddled into the kitchen and I shook a finger at her. "You don't have to go as soon as I clean your box." She expressed her disagreement by walking into the closet.

"Sheesh." I gave Jazz a pat as she sat on her carpet-covered stand near the window. I could put a little weight on my foot, but not enough to abandon my crutches. I slung my purse over my shoulder and made my way to the library. It is not a large building, and looks very different than when I went to eleventh grade in Ocean Alley. In addition to bright hues on the walls, the large wooden card catalogs have been replaced by a bank of computers. Two are to search the collection, and the rest are for Internet use.

Aunt Madge does not have Internet in the B&B. She maintains her guests come to get away from the real world. I used to check email at the library or Java Jolt, the coffee house where we all hang out, but not since I had Internet installed in my bungalow. Now I mostly come to the library to look at back issues of the *Ocean Alley Press* or other local publications. Or talk my former classmate, Librarian Daphne, into posting flyers about a Harvest for All fundraiser.

She greeted me with her typical half-breezy, half-skeptical look. "What are you up to today, Jolie?"

"I'm not *up to* anything."

She smiled. "I'm not sure I believe you when you're that definite about it."

"That's not nice." I returned her smile, but was careful not to say what I was doing. How do you explain looking for information on a family that lived in Ocean Alley less than one year and moved away twelve years ago? And, by the way, was in the witness security program, or whatever it was called.

It was Annette Householder's flower arrangement hobby that had piqued my interest. Ocean Alley has a Master Gardener group. Most of its members are older, people who became gardening enthusiasts after they retired. There are always a few younger members, and I hoped she had been one.

The Master Gardeners do a spring plant sale and a fall bulb sale. At both they sell beautiful arrangements of cut flowers, and Aunt Madge always buys something for the entry hallway at the Cozy Corner. I'm not big on cut flowers, probably since I'm too lazy to grow my own and don't generally want to pay store prices for bouquets. Besides, my bungalow is too small for floral displays.

What I was looking for was the Master Gardeners' newsletter, which I knew about because the club distributes it to real estate offices. It's published at irregular intervals, but at least a few times each year. Most of the photos are of plants, but occasionally there is a group picture of members or a photo of someone in their home garden.

Copies of local newsletters or activities of groups such as Lions and Rotary are in what's called a vertical file, which means they are in a file cabinet in the library's reference section. That made my search a bit more obvious than when I look at old microfilm of the *Ocean Alley Press.* I reminded myself that no one cared what I looked at, it just felt that way because I didn't want to be noticed.

Files are alphabetical, of course, but if the first word is *the* or *Ocean Alley,* then the material is filed by the more specific name. Ocean Alley Master Gardeners was filed under M. It was a thick file, and a couple of newspaper clippings fell out as I retrieved the material.

I put the file on a table far from the reference desk and retrieved the clippings. It took about fifteen minutes to organize things by date, and I didn't hear Daphne when she first walked up.

"Girl, you are concentrating," she said.

I thought fast. "Oh, I am. I'm, uh, looking for examples of gardens that have things that grow well at the beach."

Daphne's look of suspicion lifted. "There are a bunch of articles about that in those files. Are you going to start with what your aunt has at the B&B?"

Aunt Madge has flowers? Of course she did. I weeded the patches a bunch of times when I lived there. I mostly remembered bushes. Azaleas, I thought.

"You know, those decorative grasses that grow well in soil that's part sand," Daphne continued.

"Right. I was hoping for some color, though."

She started to reply and then there was a ding from the front desk. *Saved by the check-out bell.* That would keep me from pretending I knew about flowers other than tulips and marigolds. I'd have to remember to actually plant something in my small patch of front yard.

I was most interested in the newsletters, but tried to be careful to keep all of the items in their approximate chronological order. The Finches had moved to Ocean Alley the summer before my junior year, and left before the end of that school year. It wasn't a long span of time, and I wasn't surprised to find no mention of Elizabeth Finch. I stood, ready to refile the material when I thought to check a couple of issues after they left. Photos weren't published immediately.

And there she was, in the May newsletter, just as my junior year was ending. The caption read, "Elizabeth Finch shows her variety of spring flowers." She was kneeling on the brick path that led to their front door, and on either side of her was an array of daffodils, tulips, and hyacinths. I hadn't remembered her flowers, but I usually went in the kitchen door.

My eyes went to her face. She literally beamed happiness. I could imagine a transplanted Elizabeth realizing she could find happiness in her new identity and anticipating a summer of planting flowers and maybe harvesting vegetables. None of that came to fruition.

I wondered if the newsletter had contributed to the Finch family's discovery and quick removal from Ocean Alley. But it appeared after they left. No one would have seen it before then.

Daphne looked over my shoulder. "I don't think I know her."

I kept from jumping in surprise. "I used to babysit for her kids. They moved even before eleventh grade ended."

"She's really pretty," Daphne said. "So are her flowers."

"Hard to really see in this photo," I said, trying to pretend I knew what I was talking about.

"Master Gardeners and Lions were the first two local groups to have websites. Maybe the newsletters are there."

I turned to look fully at Daphne, who was standing just behind my right shoulder. "Great idea. Thanks."

"Sure." She walked toward the stacks with a few books she was probably reshelving.

I put the large folder back in the vertical file and signed onto one of the computers with Internet access. There was no line of patrons waiting for one, so I'd be able to look as long as I wanted.

After a couple of quick searches I came to the local group's website. The Master Gardeners were colorful in every sense. There was every kind of flower, and a man who figured prominently in several photos from ten years ago had on a tee shirt with a huge peace sign. A woman wore a Support Our

Troops shirt. *Not mutually exclusive.* Even so, I bet their meetings had talk about more than flowers.

Finally I figured out the link to past newsletters. Elizabeth Finch was in two newsletters. One in late fall had her demonstrating how to condition the soil so bulbs would do well in the partially sandy soil. That explained why her garden was featured so prominently after she moved.

Elizabeth Finch did not keep a low profile in her garden club. I wondered if the fall picture had helped lead the bad guys, as Lucas called them, to her family. It seemed far-fetched. However, if whoever they were had people who read obituaries, why not web pages? If they knew the Finches' hobbies, maybe they did some targeted searching.

Daphne was right about the Lions being the only other Ocean Alley club with a strong web presence when the Finch family lived here. No Nicholas Finch that I could find. Even if he did belong to a group, my guess was that he would have been much more circumspect about his participation.

I picked up my purse to leave, and then remembered that Mr. Finch sold cars in his life before Ocean Alley. I didn't know what he did when they lived in Ocean Alley. He wouldn't have been in the same profession, but maybe he did something with cars. I had a vague memory of antique cars being displayed at some local dealerships, and maybe the county fair. *Surely he wouldn't have been that dumb?*

An Internet search found the Ocean Alley Old Time Car Club, but the only other car-related organization was Triple A. In a spurt of rational thought, I decided to be satisfied with what I had found. For a while, anyway.

THAT EVENING, LUCAS told me about his walk through the hospital with Sergeant Morehouse, complete with several comments about how it had been a waste of time. "He kept asking me to think about whom I saw when I was in different parts of the hospital. I know it's important, and I get why. But I was totally focused on Kim. I wish I hadn't noticed that woman's cape."

"What do you mean?" I asked.

"He thinks because I noticed the cape that I paid attention to a lot of other stuff."

I smiled. "The sergeant is persistent."

"That's mild."

"It's a trait you should recognize. While you are so persistently looking for Kim, do you check with your dad to see if he's heard from her?"

"He promised he'd call if he did." Lucas' tone said to not discuss the topic further.

I didn't want to talk about Kim. I wanted to hear more about Douglas Householder, and looked for a way to bring the conversation to him. "You said you worked in a hospital, but I don't think you said what your dad does now."

Lucas looked as if he didn't see why I cared, but he answered anyway. "He had to do something really different than selling cars, of course."

"Oh, sure."

"He got trained to be a plumber before we came to Ocean Alley. Mom hated that because his clothes got dirty. When we went to Atlanta, he kept track of inventory in a department store. Mom liked that." Lucas shrugged. "We got discounts."

"Sounds like a good deal. You know, it occurred to me, I wouldn't know how to contact your father."

Scoobie's voice came from his bedroom, where he was studying. "Why would you need to?"

Lucas grinned at me. "Yeah, why?"

I feigned total surprise that they questioned my motive. "You're healthy, but if...your appendix burst or something, I don't know who to call."

Scoobie grunted, still staying in his room.

I looked at Lucas. "You can leave it in a sealed envelope in the kitchen if you want."

"I'll put it in a safe deposit box and give Scoobie the key."

HE DIDN'T, OF COURSE. Thursday morning I found Douglas Householder's name, address, and home phone number on a card on the kitchen table. I copied it into my address book, but called the name Douglas Sandman.

I had showered and was getting an apple from the fridge to take with me, when I saw someone had added a note to the card. "You forgot his blood type." Scoobie's handwriting, of course.

CHAPTER THIRTEEN

I DROVE to Harry's home office to work on a report and check for new requests for appraisals. My mind would not concentrate on work. What did I really know about the murder? Nothing, except that Tanya Weiss was still dead and Lucas had been in the hospital at the time but still couldn't find Kim.

I had begun to think that there was not a likely connection between Kim coming to Ocean Alley and irate mobsters - or whomever - looking for her father. So they knew her mom died, and maybe even knew that she had more or less run away from home. So what?

Once they had seen the obit, whoever was mad at Douglas Householder could probably have gotten at him anytime they wanted to. And if they wanted to use Kim as some kind of leverage, her behavior had been so erratic it would almost make it easier to find her.

That doesn't make sense. Yes it does. No routine, so no one to notice if she doesn't make it home, or wherever. In a way, Kim had made it easier to find her. And Lucas made no secret of his search for her. Bad guys sophisticated enough to find the Householders because of the mom's obituary would have more resources to search for Kim than Lucas had.

I let myself into Harry's house and was greeted by its now usual cold silence. Within a few seconds, the fax machine rang and started to spit out paper. The person most likely to send a fax about a potential appraisal, rather than an email, was Ramona's Uncle Lester. He'd finally graduated to a smart phone, but I'd seen him in Java Jolt trying to respond to a text and figured he'd stick with fax machines for a while.

The words were pure Lester. "Harry, you old fart. The Watkins' place is worth seven grand more than your dim glasses could see. You need to send Jolie back over there."

Lester knew I had done the appraisal, but he doesn't like to criticize me directly. Scoobie says it's because Lester wants me to say yes if he gets up the courage to ask me out. I think he simply doesn't want to argue with me. Harry is more polite.

I took the fax and wrote on it, "Are you guaranteeing the mortgage for the bank?" and faxed the page back to him.

The microwave hadn't finished warming the water for my instant coffee when the office phone rang. Without looking at caller ID I picked up the receiver and said, "Hello, Lester."

Ramona laughed. "My dear uncle called me to see if you're mad at him. If you tell him you are, he might quit sending those faxes."

Someone near Ramona said, "Excuse me, Miss?" She said she was at work and had to help a customer.

I let Lester stew for a few minutes and then called him on his cell. He's rarely in his office. It's a small space on the second floor of a two-story building with no elevator. He meets most customers at Burger King, or occasionally Java Jolt. Owner Joe Regan discourages the latter because Lester buys one cup of coffee and sits there for hours.

"I'm not mad, Lester, but I can't say the house is worth more than the comps will support. Unless you know of some recent sales that I didn't find."

"What about the Riordan place?" he asked.

"You have to be kidding. That was more than two years ago, and it has one thousand more square feet."

"Yeah, but the bank don't know that."

"Lester, they do. Plus, neither Harry nor I want to lose our appraisal credentials for overestimating a house's value by so much. You're just going to have to earn less of a commission."

After a couple more wildly off-base suggestions, Lester hung up. I sent Harry an email and told him he was lucky to miss Lester's fax, and suggested that Harry look again at my conclusions in case there was a chance Lester was right. Two minutes later Harry sent back an email that was a comic book-style skunk laughing hysterically. Didn't sound as if he planned to look at the appraisal for himself.

I finished entering data into the appraisal software and studied the floor plans it created for me. I love that graph paper and pencil erasures are no longer part of an appraisal.

When I was satisfied that the drawing was accurate and I had selected pictures to put in the appraisal package, I turned my attention to that night's Harvest for All Committee meeting.

I have learned to develop a detailed agenda or Scoobie, who drafted himself onto the committee a year or so ago, will hijack the meeting with some crazy fundraising idea. The varied personalities mean meetings are enough of a balancing act as it is.

Sylvia Parrett and Monica Martin are in their mid-sixties. Sylvia is a very rigid person, but she's also a hard worker. With her buttoned-up cardigans and low voice, Monica can only be described as mousy. Though they work as hard as anyone for the food pantry, they are the two least likely to get Scoobie's humor. Monica does not try to put down Scoobie's ideas though, which Sylvia occasionally does.

I know I shouldn't have favorites, but Lance Wilson, our treasurer, has become a dear friend. *Who knew I would have a friend more than sixty years older than I am?*

Aretha Brown used to be our only black member, and I asked her to help me find someone else of her complexion, as she translated my request. I know who's black and who isn't, but I also know people are more likely to join a group if they see a friend is in it. I have lots of black friends, but the close ones are in Lakewood. I was almost embarrassed that the person Aretha asked was Daphne, whom I'd known since high school. I figured that as the librarian, Daphne was asked to be on lots of committees and would say no.

Megan Ortiz was our most recent member before Daphne. It took me a couple of tries to convince her that what she knew as our most regular pantry volunteer was invaluable. Her daughter Alicia doesn't come to meetings, but she helps at every event and in a pinch can be counted on for a shift at the pantry. More important, she gets her friends to help at fundraisers.

All of us respect the retired Dr. Welby, who at times acts like our de facto chair. He speaks in a kind of formal baritone, whether he's telling someone not to make fun of his name or cajoling money from a business. He's really good at asking busy people to help us.

I went over fundraising ideas again. I meant it when I told Mr. Markle that we'd try to help his store get more customers. I was also trying to think of an idea that wasn't so, well, silly. Our spring liquid string contest was not the kind of event everyone will attend.

Plus, we would have the unusual angle of a joint fundraiser with the Shop with a Cop group. Lance said he would back me up on my deal with Sergeant Morehouse. We'd probably do most of the work, since police officers are busier than most of our members, and then we'd have to split the funds. My plan was to say we'd have a lot more publicity because the cops know everyone.

BY THE TIME OF our six o'clock meeting, I'd worked myself into a worry that a couple of members might quit the committee because I'd make the unilateral decision to work with Morehouse and his crew.

We were squeezed into the smaller of two meeting rooms in the basement of First Prez. Thankfully, it wasn't hot outside, and we hadn't had to slug through snow or rain to get to the meeting. People might be in a better mood all the way around.

"Thanks for coming, everybody," I began. No one said anything. "Um, I know it was kind of short notice, but we need to pull in more money than usual this Thanksgiving."

"Or Christmas," Dr. Welby said, in a serious tone.

Damn. He knows, and he doesn't like the idea.

"That, too, of course," I continued. "I was focusing on the first big event."

"Maybe we can patrol the town and come up with ideas," Sylvia said.

After another second of silence they all started to laugh.

"We got you," Monica said.

I leaned back in my chair and let out a breath. "Did Scoobie arrange this?"

"He did not," Sylvia said, as Scoobie walked in.

"No, but I said I'd stay in the hall until they finished giving you grief. I'd never have kept a straight face."

"It was Monica's idea," Lance said.

"Oh, dear." She looked stricken.

"Don't worry, Monica, I don't believe it."

"It was mine," Aretha said. "I like the idea of working with Shop with a Cop. I try to get a couple kids at the community center to participate in that, but they say it isn't cool. If we have an interesting fundraiser, maybe they'll come to that and get to know a couple of cops."

"Now, what ideas do we have?" boomed Dr. Welby.

"We'll do the treasurer's report first," Lance said, and began his recitation.

I glanced at Scoobie and he silently mouthed, "Not me this time." I rolled my eyes at him.

I took the chair role back from Dr. Welby. "It would be a good idea if whatever we do places some kind of spotlight on Mr. Markle's store. He said business is down after that robbery."

"Does he still give a discount if people say they are buying food to donate to us?" Sylvia asked.

"At designated times," I said.

"My sorority raffles off big baskets of goodies, even if it's not the main part of one of our fundraisers." Daphne thought for a second. "We could give a raffle a lot of publicity and get a few prizes from local businesses. And say Mr. Markle will give people a discount if they donate a food basket and buy the contents at the In-Town Market."

"And they can get all their ingredients for the bake sale there," Monica threw in.

"Those would work," Scoobie said, "but Alicia and I had an idea that would get a lot of free publicity."

The group was too polite to do a collective groan, but Lance did ask, "Is there any risk of falling at this one?"

"You'd have to try pretty hard," Scoobie said.

"I'll have my orthopedist friends on stand-by," Dr. Welby said, dryly.

"Have you guys heard about the big craze for bean bag game contests? Only the bags are filled with corn, and they have to be an exact size."

"You mean like at the Saint Anthony's carnival, a clown with holes where the eyes and mouth go?" Sylvia asked.

"Not hardly," Aretha said, and she gave Scoobie a grim smile. "The boxes they throw into are made to exact measurements, and slanted off the ground, not upright. A couple corporate groups I know have competitions, paint their boxes in company colors, things like that."

"Do we have to make the boxes?" Lance asked.

"You can buy them plain, and paint them, or use them plain," Aretha said.

Daphne said, "Maybe we can generate publicity by having a day to paint them."

From the looks Aretha and Scoobie exchanged, I felt as if I wasn't getting something. Plus, I had a lot of questions. "Where do you get the corn, and are there patterns to make the bags?"

"Seed corn," Megan said. "And they have to be six inches by six inches and weigh the same. We'll have to be the ones to supply the bags."

"And Alicia and her friends would help?" Dr. Welby asked.

"Oh yes," Megan said. "She and Scoobie had the idea. Alicia and her friends are looking forward to it."

We set the date, which was earlier than I was comfortable with, but the time that was best-suited to everyone's schedules. Before we left, Sylvia agreed to contact local media with the initial information and Aretha said she would take the lead on getting and coordinating volunteers. Dr. Welby was to try to get a few donations to fund what we needed to buy before the event, and I would work with Mr. Markle on making his market a visible part of the event. *What could possibly go wrong?*

"I DON'T GET it," I said. I was driving Scoobie and me back to the bungalow, *our bungalow*. "People seemed to be kind of dancing around a point they didn't want to make."

"I can't imagine what it would be."

"I know your innocent act."

"When it comes to Harvest for All, I'm all business," Scoobie said.

George was sitting on my repainted porch swing when we pulled into my tiny parking area. He walked down the steps. "Where were you guys?"

"Food pantry meeting," Scoobie said. "Come on in. What's up?"

What if I wanted to go to bed early?

We went in and I said, "You want water, there are bottles in the fridge."

I sat on the couch with Scoobie while George grabbed a bottle and then sat in the rocker. He pulled out his thin reporter's notebook. "Okay. I heard there was a second set of proposals for budget cuts at the hospital, and this time it gave names of people to get rid of."

"It says that?" I asked.

"No, Nancy Drew, I haven't seen it, but it would say stuff like *redundant positions* and *opportunities to economize*."

"When did you learn words like that?" Scoobie asked.

"You have no idea how many rubber chickens I've eaten at Chamber of Commerce lunches. Anyway," he quelled a comment from Scoobie with a look, "I think if we could get the proposal we might have a list of murder suspects."

"Seems like between us we should know people to ask," I said, mentally running names though my head.

"Count me out," Scoobie said. "I don't defecate where I eat."

"Nice," I said.

"I'm serious," he continued. "The hospital doesn't have to let students from the college do observations or practicums there. I'm not going around asking a lot of questions about something that's none of my business."

George looked at me.

"I don't know anyone really well, but…maybe Doctor Welby has heard something."

"Your aunt knows everyone…" George began.

"Oh, that'd work," Scoobie said, with obvious sarcasm.

"I wouldn't get three words out," I said. "But I'll try to talk to Dr. Welby tomorrow. You know, it's kind of odd that people seem to assume her recommendations would be implemented. You'd think a consultant or whatever she was would have to give those to the hospital CEO or the Board of Directors. She wouldn't make the decisions."

"Yeah, I'm checking into that."

From George's noncommittal tone, I could tell he knew more than he let on.

I glanced at Scoobie and then spoke to George. "Can you find out who actually decided to hire her? Maybe whoever recommended her knew her work so well they trusted her a lot."

"Or something," George said. Then, he seemed to figure he'd gotten all the help from us that he could, and stood to leave. "How was the Harvest for All meeting? Anything we need to put in the paper?"

"We decided on the next fundraiser," Scoobie said. "A corn holing contest."

From the way George sprayed water, I figured there was some significance to the name.

I looked at Scoobie, who smiled, "You know how I love puns."

George wiped his chin and saw my puzzled expression. "One meaning has to do with, uh, one of your body's orifices."

I put my head in my hands. "How am I going to explain that to Reverend Jamison?"

CHAPTER FOURTEEN

I WOKE UP Friday morning with a tension headache that started at my forehead, traveled down the back of my head, and ended in my neck. Before I went to sleep last night, I started a to-do list for the fundraiser, and it would give anyone a headache. I had put it aside to finish today.

It also bothered me that I couldn't dump much of the work on Sergeant Morehouse. He could drum up volunteers for the day of the Corn Bag Toss (the name we were using), and get cops all over town to spread the word.

But besides the fact that Morehouse was busier than I was, I needed to keep control over tasks like ordering food or making sure we had enough corn bags or the wood boxes with holes. Scoobie's face appeared in my brain, wearing an amused expression. I could hear him say, "Control? Did you say control?"

Okay, if I talk about it out loud I'll use another word. Maybe manage, or supervise. *Who am I kidding? I'll be lucky just to cope.*

BY TWO O'CLOCK I had finished an appraisal and thought I had a good first draft of the to-do list. The next step would be to con Scoobie or Ramona into doing some of it. George has been known to use newspaper deadlines as an excuse for not following through with something, so I decided to reserve him for odd jobs.

<u>Food</u>
Permits from Health Department
Get drink and chip list to Mr. Markle
Check on Monica's bake sale progress

<u>Raffle</u>
Ad in paper for donations and ticket sales
Ask Mr. Markle to sell baskets for silent auction entries

<u>Corn Bag Toss</u>
Get sponsors for toss boxes
Get volunteers to make bags

<u>Publicity</u>
Make Scoobie write press release
Make sure press release is printable

<u>Donations</u>
All $$ donated go directly to Lance to split w Shop w a Cop
Dr. Welby for some pre-event funds

<u>Volunteers</u>
Alicia & friends to haul canned goods, pass out corn bags
See if Aretha needs help with others

I stared ahead of me, trying to think of more things we needed to do. Usually we have more time to plan an event, but our spring fundraiser kind of wore us out and before we knew it October was here, and we were coming up on our biggest distribution season. We needed to do a couple of food drives the two weeks before Thanksgiving, so there wouldn't be time for a big event then. Morehouse had also told me that the police really wanted to "get this out of the way" before Halloween, which he said takes a lot of police resources.

My biggest concern was that we wouldn't have enough time to let people know about the event, but Dr. Welby and Sylvia assured the rest of us that it's the last couple of weeks of publicity that bring in people. I hoped they were right.

I decided to think positive. It was a warm fall day and I was in the parking lot of the huge Farm, Beach, and Home Store outside of Ocean Alley to buy a boatload of seed corn.

My mobile chirped. Aunt Madge! "Hi. I think we've gone two whole days without talking."

"We have. Reverend Jamison just called to see if I needed help with the raffle tickets for the fundraiser. What am I doing that involves raffle tickets?"

I groaned. "I'm sorry. Monica wanted to be in charge of the raffle of baskets of goodies, but we didn't think she could manage it by herself. I should have called when I got up. We came up with all of this only last night."

"Hmmm. I suppose Harry and I can manage, if we don't get too much help from sweet Monica. I'll get some people to find something more to raffle. People can only use so many baskets of candles or chips and salsa."

"Umm. Lance said something about needing a license for a raffle."

"The Catholics probably have one for bingo. I'll find out what I need to know." She hung up.

With a mea culpa ringing in my ears, I went through the sliding doors into the store. A lot of people don't think of New Jersey as having much rural land. We may not be Kansas, but we have more than 700,000 acres of farmland.

Basically, we have thousands of acres of dairy cows and a lot of farmers who plant crops to feed them. I'm expecting methane jokes. The biggest difference between our farmers and their Midwestern counterparts is the size of the farms, which average only about seventy acres in Jersey.

"Can I help you, ma'am?" The speaker was a man about fifty with a weather-beaten face. Usually I take that to mean time at the beach, but his flannel shirt and worn blue jeans implied work on farm, or at least wanting to give that impression.

"You probably can. I work with Harvest for All Food Pantry in Ocean Alley, and we're having a fundraiser soon. I need some seed corn."

He looked more than just perplexed. "Ma'am, it's not the time to plant."

I laughed, really laughed, and for a moment he seemed to take offense. Then he appeared to recognize he was seeing my pressure release valve in action.

"You're so right. And I wouldn't know the first thing about planting corn. Tomato plants, maybe."

His expression relaxed and I continued. "We're having a sort of, um, bean bag contest, but using bags of corn."

"Oh, a corn holing contest." He grinned. "Funny, you look like a nice girl."

I flushed crimson. "We're saying corn toss…"

He grinned more broadly. "I'm just joshin' you. There's some guys at the American Legion who make boxes and bags for those contests."

My face probably registered delight.

"For a fee," he said, quickly.

"I'm not looking for free work, but I'd love to buy the boxes locally, rather than by mail. We have people to make bags."

"Sure. I got one of the guy's phone numbers in the back. I'll get it and then talk to you about the corn."

I followed his progress along the concrete floor and then glanced at the signs at the end of each aisle that showed what was down that aisle. At the far end of the store, the sign that hung from the ceiling said, "Seeds and bulbs." I ambled toward it, figuring the clerk would guess where I'd gone.

It was my first full day with no crutches, and I had a shopping cart in front of me to lean on if I needed it. The combination of high ceilings and concrete floors made the store cold. I pulled the zipper up on my lightweight windbreaker.

I got to the seed aisle and groaned. There were rows of burlap-looking sacks in wood barrels. A maze of signs announced various kinds of corn, soybean seeds, and bulbs for flowers. And more.

"Figured this is where you got to." He handed me a piece of paper and I saw two names and phone numbers.

"I should have introduced myself. I'm Jolie Gentil."

He nodded. "Hal Winder. I thought you looked familiar. That guy who writes for the paper likes to make you look like a goofball."

It's hard to maintain dignity when someone's frame of reference for you is as a goofball, so I decided to simply smile and ignore the comment. "I sure hope you can tell me what to buy. I'm not sure I'd make good picks on my own." *Thus reaffirming I'm a goofball.*

Fifteen minutes later, after being told I didn't need the seed with the best pesticide because it wasn't getting planted, I had two fifty-pound bags of corn seed in my trunk. Plus two rolls of duck cloth fabric, which the store stocked specifically for corn toss bags. According to my new best friend Hal, nothing less durable would last more than a few throws without coming apart.

A late-model dark green sedan followed me out of the store parking lot and back to the highway. I wouldn't have noticed it except that it passed me twice and then fell back. I try not to be too suspicious of people, but it seemed as if the driver wanted to know where I was going but didn't want to consistently drive behind me. If he had, I probably wouldn't have noticed the car.

I had planned to drive straight home, but decided to drive to the courthouse instead. If I went to the police station it could seem obvious that I thought the person was following me - unless they already knew I ended up at the Ocean Alley Police Station more often than most people.

They don't know who you are. It's just somebody who hasn't heard of cruise control.

When I pulled into the courthouse parking lot the car kept going. *There you go, Jolie. You were imagining things.*

I pulled through the lot and went out the other exit. Then I traveled down a side street until turning onto Bay Street and driving the additional block to my house. As I unlocked my front door I thought that the two bags of seed were heavy enough that they'd have to stay in my trunk until someone else could unload them at whatever location we used to sew the corn bags.

Just as I shut the door I saw a green sedan pass the house. Since I can only tell the difference between Volkswagens and big-fin Cadillacs, I couldn't be sure it was the same car. My mind played through various scenarios. Someone looking for Lucas or Kim? Someone who'd heard me talking about a corn hole contest and wanted to meet me?

Get a life.

I GOT UP SATURDAY morning determined to think positive about being able to get everything done before the corn toss contest. There was no reason to assume I'd be overwhelmed. Except maybe that it was how I felt.

I decided not to add to my stress level by mentioning the green car to Scoobie. It was probably nothing, and if he or George got wind of it they'd use it as an excuse to pay more attention to my comings and goings. I had pretty much decided I was imagining that anyone was following me.

By the time I pulled into the In-Town Market parking lot I had talked myself into a better frame of mind. I had a list of supplies we would need for the corn toss and wanted to give Mr. Markle time to order them so we could get the best price. Once the order was placed I'd feel as if I'd accomplished something.

"Morning, Jolie." I looked up to see Mr. Markle behind the customer service counter rather than at the cash register.

"Get some of your help back?" I asked, and laid the list on the counter.

"Yep. Clark and one other high school guy. Their parents didn't like the hours their kids would have to work in a fast-food place."

I glanced over my shoulder. Clark was tidying a display of diapers that sat across from the two cash registers. He noticed me and paused long enough to wave. I turned back to Mr. Markle. "Good. I hope they apologized. The parents, I mean."

"No, but the mother did come in with him when Clark asked if he could reapply for the job. I didn't tell her I never took him off the payroll."

"Smart," I said.

He shrugged. "I was too busy for paperwork. Now, let's see your list."

Mr. Markle reads and thinks fast, so I didn't bother to move away for a minute. I used the thirty seconds to obsess about how much there was to do.

He looked up. "I can get you a better deal on cups if you use foam instead of those heavy paper cups."

"I know." I was proud for not sighing. "Sylvia and Dr. Welby say foam is hard for the environment, so Dr. Welby's donating an extra twenty dollars for supplies."

"Always happy to take more of the doctor's money," he said, and put the list in his shirt pocket. "You want me to hold the stuff until the day before your shindig, right?"

"That would be great. Just let me know what we owe when it comes in, and I'll bring a check to you before the big day."

The mention of Dr. Welby reminded me that I wanted to ask him for names of people at the hospital who might talk to me. I figured he'd be at the golf course outside of town or the Red Cross office, where he has been a medical advisor of some sort since Hurricane Sandy. He wasn't happy with the supply of tetanus booster shots on hand when he volunteered to give shots to people who were cleaning up muck for the first few weeks after the storm. Because he groused about it, the local Red Cross director put him to work as a more regular volunteer.

I gave a grim smile to myself. I hadn't made suggestions for the food pantry, but that hadn't kept Reverend Jamison from requisitioning my help.

When I called his cell, Dr. Welby, probably assuming I wanted to talk about the fundraiser, told me to stop by the Red Cross office.

I waited in the tiny space just inside the front door and amused myself by trying to count the number of pieces of candy corn in a large canning jar on the counter. You could guess the number for free, but there was also a donation jar on the counter, so I guessed 343 and put a dollar in the jar.

"Come on back." Dr. Welby stood at the entrance of the narrow hall. I followed him, and he lowered his voice. "If you win those, don't eat any."

"Why not?"

"I watched one of the kids load the jar," he said and gestured to a card table chair that sat next to his desk. On the desk was a sign that had a list of titles, stacked one on top of the other. Medical advisor, volunteer coordinator, disaster donation coordinator.

"You all share this desk?"

"Not at the same time," he said. "I think it's the director's hint to the local board that we need another desk or two. No idea where we'd put them. What can I do for you?"

I'm used to Dr. Welby's rapid-fire sentences. "I wanted some ideas," I began.

"Don't know much about corn hole contests," he said.

"Corn *toss*," I emphasized. "Not about that. It's about the hospital." He raised an eyebrow. "About whom I can talk to there."

"About what?"

"Well, you know I found that woman's body."

He didn't say anything.

"I want to know who did it."

"Not on my radar." He eyes belied humor. "The police don't want to tell you?"

"Nope. And they've talked to a kid I know a couple of times. I want to be sure he isn't charged with anything." This was not true. I didn't want Lucas charged with Tanya Weiss' death, but I wasn't worried that it would happen.

Dr. Welby was sitting in the kind of office chair that's on wheels. He leaned back in the chair, which squeaked. "I figure it was somebody she was about to lay off. Lots of people didn't like how she did her efficiency studies." He placed air quotes around the last two words.

I leaned forward. "Like who?"

He shrugged. "Everybody. But let's see…the Board probably wouldn't have gone through with it, but I heard she recommended that there be no surgeons on call between midnight and six A.M."

Something nagged in the back of my mind. "So, the hospital wouldn't be able to find someone if a person needed more than stitches?" *Where had I heard someone say that?*

"Several surgeons live in town, of course, but if no one is officially on call, they could all be down in Atlantic City. And of course, people on call get paid a little, so the younger docs would lose a bit of money."

"Why younger ones?"

"They volunteer more to be on call. Helps pay student loans and they hope no one needs them when they're on call."

"Sounds like fire fighters," I mused.

"People die when they can't get either one," Dr. Welby said.

"Good point. So, do you know some of these doctors?"

"Not well. But if I was doing what you want to do, I'd talk to someone who works there full-time. Doctors generally don't."

He paused, thinking. "Maybe, oh, a senior nurse, or what's that guy's name from church?"

"Nelson?"

Dr. Welby snapped his fingers. "That's him. He buys supplies, so he talks to everybody."

I didn't want to say Nelson didn't want to have much to do with me, so I asked, "Anyone else come to mind?"

"Sandra Cartwright goes to First Prez. She's a good charge nurse, and a friend of my wife's." He pointed an index finger at me. "But don't bug them. People who work there have had a lot of stress since the hospital merged with that for-profit group."

I thanked him and sidestepped a request that I attend the next CPR course by saying I'd taken one. Ten years ago, but I didn't say that.

Within a few minutes I had a plan. Reverend Jamison always makes a big pitch for our fundraisers at First Prez the weekend prior to one of our events. A lot of churches do this because they all send people to Harvest for All. I knew this mostly because Lance tells me. I haven't gone to church regularly since my sophomore year of high school. I didn't have some big rift with a minister, I was avoiding a boy I had a crush on who kind of dumped me, and never went back much. Scoobie goes regularly, but to various churches. I'd have to hope he wouldn't be at First Prez this Sunday. He'd figure why I was there and rat me out to Aunt Madge.

CHAPTER FIFTEEN

ON SUNDAY I got up in plenty of time to get ready for the ten-thirty service. Scoobie had gone to Saint Anthony's for the nine o'clock Mass because it was the third Sunday of the month and the Knights of Columbus have a monthly pancake and sausage breakfast.

The last three days had been a balancing act between appraisal work, the fundraiser, and staying aware of Lucas' actions. I didn't want him ending up with some enemy of his father's and me not notice for a day or two.

Lucas was already in the kitchen when I got there and had made coffee.

"You want to come to First Prez with me?"

"You think Kim'll be there?"

"Um, not really. Just thought you might want to do something besides hunt for her."

He shook his head. "I'm going over to Asbury Park today. She's a Bruce Springsteen fan. Maybe she'll want to see where he used to hang out."

I wished him luck, thinking that the town, at least the part that ran along the ocean, looked really different than it did when Springsteen grew up there. It had undergone a couple of economic development attempts, the first somewhat centered around a casino that had gone under. I heard more recent efforts were working out better.

Reverend Jamison knew I planned to be at First Prez. He said that he would direct people to me so they could ask questions about the corn toss as they ate donuts and coffee after the service. I had not mentioned my plans to Aunt Madge, who would accuse me of having an ulterior motive that went beyond publicity for Harvest for All. And would be right.

At the end of the service, I seated myself as far from the donuts as possible and told myself a cup of coffee would sate my hunger pangs. It took about two minutes to figure that no one would seek me out, so I stood and began to move among the eight tables of congregants who had found their way to the community room.

I knew they were familiar with Harvest for All. Since it shared a wall with the room we were in, it would be impossible not to know. I stared at the part of the room opposite of where Aunt Madge and Harry were eating. He had given me a jaunty wave as they sat down, and Aunt Madge a not-so-enthusiastic nod.

The first people to seem interested in the corn toss were a couple in their late twenties or early thirties. The wife looked ready to deliver a baby on their way home, and they promised to come watch the corn toss if they weren't otherwise busy. This brought laughs from two other young couples at their table. They did not promise to attend.

I was trying to make my way to Nelson Hornsby. I thought I knew who Sandra Cartwright was, and saw her several tables away. But Dr. Welby's view was correct. Nelson would know a lot of hospital employees because he organized purchases for every unit in the hospital. He had to have an idea about who hated Tanya Weiss enough to kill her. Besides maybe himself.

The poor man almost escaped my questions, but Reverend Jamison was talking to the woman next to Nelson and it would have seemed rude for him to leave.

"Jolie, you know these folks, right?" Reverend Jamison gestured at the four people at the table.

"I know Nelson, and I bet you're his wife." I leaned across the table to shake her hand.

"Yes, Erica Hornsby. And these are our friends Peter and Arlene Macomb."

I greeted them and slid into a vacant chair next to Nelson. "I know it sounds like a silly fundraiser, but those are the kinds that bring in the most donations."

The four of them asked a couple of polite questions about timing and the location. Then a woman at the next table called to Erica and Arlene and they half-turned to talk to her.

Peter stood and gathered napkins and cups. "I'll take these to the trash. Be right back."

Nelson looked at me, eyebrow half raised.

"I'm sorry to bother you, but the police keep talking to the young man staying with me."

Nelson nodded. "The famous guy in the hoodie."

I forced a smile. "I've known him since he was ten." No need to mention I'd had no idea where Lucas was for years. "I hope they don't really think he killed her, but it's hard on a guy in his early twenties to deal with all the questions. So, I'm asking people if they have any ideas they didn't share with the police." When he seemed about to dismiss me, I added. "I think people will sometimes talk to someone not in law enforcement more easily than to the police."

Nelson frowned and spoke in a low tone. "I know people in every part of the hospital. It would be easier to figure out if anyone *liked* her. It wasn't just what she was tasked to do. She was condescending and thought anyone who worked there didn't have what she called *enough distance* to see how things could be different."

"I heard there is a list floating around of who she specifically recommended be fired."

His tone held barely hidden sarcasm. "No doubt if such a document exists the police have it."

I frowned. "How widely was it distributed?"

"I never saw it, if it even exists." Nelson's wife seemed to have realized our conversation was strained. With a slight pang of guilt when she gave me a puzzled stare, I remembered she was ill.

"I'm bugging your husband," I said. "I shouldn't bother him on a weekend."

At my friendly tone she smiled. "He needs to be bothered." She turned back to her friend as Peter walked back up from trash duty.

I stood. "I'll probably be over there this week. I'll stop in."

A familiar voice next to me said, "No doubt he'll change his locks."

Nelson relaxed as he looked at Aunt Madge. "It's a thought."

I nodded at Nelson and watched Aunt Madge for a second. She was heading for the exit and probably thought I'd follow her. Instead I scanned for Sandra Cartwright. She was putting on a light-weight fall jacket as she said good-bye to a friend she had been sitting with.

I took more time than needed to collect my paper napkins and coffee cup, and tossed them in a trash can and followed Sandra into the hall.

She surprised me by turning her head and smiling at me. "Doctor Welby warned me about you, you know."

I stifled a groan. "He did say he thinks highly of you."

Sandra Cartwright had a laugh that was kind of like a soft wind chime, and the lines on her face were smile creases.

Having apparently seen that Sandra did not consider me a bother, Aunt Madge called, "See you later today, Jolie?"

"Scoobie and I might be over for afternoon bread."

"Bring the kids." She sped up to join Harry.

"You have children?" Sandra asked.

"No. Two young people who used to live in Ocean Alley are staying with me for a few days. Late teens/twentyish." I hoped it would be both of them again soon.

"Ah. Now, as I understand it, you want me to think about possible murder suspects."

We had reached the door that led outside. I leaned forward to push its handle and let her walk out ahead of me. "You could say that. Mostly I'm looking for people who were especially angry with her. Maybe she recommended their jobs be eliminated."

Sandra didn't say anything as we walked a few steps in the parking lot, then she paused and looked at me. "All because someone you know is a suspect?"

I thought fast. No need to tell her Lucas was more of an excuse than a reason to talk to her. "He isn't a suspect yet, but he's been questioned a couple of times. He doesn't have lots of money for a lawyer, and if they call him in again he really would have to hire one." *Sounds good to me. I hope Sandra agrees.*

"And you are sure that person is innocent."

"I think it's more likely I killed her, and I never met her either. Until I found her body, which is another reason I'm...intrigued."

"People talk about how she focused so many of her recommendations on the nursing staff. She did, but in some ways it was not as hard for us as some of the specialty positions."

"Why do you say that?"

"A couple of reasons. We're the largest cohort of hospital employees, and we sort of form our own support group. It was kind of us against Tanya. And there are also lots of other jobs for nurses in town. Or at least within ten miles."

"But not for other people who might have been laid off?"

She nodded. "I've heard, no verification of course, that she thought some units could be run by contractors. Some of the people whose jobs would have been eliminated might have been able to come back as contractors, but not everyone." She gave her soft wind chime laugh again. "Those HR folks had to give her information about salaries and staffing levels and such. I heard some of them were really ticked that they had helped her and she might stab them in the back by saying their work could be contracted out."

"That's…interesting. Did you hear anything about a memo that lists jobs, or maybe hospital departments, to be cut?"

"There are two dozen rumors, and I doubt many of them have a lot of credence." She thought for a moment. "I think the folks in the ER were angriest, as a group. They know how much difference a minute or a certain piece of equipment can make. They and Sam Dent, you know him in Radiology?"

"Met him briefly, but I don't really know him." *Not that I'd forget anyone that rude.*

"I can't think of the name of the equipment he and the ER docs wanted. It was an ultrasound that would help diagnose injuries without having to transport the patient to x-ray. We have some portable x-ray equipment already, but only for bones, nothing like the machine they wanted. Sam and a couple of ER staff were furious at the idea that could be cut."

When I started to say something, she raised a hand to politely silence me. "Frankly, not all hospital administrators are money-fanatic idiots. If the equipment would do what they said, I can't imagine it would be taken out of the budget. I was hoping to lose a couple hospital deputy CEOs."

I laughed. "No wonder Dr. Welby likes you."

"I'm not one for mincing words. And I can retire in a couple of years. I'd rather retire from Ocean Alley Hospital, but I know a lot of people in the region. I could get a job in a snap."

I thanked her for her candor, and walked to my car. Sandra had some interesting insights, but did I really know more than I did before? Maybe not, but she had put some things in perspective for me.

I had thought Weiss' recommendations would be strongly considered by the Board of Directors or whoever made budget decisions. But maybe the key decision makers would see most of her recommendations as too harsh. Maybe she even made a lot of unrealistic proposals expecting that when some cuts were made they would seem reasonable. Though I couldn't imagine why she would care. It sounded as if she went from hatchet job to hatchet job.

Perhaps the murderer didn't know much about how the hospital worked. Maybe the killer thought if he, or she, was on some list for job elimination that it would definitely happen. That made me think that maybe the killer was not a senior staffer. Of course, they could be very senior, and just enraged.

ON MONDAY I NEEDED TO visit businesses around town to cajole them to form teams for the corn toss. Or just give money. Because it is hard for me to go around town asking for money, directly or indirectly, I decided to visit Todd Everly at the hospital.

His office door was ajar, and I knocked lightly. I heard the squeak of his chair and he looked from his office to the doorway. "Hello, Jolie."

At least he's always glad to see me.

"Hi, Todd. I guess I'm still minding your business."

"No problem. Come on in."

I walked into his office and he cleared a couple of binders off the chair next to his desk and we both sat down. He appeared to be trying to hide a smile.

"A couple of people have told me there was a second memo that lists specific jobs to be cut, or maybe contracted out."

He nodded. "I only just saw it. Our fearless leader showed it to senior staff in a meeting this morning."

At my puzzled look, he said, "Our CEO, Quentin Wharton. He said he was tired of being asked about it, and it wasn't something that would be considered now."

"Really? No more cost cutting?"

"Oh, there will be. They're going with this amazing innovation called employee focus groups."

I laughed. "Amazing?"

He grew serious. "Apparently everyone has told Wharton and Logan that there are plenty of good ideas to make this place more efficient, and the people who have most of them are the people who work here." He shrugged. "I'm sure they'll get outside advice, but if nothing else we'll all feel better if we know our ideas will get to management unfiltered."

"Makes sense. Does that mean management, or you, thinks that the murderer was someone on staff?"

"We all talked about that, but certainly not in a staff meeting with the bosses, and not so much now. I suppose hospitals are no different from other companies. People focus most on what's going on now. No one's going to forget the murder, but we're almost talked out."

He shrugged again, reminding me of Lucas. "And Tanya Weiss was not someone we knew well. If there's an arrest or more press coverage about the investigation, I'm sure it'll all be front and center again."

"Do you feel like the police keep you in the loop?" I asked.

"As far as I know. I was pretty ticked that they hadn't told me it was your friend on the cameras, but Morehouse, or maybe it was Tortino, called later that day to tell me." He saw my expression, and smiled. "And no, I wouldn't tell you if there was a lot of information that's not in the press. But I don't mind telling you there's probably not a lot you don't know."

For a second Tanya's vacant eyes came to me, and I pushed her face out of my mind. "It's just hard not knowing. Since I found her."

He nodded. "Do you think you're in some kind of danger from the person who killed her?"

I was surprised by his question. "You mean, like the killer thinks I may have seen them or something."

"Right. I can't help but wonder why you're so…persistent."

"That's because you don't know me well."

He laughed, and it gave him an almost boyish air. "Probably."

"But, no. I didn't see anything, and if the killer was in the area when I went into the restroom, he knows that."

"Good. No point worrying about something that isn't going to be an issue."

Scoobie came to mind. "I hear that a lot."

"So…is there anything else?"

"Can I see the memo? The proposed cuts?"

Todd gave me a look of amusement. "How long do you think I'd have my job if I showed people internal documents?"

"Oh, sure. I get that." I did, but I didn't like it. "Who else has seen it?"

He laughed, hard. "You're friends with the guy doing the practicum in Radiology, Scoobie, right?"

"Yes, but he won't snoop for me."

"He doesn't have to. Sam's apoplectic about what's in the proposals. He's running around the hospital shaking the memo in people's faces."

I WAS SURPRISED THAT Scoobie was willing to talk about what was in Weiss' proposals. He said it wouldn't be revealing secrets because Sam had pinned the part that dealt with Radiology above that office's coffee pot with a note that said, "You get what you pay for."

"Somebody told the CEO, and he stopped by Radiology to say that no part of the memo could be made public, even if Sam was only posting what pertained to his department. I think what really got Sam to shut up," Scoobie said, "was Wharton told Sam he could be on some senior staff committee to evaluate any future proposals."

I was lying on my back on the floor of the living room, with my foot propped on my couch. It was mostly better, but still swollen at night and this seemed the best way to elevate it. Jazz was on my stomach, and Pebbles was on the floor by Scoobie's feet. She has taken to trying to eat his shoe strings.

"Why do you think she does that?"

He looked down at her. "Probably have scents from outdoors."

"Keep going."

Scoobie looked at me as if I was nuts, then realized I was still talking about the hospital not giving instructions to Pebbles. "Okay, you probably heard she recommended an across-the-board cut of two percent in all departments, and no money for training. At least people wouldn't have to take time off to earn continuing ed credits."

I reached for a notebook on the floor next to me and wrote that down. I hadn't heard any of this, but didn't want him to know he was my primary source. "You didn't talk about the training stuff before."

He shrugged. "Not so much discussion about that. I haven't seen the full memo, but everyone's saying that Weiss recommended contracting out nearly all of the human resources stuff, and even more equipment cuts than we talked about before."

"Such as…"

"Let's see. Delaying buying some fancy new MRI machine for a year at least, no new tables for the operating suites—that really ticked off a lot of doctors, even the ones who aren't surgeons."

"What else to hire contractors for?"

"I heard a lot of your buddy Nelson's Purchasing Department. His job would stay, but he'd get a pay cut."

I craned my neck to look directly at Scoobie, who was finishing a sandwich. "Do you have any idea what Nelson thought about that?"

"Nah. There were other admin departments in the same situation. Accounting I think, or maybe that's one where she wanted to replace more people with computers. Like I said, I didn't see all of it."

"Do you know how frustrating you can be?"

"Do you know what it means when the pot calls the kettle black?"

The front door banged before I could answer, and Lucas called, "Sorry. Wind."

Sounded more like a slam of irritation to me, but I didn't say so. "Any luck?"

"No, and I'm running out of time."

"What do you mean?" I asked. He sat in the rocker and I tilted my head backwards to look at him.

"Like I said before, the hospital I work for has been really good about all this, but if I don't get back to work soon I could lose my job. Or I have to go on some kind of long-term leave without pay and I lose my health insurance."

"I guess you could buy it on your own," I said, hesitating.

Yeah, but where I work my share of the monthly insurance is cheap. On the private market with no employer contribution, I'd pay three times as much."

"And have no income," Scoobie said.

"Do you really think she's still in town?" I asked.

"Yeah, I do. I stop by Harvest for All two or three times a week. Your friend, Megan, says she thinks her daughter Alicia has seen Kim a couple of times, but not up close."

"Seems like Alicia could catch up with her if she really wanted to," I said.

"Chasing people doesn't always turn out the way you think it will," Scoobie said.

"Thanks, Mr. Zen," Lucas said. He sighed.

"Why don't you go to All-Anon with Jolie tonight?" Scoobie said, half smiling.

"I think I'd rather eat sea nettles."

"Hey, I think I resent that," I said.

Lucas gave half a grin. "I might go. But alone."

CHAPER SIXTEEN

I HAD SPENT THE LAST TWO days obsessing over how much I had to do and calling the others on the committee to see if they were doing what they said they would do. Of course, I said I was calling to see if they needed any help. Now that it was the Thursday before the corn toss, I was officially crazed. Talking to the other committee members was reassuring.

Aretha could organize a fishing fleet at the height of the season, so rounding up volunteers was not as tough for her as it would be for me. Daphne had plastered the library and city and county office building with signs, and Scoobie had promised he'd have a draft press release to me by the Wednesday prior, which was today. We already had the corn toss on every TV and radio station's online community calendars, and George had mentioned it in his About Town column twice.

Tomorrow would be our major media day on the radio and in the *Ocean Alley Press*, which is always our biggest promoter. The editor knows our antics sell papers, so he likes to get his audience prepped for the post-event coverage. Since the corn toss was on a Sunday afternoon, we had one more set of church services around town to publicize it. That would be late to form teams, but could still attract spectators.

I had an appraisal to write up and made my way to Harry's home office. I pulled my car to the curb in front of Steele Appraisals and fumbled in my purse for the office keys. Then I realized they were in my hand. "You're getting pretty ditzy," I said.

As I got out of my car, I saw that a green sedan had just driven by me. No amount of squinting could tell me whether it was the car I noticed a couple of days ago.

"Good, Jolie. Now stress is making you paranoid."

Still muttering to myself, I walked onto the porch and unlocked the door to Harry's house and started for my computer. I stopped because a bright yellow piece of paper was on the entry way floor. Someone had apparently pushed it through the mail slot. I stooped to pick it up and groaned when I turned it over.

In the middle of the eight-and-a-half by eleven page was a large ear of corn, with kernels that were each about an inch square. Each square had a photo of a committee member, thankfully without names next to the photos. *George had to be in on this.* I knew Scoobie wouldn't have had pictures of everyone. In fact, the only camera he used was mine.

I studied each photo. Though someone might not find an image their favorite photo of all time, none of them did what Aunt Madge would call an injustice to anyone. It was the wording on the flyer that made me cringe.

The Harvest for All Committee and the Ocean Alley Police Department's Shop with a Cop Program invite you to their first annual Corn Toss Contest, open to all Ocean Alley area residents over the age of 16. Bring your throwing arm and ability to duck to the Community Center Parking Lot on the Sunday before Halloween. Form a four-person team or join others you meet on Sunday. Or just come and watch. There is a suggested entry fee of $5 per person; no charge to watch.

The flyer described the time and gave a rain date, and ended with committee member names, more or less.

Jolie the Jinxer
Dr. Welby the Wise
Aretha the Assertive
Sylvia the Self-Confident
Monica the Mouse
Scoobie the Scallywag
Megan the Master
Lance the Lucrative

I sighed. "Could be worse." I made a mental note to be sure that Monica was okay with being called a mouse. I reread Scoobie's flyer. He probably designed it to attract younger people than those of us on the committee. I didn't know where he planned to post it, and didn't think I wanted to know.

Taped to the bottom of the page was an envelope the size I use to mail checks. I felt it. Probably the draft press release. It was.

> *"The Harvest for All Food Pantry invites local residents to bring their competitive spirit and throwing arm to the Ocean Alley Community Center on the Sunday before Halloween from two o'clock until about five o'clock.*
>
> *Why, you ask? Because more than a dozen teams of local residents will compete at the first annual Corn Toss Contest. Each team member will be asked to pay a $5 entry fee.*
>
> *Similar to a bean bag game, this adult contest has people plopping six by six bags of corn seed into a regulation-size corn toss box. Four-person teams can be prearranged, or if you don't have a group of friends with enough nerve to form a corny team, Harvest for All can help you join a team.*
>
> *A bean-bag toss will be available for children ages two to ten. If you don't want to play or urge on a team, come to bid on lavish baskets of food and gift items, or enter the raffle. Attendees are asked to bring at least one canned good (no sauerkraut, please) or make a monetary donation."*

Next was the phrase, "Co-sponsored by the Ocean Alley Police Department's Shop with a Cop Program." I remembered Sergeant Morehouse had said he wanted their role downplayed in the publicity, so no one would call him.

So far the press release seemed harmless, though I wasn't sure what Scoobie had against sauerkraut. Then I read the last part.

Members of the winning team will be designated Ocean's Alley's Supreme Corn Holers for a one-year period. The title must be defended at next year's event.

I reread the text of the press release. George had said that the term corn hole had a rude connotation in some circles, but how many people would know that?

A LOT, AS I found out at that evening's final Harvest for All planning meeting.

"Jolie Gentil, how could you?" Sylvia's face was red, and she shook a flyer at me. "This appeared all over town this afternoon. None of my friends will come."

I realized Scoobie must have turned the flyers over to Alicia and her friends to distribute.

"They don't have to play," Scoobie offered.

Dr. Welby's tone was serious. "Did you know what this term meant?" He looked at me. Scoobie did not.

Scoobie is a chicken. I cleared my throat and responded. "Not when we scheduled the event. Later, George told me some people, people without very good manners, sometimes attach a…vulgar meaning to the term."

"I have excellent manners," Monica said.

"You do," Aretha said. I could tell she was trying not to laugh. She spoke directly to Sylvia. "I suggest we not be defensive. We simply continue to call it a Corn Toss Contest."

"That would be fine," Sylvia snapped, "if our own press release didn't call it something else."

"Technically," Scoobie said, "The press release only calls it something else in describing the winners."

Her face beet red, Sylvia stood and started for the door.

I rose to follow her, but Lance gestured that I should stay in my seat. "I've got this." He walked to the hall and called her name. I held my breath for a moment. The door to the street did not open or, more important, slam shut.

A couple of Lance's words reached me. They included "young people," and "used to that kind of humor."

I decided I needed to keep the meeting on track, even though what I wanted to do was throw a bag of dead fish at Scoobie.

"Okay, Megan, how about you let us know how the teen group did sewing the bags of corn."

I half-listened as she described how the high school consumer economics teacher had let them use the machines in the sewing class room. The male high school volunteers had apparently assumed only the girls would operate the machines, and the girls had a very different opinion. The only apparent casualty was a lot of twisted thread in a couple of the machines' bobbin housings.

"So, how many did you make, all total?" Dr. Welby asked this, and I realized I was paying too much attention to the hallway.

"We made forty-four, but some of the teams will bring their own," Megan said.

By the time we finished a brief conversation about making sure all bags weighed the same - to be accomplished by borrowing a set of postal weight scales from the Purple Cow - I heard Lance and Sylvia walking back toward us.

Scoobie looked at me and gave a small shrug. He and Sylvia have never gotten along, and this was at least the third time she'd gotten really upset at something he had done. And he had done it. He knew some people might not like the words corn hole. I felt ambushed, but it was at least partially my fault. I had approved the press release.

Lance and Sylvia walked in and he winked at me - behind her back.

"Okay, I understand." That's all Sylvia said before she sat back down. I wasn't about to ask what she understood.

"Aretha," I said. "Let us know how the volunteer cadre is shaping up."

THE MEETING BROKE UP a few minutes later, and I walked out between Lance and Scoobie. Megan and Aretha were just behind us.

As the door to the street shut, meaning Sylvia, Monica, and Dr. Welby were out of earshot, I looked at Lance. "What did you tell her?"

"After a general comment that we should rise above disparaging remarks, I said that most people know that the term refers to the holes some Native Americans used to dig holes to store corn over the winter, so it would be below the freezing line in the soil."

"Is that true?" Scoobie asked.

"I doubt it," Lance said.

Megan laughed, and I patted Lance on the shoulder. "I learn from you every day."

CHAPTER SEVENTEEN

I HAD TO FINISH AN appraisal Friday afternoon so the bank would get the results quickly. The buyer and seller were hustling to get to settlement in less than a month because the people who made the offer on the house wanted to avoid moving out of their house into an apartment and then into their new house.

A list of chores for the Corn Toss was racing through my brain, but the fact that the courthouse shut at five o'clock made up my mind for me. I walked into my bedroom, took my camera out of the top drawer of the chest, and grabbed my notebook from the bedside table. It was three o'clock, and if I hustled I could examine the house and do the courthouse research before five.

I drove toward Ocean Alley's Popsicle District, so named for the bright hues its residents began using to paint their houses a few years back. Still, I gaped at the house. It was the only one that looked like a lemon bar, complete with bright yellow porch furniture. *To each her own.*

I gathered my notebook and camera and walked to the front door, still limping a bit on the steps. The man who opened it was dressed in contrast to the house, all in black with a long ponytail that was a mix of brown and grey. I judged him to be about forty.

"Yeah?"

"I'm Jolie Gentil. I'm supposed to appraise your house today."

"Next week." He started to close the door, but I put my palm on it as it swung to me.

"If you wait until then you might lose the sale. It's contingent on the buyers being able to go to settlement in a month."

"Fine by me." His thin-lipped grin showed a missing tooth on top.

"But not with me. Let her in, Ogden." The woman's voice was authoritative.

"Humph." He stepped aside.

"Come on in Jolie. My son isn't looking forward to getting his own place."

I wouldn't touch that with a long oar. I smiled at the woman as she ushered me in. Ogden went toward a loud TV in the back of the house.

"I'm moving into an independent apartment at Silver Times Senior Living. Just one bedroom. I can't wait."

I exchanged pleasantries as I pulled out my tape measure and got to work. If Ogden was as charming to her as to me, I figured she would do cartwheels on the way out the door. Or into the apartment.

From the front, the full size of the house wasn't obvious. The three bedrooms were not large, but there was a huge three-season room at the back that served as a family room of sorts. Judging from the space heater, it was used year round, and appeared to now be Ogden's space. There were half-packed cardboard boxes that, on second look, were probably still packed from when he moved back home. DVDs spilled from one, and a couple of empty beer bottles sat on a closed box. *No wonder she wants a one-bedroom place.*

I did my work as quickly as possible, angling the photo of the family room so there were no boxes in it. I trudged through the yard, which was a mix of gravel and sand, taking photos of each side of the house.

It was four-twenty and I was in a hurry to get to the courthouse when I remembered I had not checked Pebbles' litter box that morning. If it's not up to her standards she uses Jazz's box. It's waaay too small for the skunk.

I hurried up the front door and half-jogged through the kitchen, which was a reminder that I shouldn't do that to my foot. A peek in the closet told me I owed thanks to either Lucas or Scoobie. I walked back through the house and was almost to the front door when I saw a note from Lucas taped to the inside of the front door, where I couldn't miss it.

"She's at the hospital. They're going to meet me and take me to her room." I studied Lucas' scrawled note, which was punctuated with a huge smiley face.

If they're meeting him, she must be badly hurt or something. I glanced at the clock, which said it was almost four-thirty. Lucas had not written the time that he wrote the note. I wrapped my hands around the car keys in my pocket and then slowly released the keys. Lucas had my mobile number. When he wanted me there he would call. *He probably already called Scoobie.*

Ten minutes later I had one eye on the clock in the Register of Deeds office as I searched for similar houses that recently sold for prices comparable to what the buyers and sellers had agreed to for the lemon drop. I never knew how the negotiations went. Wherever they started, this one seemed to have ended up with a price about three thousand dollars more than I would be able to justify, and even that was a bit of a stretch. *That'll give Lester something to go ballistic about.*

A tap on my shoulder made me jump and turn.

George had a large grin. "I found something you want."

"Would that be peace and quiet to do my work?"

The young woman behind the counter in the Registrar of Deeds' office snickered and then turned away quickly.

"Nooo, Miss Priss. It would be," he lowered his voice, "information on a probable affair between our Ms. Weiss and the hospital Board's president."

"Wow. Give me two minutes and I'll meet you on a bench on the north side of the courthouse."

He loped out and the woman at the counter caught my eye. "Sorry."

"No problem. Maybe it'll make him mind his manners."

"Not likely," she said.

It took fifteen minutes to get the rest of the information I needed, and George was pacing around the bench when I walked out. His excitement overcame his irritation. "It's not one hundred percent, but two people told me Weiss and he slept together for at least the last few months she worked at Freehold."

"But not here?" I sat on the bench and extended my foot.

"Haven't heard anything. If she was smart she'd keep her sex life to herself in a town like Ocean Alley."

"Yes, you never know when a nosy reporter's going to be checking out your love life."

"Very funny. I wrote out a timeline for her last few years." He held out a piece of paper. "She was at a large hospital in Trenton, then the kind of small hospital in Freehold, and most recently in Perth Amboy. That was a short one." He consulted his notebook. "Only two months."

Weren't those jobs in one of your articles, or her obit?" I asked.

"Yeah, but not in order and not really discussed. And here's the good part." He flipped a page in his notebook and showed me where Jason Logan worked during the same timeframes.

"Not at any of the same hospitals," I said.

"True, but he was on the Board of the Chamber of Commerce in Freehold when Weiss was there. He would have met her then. Someone told me that Logan met Wharton and a couple of bigwigs from Ocean Alley Hospital when Logan worked in Freehold. Apparently Logan got the Chamber there to help the hospital raise some money from the business community."

"And the new partners at our hospital liked those fundraising skills and asked Logan to chair this Board?" I asked.

George shrugged. "Could be. Not important. What does matter is that Logan supposedly recommended Tanya Weiss for her job at the hospital here."

I thought for a moment. "It doesn't mean they slept together. Or that it matters if they did."

"No, but when I drove up to Freehold and asked around, the hospital PR office had copies of old newsletters, and look at this photo."

The glossy newsletter had photos of a fundraiser for some new mammography equipment. In the middle of the page was one of Tanya, and next to her was Jason Logan, with his arm casually draped over her shoulder. They both had hundred-watt smiles for the camera.

"Did you ask anyone about them?" I asked.

"Tried to. The head of the press liaison office threw me out. Unless I'm up there and need medical care. He was careful to say that." George grinned. "So whaddya think?"

"Not enemies, certainly." I studied the photo for a few more seconds. Office romances are everywhere. They generally didn't provide motives for murder.

As if anticipating my thoughts, George added, "Here's the really good part. A woman in HR here told me that Logan and Weiss broke up just four days before she was killed."

"Like with a huge fight in front of a lot of people?"

"Nope. She told me Tanya came in with red eyes one morning. When the woman in Human Resources asked if she was okay, Weiss spilled her guts. Something about she initiated the break-up because she found out he was cheating on her."

"Whoa, George, that's pretty scurrilous stuff. How sure are you about this?" What I was also thinking was that it was the first time anyone had put a human face on the seemingly ruthless budgeteer.

"She's always been my best source at the hospital."

I raised an eyebrow and George interpreted it correctly. "You know I won't give you her name. Crud. Could be a he, you know."

"No it can't. No woman would tell a guy that unless it was her best friend or something."

George looked away and then back to me. "If he recommended her for this job and she dumped him..."

"Which he might have deserved."

"Even so," George continued, "if she dumped him he'd feel like he did her a big favor for nothing."

I shrugged and dug in my purse for my chirping phone. "Unless she put pictures of him on the web, I can't imagine he'd do much other than ignore her." I looked at the caller ID. "It's Scoobie. Hello Mr. X-Ray."

"Yo, Jolie."

"And George."

"My lucky day. Hey, did you talk to Lucas?"

"No, but he left a note..."

"Yeah, I saw it. I checked here at the hospital. Kim hasn't been admitted, and no one in the ER treated her."

"That's weird. Are you sure?"

"Yep. Told the ER people I was checking on behalf of her brother. They know me, so they checked."

"He didn't say who called him, did he?" I asked.

George was looking at me intently. He had the I-smell-a-story look he gets.

"No. I think you should come over here. Since you have an in with Mr. Security."

I ignored the dig. "Sure. " I hung up and looked at George. "Uh…"

"You're so elegant."

"It's not really something I can talk to you about."

"Where have I heard that before? Except I usually hear it after you haven't told me something that would be good for a story."

He said it half good-naturedly, but I still did an inward wince. "Honest, this involves someone's well, well-being. Mental health, even."

I started to walk to my car and he fell into step beside me. "Scoobie okay?"

"Oh, sure. His usual self, anyway."

We walked a few steps in silence, and he said, "Look, if you and Scoobie say something's off the record, it will be."

I got to my car and paused with my hand on the door handle. If we needed to find Kim, there was no one in town with more spies than George, and they seemed to know not to let on that they were doing him favors. "If I tell you what we're talking about, you won't use *any* of it unless Scoobie and I say it's okay?"

"Is that an *and* or an *or*?"

I rolled my eyes and opened the car door.

For a second it looked as if George was calculating how much leeway he had, and then he said, "Okay, both of you have to say so."

I faced him. "Remember that day you called because one of your spies said I was at the police station?"

"Damn! I knew you weren't there because a kid wanted company. They'd have called Scoobie."

I eyed him. "Okay. When we were in high school, a family Scoobie and I knew had to leave town fast." I let that hang between us and watched George get excited.

"What? Criminals? You gotta be kidding." He groaned, then added in an almost hopeful tone, "But that's old news."

"It relates to today. You can't write about it."

"All right, all right."

"Anyway, the son is in his twenties now, and he came back because he thought his younger sister might be here. She ran away or something."

His hand went, by instinct, to the pocket of his Hawaiian-style shirt, where he keeps his notebook. I glared at him. His hand went back to his side. "Or something," he said.

I nodded. "She's upset. Their mom just died, and she's really depressed. He found her, and she came by the house…"

"Your house?"

"No, Scoobie's. The problem is, she didn't stay. Left by the bathroom window, actually."

"No way."

"Way. So this afternoon the brother, Lucas, left a note saying someone called to say she was at the hospital, but Scoobie says she's not there. And neither is Lucas."

When I didn't add anything else, George looked disappointed. "Oh. That's too bad."

"I guess I forgot to say Lucas was the guy in the hoodie. On the hospital security tapes. When Tanya Weiss was…"

"Murdered. Yeah. I'll meet you at the front door of the hospital." He turned and walked to his car.

"YOU BROUGHT GEORGE?" Scoobie said this as if I'd brought Pebbles and she'd pooped on the hospital floor.

"Good to see you, too," George said.

I motioned that we should move to the seating area in the hospital's main lobby, and I sat and crossed my leg so I could rub my ankle. "He promised not to tell, and I thought if Kim's really missing he might help us find her."

George reached for his notebook and I swatted at his hand, missing by several inches. He grinned at Scoobie.

"So, what's going on?" I asked.

"I'm not sure anything is, and if I didn't work here I wouldn't have access to who was treated here. But I do, and there's no record of Kim being here."

"So who would have called Lucas?" I mused.

"I don't know," Scoobie said, "but I don't like it. No name of the caller on his note, and no Kim here."

"How many people know he was the guy in the hoodie?" George asked.

"You told him that?" Scoobie was bemused. "You must have gotten him to sign in blood."

"George is big on trust," I said, sweetly. "You know that security guy, Todd Everly? He might be willing to look on security tapes to see if Lucas was here. Or Kim."

"Why would he do that for you?" George asked.

"They're best friends," Scoobie said.

I flushed. "We are not. He asked me to walk him through the day I found Tanya. He let me look at a couple of the tapes from that day to make sure it was Lucas on the footage."

"He didn't know?" George asked.

"Police hadn't told him yet. He was ticked, which is probably why he let me look." I thought for a couple more seconds. "Come on, let's go to his office." They followed me to the elevator and we rode to the third floor in silence. I figured George was so excited at the thought of hospital security tapes that he couldn't speak.

Todd Everly's door was shut, and there was no glass in the door, so I couldn't tell if he was in there. I realized it was close to six, so he had probably left for the day. I knocked anyway.

A chair scraped on the floor and the door opened. Todd looked at each of us, his gaze resting on George for a couple of seconds before he looked to me again. "What can I do for you, Jolie?" He was dressed in sweats. A duffle bag and a pair of running shoes sat on the floor near where we were standing.

"Sorry to bother you, but I'm worried about a friend, the guy who was…who we talked about before. His sister might be hurt, and he came over here to check on her."

Todd opened his door and we walked into his outer office. "You're fairly sure he came over here?"

"Yes," George said, "and I should tell you I'm here as Jolie's friend, not as a reporter."

Todd's concerned look lessened and he nodded.

"I know it's unorthodox, but I wondered if we, or maybe just you, could see if he was on your tapes in the last few hours."

Todd looked skeptical, and Scoobie added, "He left a note saying someone from the hospital asked him to come over. I've checked in the ER and admissions. Neither he nor his sister has been here today. Ever, actually."

Todd frowned lightly, "Be careful where you repeat that."

Scoobie nodded. "Will you look?"

"You have a photo of the young man when he's not wearing a hoodie?" Todd asked.

"No, but we have one of his sister." Scoobie took a folded piece of paper from his pocket and handed it to him. "And I think Lucas was wearing a Harvest for All tee shirt."

Todd took Kim's photo and nodded. "Have a seat. It takes a long time to go through a lot of tape, but I can look fairly quickly at the ER and other entrances. What was the timeframe?"

It took a minute for Scoobie and me to reach agreement. This was partly because we had to figure out when Lucas would have changed Pebbles' litter box, because Scoobie hadn't done it. We finally agreed, much to Todd Everly's amusement, that because there was no evidence the box had been recently used, Lucas cleaned it before I got there at four-twenty, but likely not long before that.

"Have a seat. I'll do some checking and come back out in a few minutes."

The visitor chairs were straight-backed with lightly padded seats, and they were close together in the outer office, which was only about ten feet by ten feet.

George spoke first. "So, are you worried that she might hurt herself, or that someone might want to hurt one or both of them?"

"It's hard to know," I said, in a low voice. "Maybe they've just gone off to the beach or something."

"Yeah, right. If you thought that, one of you would have talked the other out of coming," George said.

Scoobie gave a half-smile, half-grunt, and looked at me. "Exactly what did you tell him?"

"Probably too much, but he promised." When neither of them said anything, I added, "I said they were here in high school and had to leave..."

"She said something that implied witness protection," George said, looking at Scoobie.

"Did she?" Scoobie grinned.

"And I said Kim was upset because of their mom, and Lucas was worried about her."

"And something about an exit through her bathroom window," George added.

Scoobie shook his head lightly. "I never get you two."

George and I spoke together, "Me, either."

George had kind of a hopeful look. "Don't go there," I said.

Scoobie leaned forward in his chair so he didn't have to talk too loudly. "I'm not worried about Lucas' mental health," he began.

"Wait, was he the guy you brought to the meeting on a few days ago?"

Scoobie nodded. "So you know he's frustrated about his sister, but other than having the Serenity Prayer backwards, I think he's okay."

I smiled.

"Like our friend here," George said, kind of jerking his head in my direction.

"Hey. I'm the one who told him to take Kim to a movie instead of talking about meds."

"Yeah, yeah," George said.

"I'd say," Scoobie continued, "that she's sad, and uncertain, and wants what she didn't have, which is a supportive mom and a home she likes."

"Lot of that going around," George said, with a kind of knowing look at Scoobie.

I added, "And she hasn't learned to be happy with what she has or to change herself. Problem is, Lucas thinks he can make it right, or make her right, and she doesn't want to talk about it."

"Damn," Scoobie said. "You do listen in those meetings." He looked back at George. "So she spent the night, but when he pressed her she left."

"Out the bathroom window. But why would you worry if there's a mix-up about whether they were over here?" George asked.

Scoobie and I looked at each other. "Because they had to leave here twelve years ago when some people their father ticked off found out they were in Ocean Alley," I said.

George groaned. "This might be the best story of the year."

"You promised," Scoobie and I said.

He nodded. "I meant it. But, you never know, one day they might want to talk..."

George stopped when Scoobie and I stared at him. He put his hands, palms out, toward us. "Uncle."

The door to the room with the cameras opened, and Todd motioned to me. When all three of us stood, he pointed at me, and I followed him toward the monitors.

"This him?" Todd asked.

I squinted at the screen, pleased to see it was Lucas. "Yes. This was today?"

"It was," Todd hesitated, "the thing is, it almost seems as if whoever was greeting him knew to stand out of the range of the camera."

I felt my heart beat faster. "What do you mean?"

"Lucas and the other person are just inside the door by Physical Therapy at...let's see, five-o-four PM." Everly pointed at part of a shadow just to Lucas' left. "The camera by that entrance takes in the area just outside the exterior door and a few feet inside. The ones in the lobby are part of a group, so we can see the full lobby by switching to another camera view. I think the person who greeted Lucas knew to stand just out of the sole camera's view."

I shivered, but before I could say anything, George stuck his head into the room and asked, "Where would a camera next pick up the two of them?"

Todd frowned at him, and George took this as permission to come into the room as Todd spoke. "About twenty meters away, where the hallway merges with another one near the main lobby. They never appeared on that camera."

"What offices are along the way?" I asked.

"Just PT and the back exit that leads out of Administration. There's a security pad on both of those doors. If someone opened the admin door there'd be an alarm, because that door's only supposed to be used if there's an emergency.

"Is the PT door alarmed after a certain time?" George asked.

Todd shook his head. "Locked, but no alarm. There probably wouldn't have been anyone in PT then. Their last patient is at four. If some staff were still in there, the door could even have been unlocked. That would mean no need to use the security pad to get in."

"So, maybe they went into PT," I mused. "I was in there a couple of days ago. It looked like there were doors in the back that went to other hallways."

"Yes, I'll show you those. They lead to a hallway behind PT. Nothing there." Todd continued. "Think some more. I know that image of Lucas and the guy's shadow was just a vague impression. But are you sure you don't recognize the shadow of the person your friend was talking to?"

"The Shadow knows," Scoobie said, from the doorway. But he looked at the image and shook his head. I had already looked, and George must have looked over my shoulder. He said nothing.

Todd gave Scoobie a raised eyebrow and went back to his computer screen. "Makes sense for you guys to walk around a bit, and I'll pull material from other cameras."

"Can't we look at footage from inside the PT suite?" George asked.

"Again, the person knew his or her way around. I'll check, but the only camera on in there is at the PT registration desk. People don't necessarily want to be photographed getting treatment, and in some of the treatment rooms they might have a shirt or pants off, or something."

"Swell," Scoobie said.

"Good to know," I murmured.

George grunted a laugh, and we said thanks and walked into the third-floor hallway.

"I guess we could each pick a floor," I said.

"I should probably do first," George said. "I get thrown off of other floors sometimes."

Scoobie nodded. "I'll do this floor, since it's the main patient floor and I'm still in scrubs. And I'll walk through the ER."

George pointed a finger at me. "The important thing is to look like you know where you're going. Nobody'll stop you."

He walked toward the elevator and I looked at Scoobie. "That leaves me the second floor. I'm not going in the ladies' restroom near Radiology."

CHAPTER EIGHTEEN

IN ALMOST EXACTLY half-an-hour, the three of us were back at the Security office. No one had seen any sign of Lucas or Kim.

Todd stuck his head out of the room where he was reviewing the computer screens. "I've been through the stuff. You won't like it."

I had been seated and rubbing my foot, so I trailed George and Scoobie into the cramped office space and looked at the screen as Todd clicked his mouse from blank hallway to hallway. "You can see how often people pass through the lobby all afternoon—I have this on a fast speed for viewing. Your friend never went back out the doors near PT, and I'll have to study the lobby a bit more, but I don't think he was in there."

"So, he stayed in PT?" I asked.

"Doesn't seem likely," Todd said, still scrolling through screens.

"Can we go down there and look?" Scoobie asked.

Todd gave a somber nod as he stood. "You're with the right person."

We didn't talk as the four of us took the elevator to the first floor, except that George tried to get Todd to tell him how many security cameras there were throughout the hospital. "Don't push your luck," was Todd's only reply.

There was little light in the hallway leading to PT, but the lighting rose as we walked. "This exit door is locked after six PM, so we put most of the lights on motion sensors."

When we got near the entrance to Physical Therapy, George walked to the door where Lucas had stood with whoever phoned him. George pointed up, and we all followed his finger. The camera sat at the top of the wall, and was easily spotted.

"People could figure out the range of this camera," George said.

Todd nodded. "Not precisely, but enough to know how to stay out of its view. The thing is," he paused, "ten days ago most people who worked here wouldn't have paid any attention to where we have cameras and where we don't. People expect them."

"Are you saying that since Tanya's murder," I asked, "people are more aware of them?"

"It's more than that," Todd said. "I've been asked to suggest locations for additional cameras. My guys and I have walked throughout the building testing the range of the cameras and developing recommendations. We talked to lots of staff as we did this."

George looked up at the camera for a second and back at Todd. "So almost everyone who works here is better briefed on camera locations. A lot of people would know where to stand to avoid the ones you have now."

Todd nodded. "I'm afraid so."

"Okay," Scoobie said. "That's good to know, but it doesn't help us find Lucas. Let's look in PT."

"Of course." Todd took a key from a buttoned pocked near his belt. "Master key. Saves me memorizing a lot of security pad passwords. They change a lot."

"Good to know," Scoobie said.

George met my eyes, but I couldn't read his expression.

"We'll need to walk through together," Todd said. "I can't let visitors wander in secure areas alone."

There was the large treatment space with equipment, weights, Pilate's balls, and some low tables I'd seen patients lie on to exercise. For some reason, the intense quiet of the normally busy area made me uneasy.

We said nothing as we walked to the hallway that led to the individual patient treatment rooms. These were unlocked, and

Todd opened each door wide enough for himself and whoever was right behind him to look inside.

"It doesn't make sense," George said.

"No, it doesn't. Come on, the staff area is back here," Todd said.

We traipsed the short distance to an office on the left. It held only a fridge and break-room furniture. We left PT. I hadn't really expected to see Lucas riding one of the PT bicycles, but I had no idea where to look next.

"Did you look in the cafeteria?" Todd asked as we walked toward the lobby.

We were passing a closet marked Electrical when a noise made me stop. "What was that?"

Todd turned sharply to stare at the door. "You hear something?"

I nodded and Scoobie said, "A groan. Hurry, open the door!"

Todd almost plunged his master key into the lock and then swore. "It's supposed to work everywhere."

George walked about five paces down the hall, picked a fire extinguisher out of its slot and walked back toward us. "Stand back."

"What are you…?" Todd began.

George brought the extinguisher down hard on the door knob, and there was a splintering sound. He did it a second time and the knob hung loosely from the door. Before he could put the extinguisher down, I pulled open the door. Lucas was seated on the floor and gagged. His head almost touched a large circuit breaker box that was on the wall, and he blinked at the light. There was blood on the front of his shirt.

WHEN THE HEAD OF Security calls the ER and says he needs immediate assistance, the staff haul ass. It was less than a minute until we heard footsteps running full tilt toward us. Scoobie and I were kneeling by Lucas and George had walked a few feet away from us.

Todd seemed to have vanished, but a couple of seconds later he walked out of the door that led to the back of the administrative offices. "I wanted to be sure no one else was near here," he said. He walked toward the lobby, I assumed to check other hallways.

Scoobie had taken the gag out of Lucas' mouth. "You're okay now, buddy."

"You'll be home in no time," I added, then remembered I was talking about my house.

Two EMTs, whom I knew usually worked on an ambulance, were soon running their hands up and down Lucas, probably checking to see if anything was broken before they moved him. One of them shone a pin light into Lucas' eyes, and he reacted by turning his head and groaning slightly.

"I think we can move him," the taller of the two men said. Carefully they helped a groggy Lucas half stand. One of the EMTs reached under his armpits and the other behind his knees and they placed him on the stretcher as Scoobie steadied it. It took less than ten seconds to strap him onto it and they moved briskly toward the ER.

George and I trailed the gurney and I wondered why Scoobie almost sprinted ahead of us. As George and I reached the ER, a tall nurse with a huge bun on top of her head raised her arm, palm out, to prevent us from following Lucas.

"But, we're…" I began.

George grabbed my elbow. "Let's go sit."

I turned to tell him to leave me alone, but when he nodded toward the waiting area, I figured there was some reason for his behavior.

He leaned toward me and spoke quietly. "Scoobie went ahead to be sure he would be in there. He'll stay out of the way so they don't throw him out."

I nodded and limped to a chair and sat to massage my ankle, which was sore after walking quickly to the ER. "I thought he looked as if he'd be okay, didn't you think?"

A thin, elderly man across from me said, "Whoever he was, he butted in line. I was supposed to be next."

"I'm sorry," I said, not about to explain the concept of triage. "He was mostly unconscious, so I guess they wanted to check him out fast."

"Humph." He went back to a battered copy of *Field and Stream* magazine, tilting it toward a lamp on the table next to the plastic couch he sat on.

George gave the man an impassive look and turned to me. "He's young. He'll be okay." As if to indicate he wasn't sure about this, George moved away from his chair and began pacing on the vinyl floor.

I told my mind to calm down so I could think. It seemed highly unlikely that the mystery person on the security screen really had news about Kim, but he must have said something for Lucas to follow him partway down that hall.

Who could I call to see if people were in PT or Admin and saw Lucas today? Bob Ellis, whom I thought of as my therapist, might know. I pulled my phone from my pocket ready to call information, and paused. It might not be smart to telegraph that there'd been an injured man in the hospital electrical closet. Then I realized that Lucas might not have ended up in that closet immediately. Maybe the PT office was empty and he and the other person went into the PT rooms for a while. Then they might have gone back to the hallway where we found Lucas quite a bit later. That made more sense. Still, someone *had* to have seen the two of them.

"Jolie." When I glanced at George he had a look of impatience that said he must have called my name a couple of times. "We can go in."

I walked into Lucas' cubicle in front of George. Scoobie was standing next to the gurney and looked up as George and I entered. Now that his head had been cleaned and he was in a hospital gown, Lucas didn't look as if he had any grave injuries. His face was as colorless as the sheets.

I went to the other side of the gurney and put my hand on Lucas' arm, which was lying across his chest. He opened his eyes. "Jolie. Did you find her?"

I shook my head. "What made you come here? Your note said someone contacted you."

"Called on my mobile." He closed his eyes.

"Someone you know?" Scoobie asked.

Even lying down Lucas shrugged. "Didn't know him. I've left my number a lot of places, in case they see Kim." He opened his eyes and looked at me. "He said his name was Alfred, and he told me to meet him at the side door."

"Alfred?" George asked.

I ignored George and spoke to Lucas. "You're on the security tapes coming in that door, but the person you met seemed to know to stand away from the camera."

"Huh." He looked from Scoobie to me and then his eyes rested on George. "He kind of looked like you, but it wasn't you."

George has auburn hair and is maybe five ten. "Same height and coloring?" he asked.

"Mmm, sort of," Lucas mumbled. "Maybe more brown hair."

"What was he wearing?" I asked. If we knew that maybe Todd could check other cameras for the guy.

"He had a white coat, like a doctor, but not scrubs." Lucas shut his eyes for a second and opened them again. "White shirt, burgundy tie."

"I'm gonna find Everly," George said, and left the room.

Before Scoobie or I could say anything else, a guy about twenty-five pushed a portable x-ray machine into the room. He looked at Lucas. "Scoobie hit you?"

Lucas smiled weakly. "Not this time."

"We don't want to move you a lot until we x-ray your head," the man said.

"Behave yourself Kevin," Scoobie said, and nodded toward the door. He and I walked into the hall and Scoobie pulled the door shut behind us.

"He'll be okay, right?" I asked.

"Kevin's a good guy. He'll be careful with Lucas."

We leaned against the wall outside the ER cubicle and listened to the man explain that he was going to put a stiff piece of film under Lucas' head to take pictures.

The x-ray equipment reminded me of Scoobie's rude boss. "Do you think Sam would have been angry enough to kill Tanya Weiss?"

"You remember why we're here, right?"

I frowned. "Yes, but maybe someone heard Lucas was on those tapes and wanted to make sure he doesn't say something."

Scoobie shrugged. "Or the people who are mad at his father wanted something. We can talk to Lucas in a minute. No use specu..." He paused, looking toward the ER entry.

Sergeant Morehouse stopped and looked at the two of us. "Is this that guy in the hoodie?"

"His name is Lucas, remember?" I asked.

"Where is he?"

"In this room, getting his head x-rayed," Scoobie said.

"Have 'em do Jolie next," Morehouse said, seeming pleased with his remark.

"He could be badly hurt," I said, irritated.

"If he was, you'd be in the little room for family," Morehouse nodded to a closed door at the end of the short corridor.

The door to Lucas' cubicle opened halfway, and Scoobie angled himself in and began to move Lucas' gurney so the portable x-ray machine could come out.

I stood against the opposite hallway wall, next to Morehouse. He had on a pair of cotton slacks and knit shirt, which implied that he had been off duty when called.

"What happened?" he asked.

I went over Lucas' note and Todd Everly's help in looking for Lucas and Kim, and then finding Lucas in the electrical closet. "And Todd's key didn't work, so George broke the lock with a fire extinguisher."

"George? What in the hell was he doing here?"

"He came with Scoobie and me when we figured Lucas might be missing. He said he wouldn't be a reporter for a while."

Morehouse snorted. "Got you fooled. Where's Everly?"

Kevin and his portable x-ray machine trundled by us, and Morehouse followed me into Lucas' cubicle.

"How ya doin' Lucas? Can you talk to me for a minute?"

When Lucas gave a less-than-enthusiastic positive reply, Morehouse looked at Scoobie and me and said, "Wait in the hall a sec. I want to hear his own version."

Lucas must have asked what he meant, because as Morehouse shut the door, he said, "Sometimes a well-meaning busybody tries to prompt a person."

Scoobie looked down the hallway. "I'm going to see if Kevin will let me look at the film." He walked away just as George walked up.

"I saw Morehouse. He in there?"

"Yep. Shouldn't take long. Where were you?"

"Went back to where we found him. Everly asked me to stand there for a minute 'til he found someone from maintenance to put a new lock on the closet."

This kind of amused me. "I'm surprised you agreed to stay put."

George gave me a quick grin. "Now he owes me one."

I rolled my eyes as Morehouse came out of the cubicle and shut the door behind him. "I told him you'd be in in a minute. Step over here."

We moved to a nearby corner. While closer to the busy nurses' station, we weren't blocking the hallway.

"You came because he left you a note?"

"Because we couldn't find him or Kim after we read Lucas' note. Scoobie talked to some people here, and they said neither of them had been here. It sounded as if Lucas was telling us Kim was a patient, or at least being treated here."

"I'll need to see that note," Morehouse said.

After a bunch of questions that walked us through the last hour, Morehouse spotted Todd coming into the ER and walked toward him. His parting comment was to George. "I thought the fire extinguisher bit was only for TV."

George grinned at me and said, quietly. "Me, too, but I figured, what the hell?"

"Hey, guys." Scoobie walked up. He lowered his voice. "No skull fracture. When Lucas first got in here, the attending checked him for signs of a concussion. Looked to me as if they thought he might have a mild one. Headache, light sensitivity, stuff like that. They thought that cut on his head was from the corner of that metal electrical box."

"Will they keep him, you think?" I asked.

Scoobie shrugged. "They'll probably put a stitch or two in his head. I think they'd usually send him home, but because it happened here, I'll bet they'll want to roll out the red carpet."

"They don't do that when you find a body in the bathroom," I said, realizing that my foot was aching a lot again.

"I'm sure you put it on a customer comment card," George said.

Scoobie grinned, and I sensed that had we not been in the ER they would have high-fived one another. "I'm going back in with Lucas." I walked away from them. *They think they're so funny. This is not funny!*

I pushed the door to his cubicle and it made a gentle swoosh. "Can I come in?"

"Yeah, but could you turn most of the lights off?" Lucas asked.

I saw a light over the sink and turned that on, and then turned off the long overhead florescent light. "That work?"

"Better. They gave me some medicine for this headache. It'll work in a while. You didn't see Kim?"

I pulled a plastic chair next to his gurney. "It's not likely Kim was here. I think someone just wanted to…get at you."

He gave me an intent stare. "I only took a minute for me to see he wasn't helping Kim. The man wanted to know if I saw someone walk into the restroom where the hospital woman was killed. I told him no, and he said I did. I guess I shoved him in the chest. I told him I wanted Kim, and then…that's the last thing I remember. No, wait. The guy sprayed something in my eyes. I rubbed them, and he hit me." He paused. "Or something. My ribs kind of hurt."

"It's weird that whoever attacked you had the key to that closet you were in." *And that Todd Everly did not.* I wondered if the person who attacked Lucas was on the maintenance staff.

"You had it?" he asked. "Of course you didn't."

"George broke in with a fire extinguisher."

"Wish I could have seen that." He started to sit up, leaning on one elbow. "I need to get back out there."

I pushed him down. It wasn't hard. I figured his meds were kicking in. "It'll help a lot if you die because you didn't take it easy after a head injury."

"It's not bad."

"Maybe not, but overnight won't kill you. You'd be sleeping, anyway."

There was a light tap on the door and Scoobie stuck his head in. He looked at Lucas. "I need to borrow Jolie for maybe half an hour. Stay here, and we'll be back."

I followed him into the hall, and when the door shut he whispered. "Alicia called. She said there's someone on the pier who looks like Kim."

CHAPTER NINETEEN

WHAT ALICIA HADN'T said, or at least Scoobie hadn't told me, was that Kim was standing at the edge of the pier, seemingly thinking about jumping off. It was probably fifty degrees with a light wind. In the daytime that might have been fine weather for fall at the beach, but not in early evening.

Ocean Alley's pier is a short one for fishing, not a big one with rides and stuff. Alicia and I stood a few feet back from Kim and Scoobie, and we shivered. "I didn't call the police," Alicia said. "Should I?"

"I'm glad you didn't. It might have made her more desperate."

Scoobie's tone sounded as anxious as I felt. "Kim, listen to me." Scoobie had tried to walk closer to her but Kim moved a few feet further down the railing, so he stopped.

"No!" This came out as a cross between a sob and a curse. "I don't need to listen to anyone. I need to do this." She was almost shaking with cold, in a short-sleeve tee shirt. The jeans I had lent her were wet at the cuffs. I wondered if she had tried to walk into the ocean to drown herself, and wasn't able to do it.

"I was where you are," he said, in a calming tone.

Kim didn't look at him, but I could tell she had heard him. Her shoulders stiffened just a bit. I tried to picture the water below the end of Ocean Alley's short pier. There were stones piled under the pier, ostensibly to protect the wood pilings. Unfortunately, they were about the size of footballs, and some of them would slide into the ocean when the waves were really rough. They'd usually wash back up in almost the same spot, but not always fully under the pier. The water was shallow. If she jumped her head would likely land on a rock.

"I was about your age. My mom was…a mess."

"At least you had one," she whispered.

"That's one way of looking at it." Scoobie lowered his voice. "Did your mom break your arm twice?"

Alicia gasped and looked at me. I nodded and we both looked back at Scoobie and Kim.

Kim turned her head to look at Scoobie and then back at the ocean. "No. Did yours take pills so she didn't have to talk to you?"

"Sometimes. Mostly it was booze and she'd sit in front of the television until she passed out. Your parents can't fix what they broke after they're gone, but you can. You and Lucas."

"Thomas Edward," she said, again almost in a whisper.

"Did you ever call one of those suicide hotlines?"

Kim shook her head, almost imperceptibly.

I turned to Alicia and spoke just above a whisper. Kim wouldn't be able to hear me above the sound of the surf. "I think you should go home. I'll call you and Megan in a bit."

Alicia looked dubious and matched my lowered voice. "She called me. I think she maybe wanted me to talk her out of it."

"You *knew* that she had…issues?"

"No, but mom had shown me her picture, and I thought she'd been at Step 'n Go a couple of times. She's loads thinner and her hair is a different color, but in case it was her I gave her my number last time she was there."

I gave Alicia a look that telegraphed my exasperation.

"If I'd told you, you would have tried to find her there. If she saw you, she'd leave. Besides, I wanted to be sure it was her."

Scoobie kept talking to Kim. "It did help. I called a couple of times. They kept me from doing it, but it didn't make me feel better. Not right then, anyway."

"So why would it help me?" Kim asked.

"Alicia," I almost hissed.

"I'm staying." She stared at Kim, not looking at me.

"Because the third time, this guy talked to me about twenty-five minutes. And then he used this one phrase. I've seen it since, but it was the first time I heard it. He said suicide is a permanent solution to a temporary problem."

When Kim didn't say anything, Scoobie continued. "I thought about it for a few seconds. I almost hung up, but he started talking again."

"What did he say then?"

Yes! She's really talking to Scoobie. I felt almost giddy.

"He asked me how old I was. Again. I wouldn't tell him before that. So I told him I was almost eighteen. Which I was. He said if there was nowhere else I could go there were places that would help me."

Scoobie looked intently at Kim, but just as resolutely she stared at the ocean. "Anyway, the guy started talking about the Salvation Army and the YMCA, Saint Anthony's here in town."

Kim turned to look at Scoobie, and then looked down at the water.

"I don't remember what all the guy said. I didn't say anything, and he finally said he could talk me out of killing myself that day, but I had to decide if I wanted to get up or stay down. For some reason, it sunk in."

Her voice was bitter. "This social worker kept telling me I was smart and had been given lots of *education advantages*. She said I should pull myself together."

Scoobie was quiet for a few seconds. "I hate that expression. It means you have to decide not to be weak, or whatever the person thinks you are. I was a strong person. I just didn't see any way out from where I was."

Kim stared at the ocean some more, but it looked as if she was thinking about what Scoobie had said, not trying to figure out how to jump.

I looked back at Alicia. "I can't thank you enough, but somebody'll see us and call the police. Do you want to have to talk to them?"

"I didn't do anything wrong," she said, in an even, low tone.

"Of course not..."

"But you mean Scoobie can take care of her." Alicia looked at me and turned and walked away.

I hoped she wouldn't be angry with me, but if Kim did jump, I didn't want Alicia to have to see it. It registered that she had said Scoobie would take care of her. *What am I, a sand dune?*

Kim asked Scoobie, "Did you have any money?"

For just a second I thought Scoobie had a smile. "Nah. There was a church that had lunch every day for people who were hungry. I finally came up with a plan, but I don't recommend it."

Kim looked at him. "What did you do?"

"I joined a carnival."

She smiled. "When I was about ten, the circus came to Atlanta. If I could have figured out how to go with them I would have."

"Would you have been willing to shovel pony poop?"

"Eww. No!"

"That's what I had to do the first couple of weeks. And that was the easiest job I had. I came back to Ocean Alley after a few weeks."

"And went back to your parents' house?"

"Nope. Slept on a friend's porch for a while. Then the guy's parents helped me figure out how to apply for college financial aid. You can use some of the money for living expenses."

"And then you were okay?"

"I did a few more dumb things, but I'm okay now.

"Like what?" Kim shivered and rubbed what had to be goose bumps on one arm.

"That would take a week," Scoobie said.

She looked at him, tears on her cheeks. "It's my fault Lucas got hurt. It was the people after my dad, wasn't it?"

"How did you?...If anyone was pissed at him, I bet it was whoever killed a woman at the hospital."

Kim looked distracted. "My mom always said her mom would wash her mouth out with soap when she said words like that."

Her tone was almost dreamy. I started to wonder if she'd taken a drug of some sort. At least she seemed to be off the Lucas topic. *How did she know he was hurt?*

Scoobie sighed. "My mom did it. It was awful. You feel like you have soap in your mouth for hours after."

"Did she say sorry?"

"Nope."

"My mom left me a note. She said she was sorry for everything. But she didn't say what."

Kim put one foot on the railing that was just a foot off the deck of the pier.

"Don't!" Scoobie said.

"Wait!" I hollered.

"I'll help you," Scoobie said. "In a year, I'll help you."

If I didn't trust Scoobie so much I'd have hit him.

She left her foot in place. "Help how? When?"

"Just give it a year. Stay here, make friends, maybe talk to a doc about some meds. Bother Lucas some more."

She gave a tiny smile, but left her foot on the rail.

"I'm serious. I eventually did a lot better on my own, but this doctor who would come to a men's shelter, he gave me some anti-depressants. It took a while, but it made a difference."

"It never helped my mom. She…hey! There's a man down there!"

Kim was so entranced by the man below her that she didn't tell Scoobie and me to stay away when we ran up beside her.

I squinted, though why I thought that would help in the near-dark I don't know. I could see the shape of a man. He was holding onto a piling and seemingly trying to walk from one piling to the next. Waves crashed at his waist and he staggered.

"Who is it?" I yelled.

"Who cares?" Scoobie looked at Kim. "Do not jump until I get back!"

He ran toward the end the pier and down the short flight of steps that went from one side of the pier onto the beach. Then he was out of sight, and I knew he would be for a brief time.

I looked at Kim, and she looked back at me. I could almost touch her if I stretched my arm, but I knew she could elude me and jump in a matter of seconds. "Please don't," I said.

She looked down. "I want to be sure Scoobie's okay."

For the first time I thought she might not jump.

We both leaned over. Scoobie had run into the water. It was almost at his knees, with waves sometimes going higher. He gestured at the guy, who gave an impatient sort of wave, as if telling Scoobie to get lost. I looked more closely. *Could that be*

George? The lights on the pier didn't reach below it, so I couldn't really tell.

There were shouts from behind us and I turned. Two women were running down the beach toward Scoobie and the man.

Scoobie held onto the outer piling and gestured to the man to walk toward him. After a few more seconds the man seemed to be nodding that he would. The tide was coming in and the water was higher than it had been even three minutes ago. The man stumbled and then reached for Scoobie's hand and let himself be guided back to the beach. They were yelling at each other, but I couldn't hear the words over the pounding of the waves on the sand.

As they moved more onto the beach, the two women walked up to talk to them and the light from the pier fell on the four of them.

"George," I said.

"That's the guy who was at your house," Kim said.

"Yeah. What was he thinking?" I looked at Kim. "You don't want to end up on those rocks. Listen to Scoobie. Give it a year."

Kim looked as if she was defeated, but she nodded and took my outstretched hand so we could walk off the pier together.

"YOU ARE INSANE." I directed this at George. He was on my sofa holding a cup of hot tea, and wearing a T-shirt and sweats he borrowed from Scoobie.

George shrugged. "It worked."

"What do you mean?" I asked.

Scoobie, also in dry clothes, came back into the room from his bedroom. "If you tell me you got the idea from *It's a Wonderful Life* I won't believe you."

"What life?" Lucas had walked into the living room. He was so pale that the bandage on the side of his head almost matched his skin. I had gone back to the hospital to tell him Kim would be okay, and he insisted on leaving. He wanted to be with Kim, whom he had just sat with as she fell asleep in my bedroom.

Scoobie pulled out a dinette chair for Lucas, but he pointed to the sofa and sat not far from George and rested his head on the back of the sofa. Scoobie sat in the dinette chair.

"You want me to drive you back to the hospital?" I asked.

"I never want to see that place again." He gave me a weak smile and then looked at Scoobie. "What did you mean?"

"Did you see the movie *It's a Wonderful Life?*" George asked.

Lucas started to shake his head but instead winced. "I think I've heard of it. Really old, right?"

"Nineteen-forties," Scoobie said. "Jimmy Stewart. A guy jumps in a river so ol' Jimmy has to jump in and save him. Keeps Jimmy from jumping off a bridge into the river to kill himself."

"In the movie, Jimmy's name was George. George Bailey," George said, grinning. He looked at me. "You got anything stronger?"

"I'll put something in with the tea," I said, and took his cup and walked into the kitchen. I looked at the back of my food cupboard for a bottle of Amaretto I keep there for Aunt Madge, and listened to the three men.

"So, you figured if she saw you...?" Lucas let his question hang.

"I thought it might distract her enough that Scoobie could get hold of her. I didn't think that Numnuts here would run in after me."

"I thought you were a younger guy, teenager or something, or I would have let you sink," Scoobie said.

"Get smashed you mean," George said.

Lucas spoke slowly, his voice breaking. "So you got in those rocks to try to save Kim?"

"They were both working on it." I called this from the kitchen as I put the alcoholic tea in the microwave.

Lucas sniffed and I heard Scoobie get up to get him a tissue.

"I, uh, may have told her something you won't like," Scoobie said.

He summarized the discussion on the pier, including his promise to help Kim in a year if she still wanted to kill herself.

"How could you do that?" Lucas' voice was weak, but still angry.

Scoobie's tone seemed meant to calm. "I'm banking on her changing her mind, with help from all of us. At the time, I thought it was the only way to keep her from jumping. She would have been killed, for sure."

"I'm not getting in the damn water again. Not with rocks, anyway," George added.

Lucas looked from George to Scoobie as I walked back into the living room and handed George his tea. "You've both got rocks in your head."

George grinned and took a sip. "God, this is awful."

I took the mug out of his hand and poured some on his knee.

CHAPTER TWENTY

SCOOBIE AND I TALKED in low tones as we sat in my kitchen. I didn't think Lucas or Kim were awake at six A.M. on a Saturday, but didn't want to test my supposition.

"You think she knew he was hurt?" I asked.

"She knew something. We looked for him for a while before we found him, but who would have told her?"

"Alicia did," Kim said. She was wearing one of my cotton nightgowns that's more like a long tee-shirt, and she looked about twelve.

"How on earth would she have known we were even looking for him?" I asked.

"*She* has a real mom. Her mom's friend works at the hospital and saw you guys there, and I guess she calls Alicia's mom whenever you get hurt or something."

Scoobie grunted in apparent appreciation and I looked at him. "I bet it was Harriet. She knows Megan, I think."

Scoobie stood and gestured that Kim should take his seat at the table, and reached for a pitcher on the counter to pour her a glass of orange juice. "So how did you end up with Alicia?"

"Her mom told her about me. I met her at that teen club. She said she wouldn't tell anyone where I was if I kept coming out there."

"Smart girl," I said. I didn't really think that, I wanted to shake Alicia. But, I had to grudgingly admit she had probably made a good decision. I looked at Kim directly. "We don't have any idea who called Lucas to go to the hospital. Or hurt him. Why did you think it was your fault?"

"He came here to look for me, and when he found me I ran away."

"Right," I said. "But you don't know who called him yesterday, do you?"

She shook her head. "But they knew he would come if they said they knew where I was."

"Who are *they*?" Scoobie asked. He sounded frustrated. I knew I was.

"The people who knew my dad. My mom said they were *everywhere.* Did Lucas tell you someone came to the house after the funeral?"

I nodded. "He thought that might be why you left."

She shrugged. "I wanted away. Just away. The guy freaked us out, Lucas and me. But I would have left anyway."

"And you thought the people who knew about your dad knew you were in Ocean Alley?" Scoobie asked.

"I thought they might figure it out. I kept seeing this dark green car."

"I saw that car!" I turned to Scoobie. "I thought it followed me one day, but I wasn't sure."

"And of course it made no sense to let anyone know you thought that," he said, irritated.

Kim gave a nervous sort of giggle. "You sound like Lucas and me."

"I wasn't keeping anything from you. I decided it was just me being jumpy."

Scoobie folded his arms across his chest. "So you say."

Kim looked between us, anxiety in her eyes.

"He's not mad…" I began.

"Just wondering if she's going to remember to tell us the important stuff," he said, seemingly trying for a light tone.

Kim looked from him to me and almost hung her head. "I'm sorry I worried you. I just didn't need to…hear about meds." She looked at Scoobie.

"Keep your options open," Scoobie said, and glanced at the clock shaped like an apple that hangs above my sink. "I gotta get to the school library, and then the hospital. You are going to hang here, right?"

She nodded. "For some reason Lucas says we're going to a movie."

I DECIDED NOT TO BE concerned about Kim. She and Lucas needed to figure out what to do next. It occurred to me that she might not want to go back to Georgia with him. I supposed she could stay for a short time. On the couch.

I sat in the parking lot of the dollar store and reviewed my lengthy to-do list. With the corn toss fundraiser the next day, I was getting my familiar panic feeling. I could hear Scoobie say, "It'll happen whether you worry about it or not, so chill."

Easy for him to say.

I entered the store to buy some poster board and markers to make signs for the corn toss, and ran into Max. He sustained a brain injury during service in Iraq, and speaks rapidly, often repeating words.

"I haven't seen you for a couple of weeks," I said.

"I've been busy, busy. I have to rake leaves at my house."

With the help of a friend, Max bought a tiny cottage, paid for with his military benefits. "I drove by there a couple of weeks ago. "It looks like you painted your porch."

"I did. I did. Alicia's friends helped."

She's a great kid. "Are you coming to the Corn Toss tomorrow?"

He shook his head, hard. "People will be throwing things. I don't want to get hit in the head."

I started to tell him it would be safe, and then decided not to. When Max is around, we all try to pay a lot of attention to him. That's fine, except at a busy fundraiser. "I'll try to remember to save you some brownies."

"You don't have to. Aunt Madge is." He smiled at me. "I liked your picture today."

"My pic…?" Damn! George probably wrote an article about Lucas and Kim. "Thanks, I'm glad you told me."

Max walked away, humming.

I bought my supplies and then put coins in the newspaper box outside the store.

Mugging at OA Hospital

A man was knocked unconscious in a first-floor hallway at Ocean Alley Hospital at approximately five-ten PM Friday. He awoke in a utility closet and was rescued by passersby. Though not seriously injured, he did require treatment in the emergency room.

The crime does not appear to have been random. The victim received a call that a relative was at the hospital and he was greeted by a white male in an area of the hospital that is little used after five PM. Information about the relative was apparently a ruse to get the man to the hospital.

The motive for the attack is unclear. The victim did not know his assailant, who is described as white, about five-ten, with straight brown hair and tinted glasses.

The hospital CEO could not be reached for comment before press time, but Todd Everly, Director of Security, said hospital staff and local police were working closely to determine who assaulted the victim. Everly stressed that patients and visitors should "take normal precautions, but do not need to fear for their safety."

The Ocean Alley Press is cooperating with local police in not naming the victim at this time. Additional details will be provided as they become available.

I scanned the rest of the paper and was relieved to see there was not an article about Kim's potential suicide attempt at the pier. George had been true to his word. The piece about the so-called mugging was to be expected, but nothing in the article indicated who Lucas was or why he was in Ocean Alley.

That was one thing I didn't need to be concerned about.

When I folded the paper I did it so that the back page was on top. There was my photo. It was from the spring fundraiser, and my hair was purple and yellow, with purple streams down the front of my tee-shirt. It looked as if I was about to sneeze.

The caption said, "Join Harvest for All and Shop with a Cop volunteers Sunday at the community center. These fundraisers draw a crowd, in part because of their zany themes. A participant in the spring liquid string event presents a colorful reminder."

At least he didn't use my name. *I'll get George later.*

I HAD A LONG list of people to contact about the corn toss and had gone back home to make calls. I wanted to be sure the volunteers weren't overwhelmed and, of course, that they were doing what they had said they would do.

Aunt Madge did not need any such conversation, but I hadn't talked to her for several days.

Harry answered the phone. "Did you get to that appraisal in the popsicle district yesterday?"

"I did, and I stopped by the courthouse to get enough info to get started on my write-up. I'll work on it for a few minutes this evening."

Harry, polite as always, said, "You're so busy, it can wait until Monday."

"Thanks, but it'll be the only sanity I have this weekend."

"Speaking of sanity." Harry handed the phone to Aunt Madge.

"Hello, Jolie. Up to your eyeballs yet?"

"Way over my head. Just wanted to see if you needed any help, or if you had everything under control, as usual."

"Probably more than you do," she said, dryly. "Don't think you'll want to do a raffle again."

"Why not?"

"Just mutterings about enough gambling in the casinos, that kind of thing. Silly, really. Tickets are only a dollar."

I filed that thought away and was about to hang up when she said, "One basket is supposed to be delivered to your house later today. From the hospital."

"The hospital! We've never been able to get them to donate anything."

"No one said this, of course, but I think it's for public relations purposes. That Board of Directors knows it's made some unpopular decisions. It isn't every day you get a senior staffer bumped off in the john."

Too true. I had barely hung up the phone before someone knocked at my door. Lucas and Kim were at the movies, and Scoobie was at the hospital until three, so I peered out the living room window. Jason Logan was balancing a huge basket of goodies on the porch railing.

It isn't every day that someone who might be a murder suspect knocks on my door. I figured if he had told Aunt Madge or someone else that he was stopping by, he wouldn't be likely to have a weapon hidden in the basket.

I opened the front door and stepped aside to let him in, noting his expensive slacks and tan cotton sweater probably cost more than five outfits in my closet. "It's too bad we don't vote on best basket. You might have a winner there."

Logan looked quite pleased with himself as he deposited the heavily laden basket on my dinette table. I followed him into the room, and he pointed to it. "We've got a mix of things to help you stay healthy—he pulled out a bottle of vitamins - things to help if you have an injury - he picked up a box of Band Aides and then an Ace bandage - and healthy snacks."

I nodded in appreciation and looked more closely. "Do I see some M&Ms down there?"

He smiled. "Yes, but they have almonds. Very good for you."

I gestured to the couch. "Do you have time to have a seat?"

"For a minute. I'm always on a tight schedule, and no doubt you are today." He sat on the couch.

His remark sounded as if he meant he thought his schedule was more important than mine, but I decided not to think that way. "It is always rewarding to see how the town helps Harvest for All. There are new donors every time we have a fundraiser."

"Ah yes, well." For a brief moment I thought he was about to raise his hand to his breast coat pocket for a check, but he stopped himself and continued. "I hope the hospital can be more active in the future. There's been so much going on the last few months, our charitable work has been reduced."

I waited. Jason Logan did not come to my tiny bungalow to profess his love for the food pantry.

His posture became a bit straighter, and he said, "We all felt terrible about you finding Tanya."

It was out of my mouth before I could stop myself. "I'm sure she felt worse."

His eyes widened for a second, then he seemed to decide I was not trying to be funny. "Yes, a great loss." He paused for maybe three seconds. "I'm told you've been talking some to Todd Everly, our chief of security."

I hadn't expected that comment. "Yes. You can probably guess that I have a special interest in that day. He's good about answering questions."

"Detailed questions?" His look was intense.

"Not really. I just feel sort of…bound to her. As if I can let go of worrying about the murder when someone is arrested."

"We will all be relieved when her murderer is found." He glanced down. Jazz had come closer, apparently to smell his shoes. I wished Pebbles would make an appearance, but knew she wouldn't.

"I've heard you were good friends."

His tone was sharp. "What do you mean?"

"George found a nice photo of the two of you at a hospital fundraiser somewhere. You know how reporters dig into every story."

He seemed to relax. "We…enjoyed one another's company."

You can't really ask whether the bedroom was the most enjoyable room, so I took a leap. "I heard you were practically engaged."

Logan's jaw tensed and he raised his voice slightly. "That is prepos…not true."

"People do infer too much, I guess." I held his gaze.

"Sometimes people don't understand that friendship can be just that." His words were spoken sharply and quickly, and I wondered if he had rehearsed them.

"Sure. I'm lucky to have a lot of friends."

He stood. "If you should hear anything you think the Board needs to know, will you contact me?"

I stood, too. "Surely, but I can't imagine what that would be."

He moved toward the door. "I guess I'm trying to say if you need more information you don't need to go to a lower-level employee. You're welcome to come to me."

I extended a hand. "Thank you. Will we see you tomorrow?"

He laughed, and it seemed he caught himself before he made it clear it was a derisive laugh. "No, no. Always a busy calendar, you know."

And yet you have time to deliver gift baskets for Harvest for All.

I stood back from my living room window a bit so I wouldn't be too obvious as I watched Jason Logan drive away. I didn't like having him in my house. Especially since I thought his motive was to see if I would be a problem to him. I had no doubt that if he thought I was about to associate him with Tanya Weiss' murder, he would be a big threat. I just wish I knew if he could be implicated.

CHAPTER TWENTY-ONE

THE HFA/SHOP WITH A COP FUNDRAISER would start in about an hour. I looked around the parking lot. Sergeant Morehouse had been right about the community center being the perfect location. We had a lot more African American and Latin attendees than at any other fundraiser, and that was a good thing.

Thanks to Lance's insistence that we abide by the *Farmers' Almanac* prediction, we had a warm October day for the festivities.

I roamed through the parking lot with my clipboard and its to-do checklist trying to strike a balance between being helpful and making sure volunteers were doing what they were supposed to do. If I ever perfect that skill, I'm going to bottle the aroma and sell it to charities. Most volunteers like to do things their way, rationalizing that since they are giving their time all choices should be theirs. In a lot of ways they can, but last year Lester stapled his business card on the back of a clue for our scavenger hunt. Now I pay more attention.

At the almost full bake sale table I had to tell two women from First Prez to put on the thin plastic gloves the Health Department requires us to use. They were both in their early forties, and the blonde frowned. Her red-headed friend said, "Oh, right. Remember that intestinal bug we all got after the Sport League picnic last year?" Her friend agreed and I made a mental note to only drink soft drinks at League events.

Scoobie and George were overseeing the set-up of the corn-toss boxes. They had to be a specific distance away from where someone tossed the bags of corn, and the hole at the top had to be an exact size. Since we'd bought our boxes from the American Legion, I knew most would meet specifications, but we weren't requiring that people who regularly played use our boxes. They did have to have them on site early, so we could inspect them.

We hadn't had time to paint our boxes, so Aretha and Daphne had the great idea of buying a bunch of static cling figures, the kind you put on window glass, and taping them to the boxes. Somehow they had found a bunch that would usually have been sold at Thanksgiving time. They had a food theme, featuring ears of corn (of course), pumpkins and squash. I'd have to remember to compliment the two of them.

The boxes need to be at a forty-five degree angle and sit twenty-seven feet apart. When it appeared there might be grumbling about the measurements, Scoobie got Aunt Madge to oversee placing tape measures so the boxes were the same distance apart. Few people argue with octogenarians, especially when their hair is a newly died carrot orange. *What's that about?*

George also said we had to be careful not to put the Lions Club and Kiwanis's boxes near each other. When he'd stopped in at the Sandpiper Bar for a ginger ale the other day, George had heard something about wagers among the players on those two teams. I was glad we didn't sell beer at our fundraisers. Father Teehan always chimed in about that and said the Knights of Columbus men wouldn't play well if we did.

Harry was overseeing the formation of teams. We asked that groups sign up in advance, but it wasn't a requirement. We just wanted an idea of how long it would take to run through the first round of games. We had plenty of boxes and bags, since teams that brought their own had to agree to let other teams play rounds at the teams' boxes, if we didn't have enough of our own. *What are we going to do with all those boxes when today is over?*

There would be a first round with probably dozens of teams (not all playing at once), and each round would have half the number of teams of prior rounds. I hoped we'd be done with all the games in less than two hours, but had no idea.

Because there were a number of single people or couples who wanted to play on a team, Harry was trying to accommodate individual requests and match singles with teams that were short a player. Unfortunately, Ramona's Uncle Lester was offering advice. His voice carried, and I was glad it was now mostly volunteers in the community center parking lot.

"See, Harry, if you make a team all men, they're sure to win. You gotta mix up men and women. To be fair, you know? And tall and short people."

I was passing the spot where Ramona was setting up her table to do caricatures for a donated fee. "How is it that you're related to someone like that?"

She stood. "I'll try to get him away from Harry."

Just then Lester saw me. "Jolie. You on a team yet?" He started toward me.

"I'm not going to..."

"You gotta play, kid. Everybody'll root for you."

George yelled from about ten meters away. "Then they don't know her." He and Scoobie high-fived, so I ignored them.

Lester had reached me. "The thing is, I'll be overseeing a lot of activities, and I don't think..."

Ramona joined us. "You know what, Jolie? I think you and I should be on a team together."

Lester's eyes brightened. "I could..."

"No, Uncle Lester," she said, in super sweet tone. "It's going to be all women."

Lester took the hint and walked back over to badger Harry.

"Good one, but I'd probably be lousy. I'm still not balancing well."

She gave a rather determined smile. "A couple women from my yoga class wanted us to be part of a team. We hadn't talked about all women, but in honor of my uncle, I think we'll go that route."

"You probably won't win with me on your team."

"No worries." She walked back to her table of charcoal pencils and art paper.

My final stop was the long row of tables that had large baskets of food and gift items. Two especially large ones were going to be raffled, and the others would be part of a silent auction. Unless there weren't many bids, then we'd push more raffle tickets.

"Aunt Madge. Wow." There were probably thirty baskets, and a couple of local florists had volunteered to wrap them in colorful pieces of plastic. She, or someone, had also rounded up a few other prizes, one of which was a bicycle from the company that rents beach gear. Could be a lot of raffle ticket sales.

"It is impressive," she said. "And Mr. Markle said that probably forty people said they were buying at his place for either the baskets or the canned food donations."

"Oh, that's great. If he goes out of business it would be a disaster for the food pantry."

"I don't think he will," she said, as she lined up the papers and pens for silent auction bids. "When Reverend Jamison made a pitch for people to come or donate, he said they should really go to Mr. Markle's store for canned goods or whatever. Because he's such a strong supporter of Harvest for All."

Scoobie walked up and caught the end of her comments. "And George said Father Teehan made some kind of joke from the pulpit about people needing to go to confession if they went to a big box store."

"Don't want to be overly critical of those stores. They donate, too." Sylvia and Aretha had walked up. As usual, Sylvia's tone was kind of like a bossy teacher.

"Good point," Aunt Madge said, quickly. "Sylvia, I'd like some help setting minimum bids for the silent auction."

Aretha looked at me and rolled her eyes as they began to walk away. "We should be good for all shifts of volunteers. I didn't get anyone for the bake sale table, though. Monica said she wanted to handle it by herself."

"Oh, boy. I'll see if she changed her mind." Scoobie left us and walked toward the large table of breads and sweets.

"Aretha, you really got a lot of volunteers in a short period of time. Thanks so much."

She gave me the kind of evil grin Aunt Madge has been known to send my way. "I told them we'd have a soup supper for volunteers. You're cooking. You're lucky your house isn't big enough."

Ohhh-kaaay. One more event.

It was twenty minutes before we would let people in to play, and probably forty people waited at the edge of the community center parking lot. Some of the people who played on regular teams had brightly colored shirts with team names, and a lot of people had on Harvest for All tee-shirts. A quick look at the parking lot showed more cars arriving every few seconds.

I had looked from the lot back toward the bake sales tables when something registered in the back of my mind. I scanned the parking area. Several cars were coming in, and a green sedan was leaving! I took several quick steps in that direction, but it was too late to catch a plate. The car had already pulled into traffic.

Scoobie and George were a good twenty meters away from me. And what would I say to them? Follow that car? *It's nothing. Someone just pulled in to see why lots of people were at the community center.*

Laughter drew my attention. Alicia and her group of high school friends were piling corn bags next to each of the boxes, four next to each. Clark and a couple other guys were pretending to throw bags at the girls, and they were pretending to be fearful. *Forget the car. Bean bags are the only thing to be afraid of today.* Or so I hoped.

I watched the teens measure between the boxes to make sure that twenty-seven feet separated the them. It would be a really long pitch, and I was glad we'd borrowed a couple clown-face beanbag toss boards for young kids. Those were on the edge of the lot, so kids didn't get hit with adult-thrown corn bags that went off-course.

I sighed. It was so much to keep track of. Plus, despite tying my sneaker really tight, I could feel my foot starting to swell a bit. I plopped on a picnic table bench and stretched my leg in front of me.

Daphne sat across from me. "Bet you wish you were at the library. Cooler than out here."

"And it would mean this was finished. I get so nervous before these fundraisers."

"Really? You always look like you know exactly what you're doing."

"What an opening." Scoobie sat next to Daphne and looked at me. "I think we're good to go. Dr. Welby's going to help Lance collect the five bucks from people who will actually play, and I gave him a hand stamp to use when they pay."

Uh oh. "What's on the stamp?"

"Not telling." He walked toward Dr. Welby and Lance.

"Do you know?" I asked.

Daphne shook her head. "All I know is he got Ramona to order it for him from one of the Purple Cow's suppliers."

My brow unfurrowed. "Can't be anything bad."

"He wouldn't do anything…untoward," she said.

"No, just embarrassing." I stood and walked toward the two refreshment trolleys a couple of the boardwalk vendors had set up. They would retain some of the money for the food they bought to sell, but planned to donate most of what they would take in. I used to be surprised that they were so willing to do this, but when I talked to Aunt Madge about it one day she said it was because they saw the contingent of hungry, homeless people on the boardwalk all summer.

"You folks all set?" I smiled at the woman who had made what looked like hundreds of candy apples. Next to her was her friend who operated the salt water taffy store. She had boxes of the stuff piled on the table in front of her. I thought that the two women were in their mid-sixties, though decades of sun and cigarettes had given them finely lined faces, so they could have been younger.

"We are. We'll have half the town on a sugar high in an hour."

Great. That should enhance their throwing arms.

Dr. Welby's booming voice quieted everyone. He had a megaphone, but really didn't need it. "In five minutes you can come up to the corn toss boxes."

Someone yelled, "Corn hole boxes," but Dr. Welby ignored them.

He continued. "We won't start the contest itself for forty-five minutes, to give everyone time to sign up for a team and read the rules, which are posted behind me. And do some practice pitches. Play nice. The ER is busy on weekends."

There was general laughter, and people came into the area with corn toss boxes and spread out to look at them, buy food, and decide if they wanted to bid for a gift basket.

I walked over to where Lance and Dr. Welby were busily collecting money from their spots seated opposite each other at a large picnic table. I caught Dr. Welby's eye and waved a thanks for his opening remarks. I hate to stand in front of crowds and talk.

"Jolie?" I looked at a woman in her early forties, who looked very fit and tall. She smiled. "I'm Ramona's friend. She said to tell you our team is the Power Women, and the most important thing is that if we play her Uncle Lester's team, we beat them."

I smiled. "Does she think that'll be hard?"

"I heard Lester got a bunch of twenty-somethings to play with him."

"I wonder how he did that?" I mused.

She grinned. "Burger King gift certificates."

"Ah." I checked out the bake sale table where Monica had finally agreed to have helpers. Daphne and Jennifer Stenner, who owns the other appraisal firm in town, were hard at work. Jennifer was unpacking a box of the over-sized chocolate chip cookies she makes. They would probably sell in two minutes. Monica had her perpetually puzzled look and walked up and down behind the table, stopping now and then to rearrange a basket of apples and bananas.

I was wiped out already, but got a spurt of energy when I saw Kim and Lucas walking toward me. Kim looked relaxed and happy, and Lucas had told me earlier that he wasn't going to mention going to a doctor.

As angry as I had been with Scoobie for his promise to help Kim in a year, I was beginning to understand that she saw Scoobie as an ally. It might have made her feel less alone. I supposed, for now, I'd have to trust Scoobie.

Lucas had accepted a ride from Harry, which I took as admission that he knew his head injury, while a bit better, was not something to take lightly. As I waved to the two of them, Lucas sat on a bench and Kim took a bottle of water from a nearby ice chest and handed it to him. *Good for her to have to help someone.*

I had not told anyone that Kim thought someone had been following her. It didn't seem like a conversation to have in a hurry. If I told Morehouse, he'd make her go to the station on a day when she could be having fun, something I though Kim really needed. I rationalized that today Lucas and Kim would be not only with us but a whole bunch of police officers. They'd be safe.

"You guys ready for some fun?" I asked.

"Kim is," Lucas said. "I don't want to be a wimp, but I'm still in chill out mode."

Kim looked around. "Can I be on a team?"

Before I could answer I heard Scoobie calling to both of them, and I told Kim I'd try to watch if she played.

She walked away and Father Teehan hailed her. By name. She gave a broad wave and kept walking. *That's where she stayed!* I should have guessed that one of the churches helped her. Kim looked too good to have been sleeping outside. I wondered why Father Teehan hadn't mentioned her to me. Then I heard Scoobie's voice saying I, and my issues, were not the center of the universe. Father Teehan didn't know who Lucas was to me, and if the priest helped Kim it was probably confidential, anyway.

My thoughts turned from Kim to someone else calling my name. It was Ramona. "Hurry up! I want you to practice."

There wasn't anything I needed to check on at the moment, so I joined her and the other two women. I'd waved at them when I occasionally dropped off Ramona at her yoga class, but I didn't really know them.

"Feel the weight of the bag," Ramona said. She handed me one and the shortest of her friends laughed at the expression on my face.

"It's heavy."

"You didn't help sew them?" the friend asked.

"Jolie, this is Suzie." Ramona nodded at the woman who was maybe in her mid-twenties and, like Ramona, in top shape. "And this is Serena."

"I didn't sew any. I'm kind of all thumbs." I hefted it from one hand to another. "It's not all that heavy, I was just surprised."

Suzie and Serena nodded as they moved a few feet away and began tossing corn bags to one of the boxes.

Ramona took the bag from me. "Since you haven't done this, we've put you as the third thrower. You can watch what we do, but you won't have the pressure of being last."

"Why is that pressure?"

"If we're down by just a point or two, you won't feel like you blew it if you miss."

"I probably will," I said, aware that I was starting to perspire just thinking of being the one to cause the team to lose.

It didn't take me long to realize why most people threw underhanded. I did several tosses, and one actually hit the box. Then I realized I needed to pay my five dollars, so I walked to the picnic table where Lance and Dr. Welby were collecting donations. Two huge cardboard boxes held donated food, and a metal money box on the table between them looked pretty full when Lance opened it to deposit an entry fee.

I pulled a couple of crumpled bills from the pocket of my shorts and handed one to Lance as I looked at Dr. Welby. "Does this cover insurance if I trip?"

Lance shook his head as he took the bill and put it in the money box. "You wish. As long as you aren't driving you're fine."

You can't make rude comments to people in their nineties.

Dr. Welby pressed the hand stamp onto the ink pad. "Let me have your hand, Jolie."

"What's on the stamp?"

"Same as for everyone else," Lance said, and smiled.

Dr. Welby carefully stamped my hand, making sure that all parts of the ink would show. I looked at it. It was an ear of corn that appeared to be sitting on a round black circle. A corn hole.

"Great. If you guys don't need me, I thought I'd play a round with Ramona and her friends. And then I need to go kill Scoobie."

It was getting close to start time, and I saw Father Teehan and Reverend Jamison talking as they looked at writing on a clipboard Reverend Jamison held. I walked toward them. "You guys are officiating? I didn't know that."

Father Teehan grinned. "We heard that impartial scorekeepers were needed. But officiating? No."

"That would be Lieutenant Tortino." Reverend Jamison nodded toward the tall police officer, whom I hadn't noticed in his painter's pants and a dark blue tee-shirt.

"I thought the police were going to do the scoring, too." I said.

"Apparently there is a four-person team of rank-and-file, and another one of officers," Reverend Jamison said.

"Rumor has it scoring might not be…impartial." Father Teehan looked as if he was having the time of his life. I remembered that half of the police force sold Christmas trees at

Saint Anthony's each year, so he probably knew most of them well.

"And I'm monitoring these two," a man's voice said.

I turned to see the Unitarian Minister, Reverend Gibson. His group has just started doing quarterly food drives for Harvest for All. "Gee, thanks."

As the three men walked toward the eight sets of corn toss boxes, I heard Father Teehan say, "I'm not sure you're holy enough."

I had to smile. Sylvia and Monica still weren't sure we should consider the Unitarians a church group.

Lieutenant Tortino picked up the megaphone that was on the table where Lance and Dr. Welby were sitting. "Okay folks, I think we have all the teams registered. Are you ready to play?"

It was a rhetorical question, which was greeted with a mix of cheers and good natured threats from the Lions to the Kiwanis. At least they seemed good-natured.

There were sixteen teams. That would go to eight, then four, and finally a playoff between the top two teams. I could see it going on for a couple of hours, and was glad it was warm rather than really hot. I grabbed a cup of water from a First Prez volunteer, whose name I couldn't remember, and walked to Ramona and her friends.

Lieutenant Tortino introduced Reverend Jamison to explain the scoring.

"It sounds a little complicated, but it's really, not," Reverend Jamison began. "Each team member throws their four bags, then a player on the other team throws theirs. After all players on both teams have thrown their four bags, we score the round. A bag remaining on the box is worth one point. A bag that went in the hole counts for three points. If it's next to a box..."

"Or five feet in front of it," George yelled.

"Or anywhere else," Reverend Jamison continued, "no points. The first team to get to twenty-one wins that game. If they are two points ahead of the other team, I should say." I listened to him explain that each player would probably throw more than one set of four bags to get a team to twenty-one points, with the opponent having nineteen or less.

Father Teehan took over the scoring explanation. "We aren't going to score exactly as they do in tournaments, because it would take more time than we have today. But the basic principal is the same, you want to get to twenty-one points—and be at least two points ahead of your opponent at that time."

Lieutenant Tortino added, "Usually, it takes two games to win a match, but we aren't going to do it that way."

There was a light chorus of boos, and I could tell Lester was among the cat-callers.

Reverend Jamison yelled, "You know who issues parking tickets, right?" A bunch of people laughed.

"Seriously," Lieutenant Tortino said, "We'd be here for hours, and for a lot of us that would take the fun out of it."

"And we'd run out of brownies." Aunt Madge said this. It hadn't occurred to me that she would play, which was silly, because she is more fit than I am. She and Harry were standing with a couple who owned one of the other B&Bs in Ocean Alley.

I looked around and saw Lucas with Scoobie with George. Scoobie saluted and pointed to the back of his hand. I raised my hand and barely stopped myself from giving him a rude hand gesture.

Lieutenant Tortino went on to describe first-round pairings. Ramona's group, which is how I thought of our impromptu team, would face a group of friends who played bridge together. They looked to be in their mid-fifties, and I felt kind of sorry for them until about ten seconds after we started playing. Then the tallest man of the mixed-gender group threw four bags in quick succession. Two went in a hole and two sat on the box.

We were alternating throws between the teams. Suzie was first on our team, then Selena then me. I did get one to hit the box. The next time it was my turn I got one in the hole and one on the box, and was as excited as if I'd won the lottery. Ramona, as our closer, usually got three in the hole.

It took almost thirty minutes, but our team finally beat out the bridge players. Little credit to me.

"It'll be at least ten minutes before the next round," Ramona said. "You probably have things to check on."

The bake sale table was swamped. Several games had just ended and watchers and contestants were celebrating. It looked as if we might run out of food. I was about to either beg off my team or find someone to run to the store when Mr. Markle pulled into the part of the parking lot that was not roped off. He was in his store's small pick-up truck, which had "In Town Market" in big letters on the door and bed cover.

Alicia's friend Clark jumped out and grabbed two boxes from the back end. He got to the bake sale table and Sylvia almost fell on the boxes to open them. I figured she had sent Clark to get more food.

I walked over to unpack, but Sylvia waved me away. "You need to rest." Her cheeks were pink and she looked, well, happy. *That's a first.*

Mr. Markle walked to me. "Jolie. I can't donate this much, but I'll sell it to you at cost."

"I can't thank you enough."

He gave one of his rare smiles. "You have already. I think it was this publicity," he nodded toward the game area, "that brought a lot of people back to the store."

I was all sweaty, so I didn't kiss him. As I walked back toward Ramona and the Corn Toss boxes, I glanced at what Sylvia and Clark were unpacking. Cupcakes, bags of potato chips and kid-size boxes of juice. *Who says food pantries can't serve junk food?*

The eight teams in the second round were a varied mix of skills. Both police teams had survived, as had the team George and Scoobie put together, which was the two of them, Alicia, and Kim. That made me feel good.

For a moment I thought Lester's team had been eliminated, but his unique bark of laughter reached me. "Like I said, the teams that were all women are gone."

"Except one," I said, as I walked by.

"What?" He stared at me, and then his gaze must have met Ramona's, because he looked almost stricken.

I glanced her way to see her rubbing her nose with her middle finger, and laughed.

As luck would have it, our team played Lester's, which was composed of two other male realtors and a tall woman I didn't know but thought worked at the Wal-Mart on the highway leading out of town. The cynic in me figured that Lester picked her because of her height, which definitely could be an advantage. Longer arms, longer throws.

I was feeling more confident, though my foot wasn't, so I sat on the grass while Suzie and Selena threw their first four bags each. As I was about to get up, Scoobie's voice said, "Coming through for invalid assistance."

Before I could wave them off, he and George each grabbed me under one armpit and hauled me up. I knew how sweaty I was, so I figured I didn't need to worry about them doing that again. They ran off, fists in the air, pretending to be doing some kind of a victory run. There was a smattering of applause, but most people were viewing the match between the Lions and Kiwanis, which involved more cross-team taunts than the other groups.

Ramona handed me a bag, and I steadied myself carefully, concentrating on staying just behind the throw line. Twenty seven feet is a long distance when you're throwing a six by six bag of corn seed. The first bag landed on the box.

I relaxed. No one was watching us, since the Lions were causing a ruckus with a horn that roared. "Knock it off," yelled Tortino, and the roars stopped.

My next two bags also landed on the box, and the fourth actually went in. From the congratulations from my teammates, you'd have thought I'd just won at least a bronze medal at the Olympics.

By the time Ramona was up on the second set of throws for our team, the score was tied at eighteen. Apparently Ramona didn't want to bend over to pick up each of her four bags, because Suzie stood next to her, kind of like a waiter at a cocktail party, except holding corn bags instead of champagne flutes.

It was over in less than fifteen seconds. Ramona must have been waiting for this moment. In four perfectly fluid motions, she took each corn bag and lobbed it at the box. Each flew into a hole. Thump. Thump. Thump. Thump.

Lester's usual unlit cigar dangled from his lips and then fell to the ground. As people cheered, Ramona bowed toward him and said, "Ash hooooooooooole."

I thought someone would have to peel Scoobie off the ground, but he got up on his own and kind of brayed at Lester.

Even Lester's teammates congratulated Ramona. Lester picked up his cigar and shook it at her, but I could tell he was more astounded than mad.

I felt kind of guilty moving to the Final Four, since the talent clearly came from the other three members of our team. But not that guilty. Then I saw who our competitor was, and I groaned.

Sergeant Morehouse was apparently part player and part coach for the officers and he moved among them, clearly advising a couple other players on how to throw better. *Oh boy.* I walked toward the bake sale table and got a cup of water. I drank all of it and took another cup back to the playing area with me.

It was almost four o'clock. In the summer that would still be really hot, but not so in October at the shore. There still wasn't much breeze, but it was getting cooler. I wished I'd brought a wind breaker. It never pays to get sweaty and then cold.

"So, the final four." George looked glum.

"Who beat you?" I asked.

"Rank and file cops. They're playing the Lions."

"And we're playing the officers," I said slowly. "So the final could be the two teams of cops?"

"Yep. I got extra batteries for my camera."

Scoobie walked up. He was doing pretend punches and dancing around like a boxer in training. "Want any advice?"

"How do we get rid of hecklers?" I asked.

"We beat them," Ramona said.

Our third round was over fast. Morehouse and company made quick work of us. They were too polite to gloat. I saw George hand Scoobie five dollars and made a mental note to find out whether Scoobie bet for or against Ramona's team.

"Good job, Ramona." I nodded toward the food selling area. "I think I need to spend some time behind the tables.

She grinned. "We won when it counted."

I had been working behind the food tables for about fifteen minutes when the game between the Lions and the rank-and-file cops ended to raucous cheers from the Kiwanis, which meant the Lions lost.

Tortino's magnified voice came again. "Okay, folks. Time for the championship. Spectators, don't stand too close to the boxes.

We don't want anyone hit with a corn bag." His tone became somewhat strident. "Especially opposing team members."

Reverends Jamison and Gibson had their arms wide and were urging spectators to back up a few feet from the boxes. Father Teehan appeared to be explaining the last round's scoring to the woman who had been blowing the roaring horn for the Lions Club. She gave a curt nod and walked off.

Scoobie's voice came from just behind me. "I hope she accepted the explanation. Otherwise, I heard the Lions were going to boycott the next can drive."

I glanced at him. "I can't believe people are that immature."

"Oh, right. Because you never used a squirt gun from under the boardwalk," he said.

"It was your idea."

"And I was the one who got you to stop." Lieutenant Tortino said that as he walked by, not even looking at us.

"I wish his memory wasn't so good," I muttered.

"Come on, I found the best place to watch from."

I followed Scoobie to one of the picnic tables. George was sitting on the table top and made room for the two of us. "I had to fight off Ramona and her friends, so I wouldn't walk over that way." George nodded to a cluster of people standing behind the box that the police officers would throw to. Ramona was looking our way and scratched her nose again.

"I never saw her do that until today," I said.

"Ah yes, the competitive spirit," Scoobie said.

THE DAY WAS MOVING from twilight toward dark. All the goody baskets had been sold before the match finally ended. Captain Edwards, whom you don't often see around town, essentially threw the losing bag. If it had hit the hole, the officer team would have won. Sergeant Morehouse looked like he wanted to punch the captain.

I watched Dana Johnson slap two other rank-and file officers on the back, and then I turned to Scoobie. "It almost looked as if the captain lost on purpose."

Scoobie shrugged. "Maybe help with police union negotiations. George'll have the photos to prove it either way."

I WAS SO TIRED when the four of us pulled into my gravel patch-cum-driveway that I was out of my car before I noticed the green sedan parked at the curb. I stopped just before I got to the porch and Kim almost bumped into me.

"What the..." Kim followed my gaze. "It's that car."

Scoobie had not heard us as he walked past us and up the steps, jiggling keys as he walked. "Why can't I find a key when I'm in a hurry?"

I spoke to Kim. "I think so, too."

Scoobie got the house door open as Lucas reached Kim and me. He seemed to have heard part of what we said.

"First dibs on bathroom," Scoobie called, and banged the screen door as he went in.

Lucas squinted at the car as the driver's door opened. "Is that...?"

Kim caught her breath. "It is!" As Lucas started for the green car, Kim turned to me. "It's our marshal. I hope dad's okay."

Lucas reached the sedan and shook the man's hand. Then the two of them turned to walk to Kim and me. I hoped the man didn't have bad news for Kim and Lucas.

The marshal gestured that all of us should go into the house.

Excuse me, it is my house.

Scoobie walked into the living room from the bathroom as I came into the room with the other three. "Doesn't look like a party," he said.

"This is our marshal, Mr. Steuben," Lucas said.

"Benjamin Steuben," he said, not looking at me.

Scoobie reached an arm to shake the man's hand, but the marshal was busy with something on his computer tablet. Scoobie pulled his arm back and waved at his face. Kim giggled.

I felt like telling good old Marshall Steuben that when people show up at my house they usually want to talk to me. I didn't.

Steuben looked up. "There's someone who has something to say to you two." He turned his phone so that Lucas and Kim could see the screen.

Lucas said, "Dad," and Kim said, "Daddy."

I took in Douglas Householder's salt and pepper hair and a more lined face than expected for someone in his mid-fifties or so.

Lucas looked guarded and spoke in a low tone. "Kim's doing a lot better. Today was…a great day."

"I can tell him," Kim said, but asserting herself, not being petulant. "I'm going to work on...some stuff Dad. I promise."

Lucas looked at Scoobie and me, and his gaze rested on Kim before he looked again at his father. "Are we…going somewhere?"

Douglas shook his head. "I am. I made a deal. You don't have to come."

Kim whispered, "No."

He looked at her. "It's time for you two to live openly. At the beach if you want." He gave a swift smile. "And I do need to go tonight. I've looked over my shoulder hundreds of times since that man came to the house. As far as I know, no one has looked for me again, but they could anytime."

"And they won't look for us?" Something close to anger had crept into Lucas' tone.

"Not likely. The people who were angriest at me know I can't hurt them anymore."

Steuben looked at Lucas with a genuine smile. "You can join the debate team." His gaze encompassed Kim as well. "You two can come, you might even be able to do that if you decide in a day or two. But you know what the rules would be."

"New names?" Kim whispered.

The man nodded, and kept his voice low. "The statute of limitations has run out on some financial crimes we're aware of. You were children. There is no reason for anyone to look for you. We have a way of letting the right people know that no one can get to your dad through you. And with the statute of limitations ended, no one really cares."

Scoobie's tone held a lot of sarcasm. "Kind of a deal with the devil?"

The marshal hesitated. "More like honor among thieves."

Lucas looked at his father. "You're deserting us."

Before Douglas could speak, Kim said. "No, he isn't. He's setting us free." Her voice dropped to a whisper. "Like mom wanted to be."

Douglas winced. "Yes. But with stipulations."

Lucas had adopted his mulish expression, and his father continued. “You can keep the names you have now, and you have to visit your aunts.”

Kim’s expression could only be described as elated. “We can? We really can?”

“Douglas,” the marshal said, “we should cut this short. You know we can't be on too long.”

Lucas’ expression had softened, but I could tell he had a lot of questions. As he started to speak, the marshal said, “Can’t tell you more, Lucas. You’re going to have to be satisfied with not knowing.”

Lucas nodded, with seeming reluctance. “But Kim will be safe.”

“And you, too, Mr. Bossy.” Kim had regained her happy expression, and she turned to her father. “I know I’ll miss you, and maybe someday we can be together. But even more than being with you, I want to be able to be me.”

“Touché,” Steuben said, but softly. He looked directly at Lucas. “We’ve never done anything exactly like this, but you guys were little kids, and the statutes are up. It can work. Now, we’ve really *got* to end this call.”

I wanted to ask why it mattered, but for a change I kept quiet.

The marshal shook hands with Lucas and me, and Kim gave him a quick hug. Scoobie picked up the phone and I wasn't sure whether it was to avoid shaking hands or if he really had a call.

"I'll, uh, fix us some iced tea," I said. "I'm still hot from all the running around."

Aunt Madge came from the speaker phone. "Not hot tea?"

I smiled at Scoobie and spoke toward the phone. "Come on over."

Aunt Madge didn't respond to that, but her voice moved into what I think of as her take-charge mode. “Kim, it’s coming on winter, and I have few guests. You’ll have Jolie’s old room for a while.”

“And I live on the roof?” Lucas said, but smiling.

"There's an extra dog bed in the basement," Aunt Madge said.

I felt the tension begin to drain from the room.

He caught the joke and grinned at Scoobie. "That'll work. Thanks."

Aunt Madge talked to Scoobie for another moment and hung up.

"Will you move up here?" I asked Lucas.

He nodded. "I have to give notice, and I should stay there a few weeks, 'til they replace me. The hospital I work for has been really good to me."

Kim looked worried. "Can you find a job here?"

"I've met some people at this hospital," Lucas said, dryly.

CHAPTER TWENTY-TWO

I DIDN'T WAKE UP until nine-thirty on Monday, and my leg immediately found a wet spot on the bed. *I have to stop going to sleep with an ice bag on my foot.*

There was a light tap on the door, and I realized there had likely been a prior tap that had awakened me. Probably Lucas or Kim, who were sleeping on air mattresses in the living room. "Kim?"

"Nope," Scoobie said. "Just wanted you to know I'm leaving for work and the kiddies are up."

"Open the door."

"If you're going to be officious about it." He turned the handle and poked his head around the door jamb.

I took in his still damp hair and freshly washed scrubs and felt that pang of… what?... again. "Thanks."

"No trouble to make extra pancakes," he said.

"You know what I mean."

"Sadly, I do get you." He grinned and left.

I stayed in bed another minute. The sense of relief about Kim and Lucas being safe was coupled with the sense of accomplishment I always feel after a successful fundraiser. But there was something else, and I was beginning to know what it was. What I would do about it, I had no idea.

Apparently certain that I was awake, Pebbles arose from her pet bed in the corner of my room and looked at me intently. Unlike with a dog, or even a cat sometimes, there is no sense of communication with a skunk. I'm supposed to know when she's hungry or…

"Yikes." I sat up and swung my legs to the floor. After assessing that I could put weight on my foot, even after standing most of the day yesterday, I stood and walked to my bedroom door and opened it. It's propped open at night so Pebbles can get to her litter box in the coat closet. Someone must have closed it so I could keep sleeping.

Since I had responded to her nonverbal instruction, Pebbles walked to the door and waddled out. As she left, Jazz's head appeared at the door jamb.

"Lucas and Kim let you out?"

"She was out here." Kim pushed the door open and looked at me. "Your skunk just came out."

I wasn't sure if she was pleased or wary. "She's getting used to you."

"Does your Aunt Madge let her visit the B&B?"

"One of the dogs has met Pebbles, but I don't think Aunt Madge would be too welcoming." Jazz came into the room and wove between my ankles. I reached down to pet her and she head-butted my wrist. "I'm getting you food."

"Lucas fed her. Do you want to use the bathroom before I jump in the shower?"

I said no and she called to Lucas to say what she was about to do.

"Keep the window shut," he said.

MONDAY WAS A REALLY busy day. Lance likes someone to be with him when he counts the money from a fundraiser, and there would be a lot of sorting to do at the food pantry. I didn't know how much food had been donated yesterday, but I knew it was at least one pick-up truck load because I'd seen Alicia and her friend Clark leaving in his truck.

I checked my email to see if any banks had let us know that an appraisal request was coming, and stopped by the Steele Appraisals office to check for faxes.

A single page was in the fax machine. "It ain't over 'til it's over."

Lester's scrawl is unique. It occurred to me that I probably shouldn't have sent him a response fax a few days ago. He'd be looking for one now.

I shrugged and wrote, "It is if you know how to keep score," and faxed it back.

I STOPPED AT THE In-Town Market. There were more cars in the lot, and I stood just inside the door to take in the people shopping. Two cash registers were open and the screech of a cart wheel that needed oil reached me.

After wandering around for a minute, I found Mr. Markle in the freezer section unpacking a carton of frozen pizza. I hoped it meant he was short-staffed because of a sudden up-tick in business.

He looked up. "Kept your promise." He went back to unpacking.

"It was more the churches, I think. I heard something about threats from pulpits if you had to shut." I leaned against the freezer door.

"Your body heat will change the freezer temperature.

Ah, the Mr. Markle I know and love. "Are you saying I have a hot bod?"

He looked startled at my informal banter, and then surprised me by smiling. "You get plenty of donations yesterday?"

"I'm heading over there now. Looked like at least one...hey, I've been too busy to read the papers for a couple of days. Did they ever catch who robbed you?"

"Funny you should ask. This morning Morehouse called to say they're beginning to think it was someone passing through."

"Hmm. Wonder why they think that?"

"Probably don't want to admit they can't catch someone," Mr. Markle said.

"Did he mention the corn toss?"

"Oh yes. I wouldn't want to be Captain Edwards today."

MONDAY IS ONE of our thrice-weekly days for Harvest for All to be open, and a lot of times it's is a hard day. People who had little food over the weekend are not happy to start the week on an empty stomach. Today there was pleasant banter among the patrons. Many had been at the corn toss, and Megan had wisely said that if someone needed a can of food yesterday, they could take it.

George had apparently written an article in the *Ocean Alley Press,* because I heard someone say they were in a photo. It hadn't occurred to me that the paper was missing from my kitchen table for any reason other than there were four people in the house. I began to think it might have been missing because of what it said.

"Do you have the paper?" I asked Megan.

"I wondered when you'd ask. George dropped one off for you."

I took it and muttered, "I hate it when they do that." At her puzzled look I added, "They coordinate. Scoobie and George. The paper wasn't in my house this morning. Or if it was it was hidden."

Megan smiled. "You'll see why."

"Turn to page three," a patron said. She was one of a group that had come together on the city bus that picks up people individually, usually elderly or disabled people. I realized she was the woman I'd seen at the hospital a couple of weeks ago who was so concerned about stool softener being available at Mr. Markle's store.

"Uh, thanks." I leaned against the counter and studied the front page. The fundraiser was featured prominently in the top right column, and a box in the middle of the story said "photos on page 3."

The article was concise.

Cops Take the Top Spot at HFA Games

Competition was friendly but in some cases intense at the Sunday afternoon corn toss contest, held at the OA Community Center. Harvest for All and Shop with a Cop volunteers and supporters either played or watched the competition, which began with sixteen teams.

The article spent most of the space on the final game between the two groups of police. Morehouse was quoted. "Some of the newer officers thought youth was an advantage, but experience tends to even things out, even if sometimes people at the top get a little soft."

Uh-oh. I was glad I didn't have to be in the police station this morning.

I turned to page three. It was all event photos. The editor is generous about this because more pictures lead to more newspaper sales. I hadn't noticed that Tiffany, the newer reporter-cum-photographer, was there, but most credits were hers. She had managed to include many teams and had a great photo of boxes of food that were piled near the bake sale tables.

It was impossible to ignore the photo in the middle of the page, which featured me, knees bent and ready to do one of my underhand throws. My arm was drawn back, corn bag in hand. My face didn't have the kind of scrunched up expression George likes to feature, but the photo did show Scoobie about five feet behind me holding a pair of long bunny ears, like kids have at Easter. He looked quite pleased with himself.

I looked at Megan. "I didn't see him with those."

"You probably weren't supposed to."

"Oh my." At the bottom of the page there was a photo that showed the expanse of the bake sale and snack table. Sylvia was at the far end, and Scoobie was a couple of feet behind her, again with long rabbit ears. George was credited with both rabbit ear photos.

Megan was already turning back to the counter, but she added, "Someday you guys will grow up."

I'm not so sure about Scoobie and George.

CHAPTER TWENTY-THREE

THERE WERE STILL boxes to unpack, but we'd have to finish another day. I was leaving for my last errand of the day when the door opened and George walked in, minus his cocky smile.

"No comment," I said. I wasn't angry, it just never makes sense to encourage him.

"That's a change. Scoobie and I wondered if you'd want to meet for coffee."

We often go for coffee, but this was almost a formal invitation. "Ramona, too?"

"Sure, so make it six and I'll stop by the Purple Cow to tell her. See you at Java Jolt." He left.

I looked at Megan and she shrugged. "Maybe he thinks you're mad."

"He knows what I look like mad," I said. "He probably wants ideas for some story he's working on."

I left and drove to the hospital. I had thought of another question for Todd Everly, and then I was going to leave Tanya Weiss' killer to the police. Lucas and Kim were fine and the memory of Tanya's vacant eyes was fading. Besides, so many people were angry with her that I'd never figure it out on my own.

However, an idea about who had hurt Lucas had occurred to me when I watched people calling friends and sending text messages during the corn toss. There was no way to trace who called Lucas the night he was hit, because Morehouse had told

Lucas that the person used a throw-away mobile phone. But maybe there would be a way to figure out whether someone in the hospital had made the call that drew Lucas there.

It was a ridiculous long shot, but if someone was on camera making a call at that exact time, then it would be worth talking to that person. I thought Todd Everly might be willing to look into that possibility. The police had asked for copies of security images when Tanya was killed, and Todd had been smart enough to keep duplicate images. He surely would have done the same when Lucas was hurt.

If he had to look at every camera over many hours, it would take a ridiculous amount of time. But if he knew to look at exactly the time Lucas got his phone call, that had to reduce the amount of time Todd would have to spend going through digital pictures. Maybe I could even help him.

The clock in the hospital lobby said five-thirty-five, and I'd be cutting it close in terms of meeting the others for coffee. I rationalized that they'd have each other to talk to and wouldn't worry about me being late.

The door to Todd Everly's office was shut, but he'd been there this late another time, so I knocked.

He opened the door and shook his head, but he was smiling. "I feel as if you should say trick-or-treat."

"That's coming up. Can I come in for a second?"

"Sure. I'll clear a spot off my elegant desk chair. Just need to finish an email."

I sat and glanced around his office for the minute he was typing. It was so small a second person would have to be wedged in. That was because of the bank of screens showing varied locations throughout the hospital. They changed every few seconds. My guess was that there were many more cameras than screens and they rotated their displays.

"Now, Ms. Gentil, what can I do for you?" He leaned back in his chair, a mildly amused look on his face.

I outlined my thoughts about someone maybe being in the hospital when they made the call to Lucas. He looked skeptical until I said I thought maybe the caller was on a security camera.

His expression changed to one that was more thoughtful than amused. "You know, that's a possibility. It seems if they were smart enough to avoid the cameras when Lucas came in, they'd stay away from them when they called him. But it's such an innocuous action, maybe not."

"And you have tape from all the cameras?"

"Digital files, sure." He frowned. "I pulled images from all the cameras just before and for about an hour after Lucas was hurt. It'll take awhile to find and download from the earlier time, but it'll be doable."

"Do you need to download them? Can't you just look and download if you see something?"

He shrugged. "I don't usually do things half-way."

I thanked him and walked back to my car feeling very pleased with myself. Maybe Todd could find who hurt Lucas and it would lead him to Tanya Weiss' killer.

RAMONA, GEORGE, AND SCOOBIE were at the Java Jolt coffee serving bar when I walked in. I noted that owner Joe Regan had added a coffee grinder from maybe the 1920s to the collection housed on shelves behind the counter where he serves coffee.

We did the usual hellos and one by one got our coffee and walked to a table near the back of the boardwalk shop. *Why is everyone so quiet?*

I sat. "Who died?"

"George," Scoobie said. I raised my eyebrows at him and looked back to George.

"I'm not dead yet, but I am fired."

I looked at Ramona. "He's serious?"

She nodded. "Tiffany came by to tell me just before we closed."

"Great," George said, looking glum. "She probably can't wait to get a promotion."

"I don't think she meant it that..." Ramona began.

"Why are you fired?" I asked, then added, "I'm sorry."

George didn't seem angry, mostly he looked tired. "Because I held back something the editor said should have been front-page news."

"Something that happened at the corn toss?" I asked.

"No." George looked at his coffee mug. "Kim. Her suicide...attempt."

"No!" I said.

"What suicide attempt?" Ramona asked.

"I guess it doesn't change much," Scoobie said, "but I think you did the right thing."

George tilted his head in an expression of agreement. "What he said was..."

"What suicide attempt?" Ramona repeated. "Someone we know?"

Scoobie spoke. "You know Jolie's had a guy in his early twenties staying with us for a few days."

Us.

"Yes, he's been looking for his sister." Ramona was impatient. "Is that who tried? He couldn't find her?"

"Actually, it was the sister," Scoobie said.

"And she's fine," I said, quickly. "Because of Scoobie and George."

"Mostly Alicia," George said.

"That's true. She called us." I looked at Ramona. "Kim, the guy's sister, was at the end of the pier Friday night. It was cool and getting dark, so there was almost no one on the beach."

"Scoobie was talking her out of it," George said, "but I wasn't sure it was working. So I got in the water under her. I thought it might distract her and Scoobie could grab her."

"It did distract her," I said, dryly, and looked back at Ramona. "Scoobie and I had no idea who was near the rocks under the pier, so Scoobie ran down there. I think it made Kim focus on the rocks around the pier pilings, and realize that she didn't really want to dive onto them."

"Why are you fired?" Ramona asked. "You should get a medal or something."

"Me, too," Scoobie said, with a smart-aleck smile.

"Because my editor thought I should have told him, asked him not to print it, and let him decide."

I studied George for a second while he looked at his fingers, which were folded in front of him on the table. "No way he'll rehire you?"

George met my gaze. "Nope. I asked if he would just suspend me or something. No dice."

"And Tiffany's been there a year," Scoobie said, slowly. "So she's learned the ropes."

Something occurred to me. "And even if the editor promotes her, he'll pay her less than you. It's like at the hospital."

"I thought about that," George said. "I've pretty much decided not to believe that."

I opened my mouth, saw Scoobie give a miniscule head shake, and said nothing.

"Can you get another job?" Ramona asked.

"Oh, sure. But I do like it here." He gestured around the pine-paneled shop, clearly meaning the town not just Java Jolt. "Except for the proprietor in this place."

From his place behind the counter, Joe Regan glanced at George. "You weren't whispering. I'm sorry you lost your job, even if you are an a-hole."

George gave Joe his middle finger.

"Okay, maybe I won't be sorry." Joe turned back to the large thermos he was filling. "You want some part-time work, let me know."

"You really shouldn't flip the bird at people if they can offer you work," Scoobie said.

George did a half-grunt, half-smile, and looked at me. "It's half your fault, you know. If you had asked me *not* to print it, I would have written the story."

"It's not funny," I said, feeling nauseated.

"I thought about writing something, but when I saw how Kim was, after you got her to your house and Lucas was with her, I realized she was so…fragile, or something. If I'd have written a story and she succeeded in a few days…Well, I would have wanted to jump off that pier."

"I wonder how he found out," I mused.

George shrugged. "Doesn't really matter. No one asked Kim, or Lucas, or Alicia not to talk about it."

"So now what?" Ramona asked.

"Do you have any money saved?" I asked.

George looked irritated.

"I mean," I flushed, "Robby took almost all of ours. It just made a hard time worse."

"Ah, I get it." He didn't look irritated any more. "If you've recovered financially, or won the lottery, feel free to support me."

"My space at the rooming house is almost done," Scoobie began.

"Yeah, that'd work," Ramona laughed.

"I meant George could live there." Scoobie gave George a pointed look.

"That's a thought. I could maybe rent my house," George said. "That could cover the mortgage payment. Or just rent it in the summer, when rents are high."

"My Uncle Lester handles rentals, too," Ramona said.

"Oh, he loves me," George said.

He and Scoobie and Ramona spent a minute telling pushy-Lester stories, but I sat very still. *Scoobie wants to keep living with me.*

IT WAS RAMONA'S yoga night and Scoobie had to study for a test, so after more words of encouragement for George, they paid and left. George and I walked out together.

"I guess your head is spinning," I said.

"Kinda. For years I've thought I should leave. I'm good enough to get a job at a bigger paper. I just really like it here. Everywhere you go…" he stopped, and I thought he sounded kind of choked up.

"You see someone you know."

"Yeah. And they're usually glad to see me. Even Sergeant Morehouse is happier to see me than you are."

I knew he was going for, if not lighthearted, at least something not too serious. I followed his lead. "If you knew the number of times he's told me not to tell you something, you'd know you aren't tops on his list of buddies."

"No kidding. Well, of course. But damn, if he told you he coulda told me."

"I think he just does it now and then to make me leave him alone."

"That makes sense."

As George finished his sentence, my phone chirped, and I took it out of my pocket and saw the caller ID. "Hospital. Wait'll I tell you." I pushed answer. "Hey, Todd."

George's eyebrows shot up to his hairline. I rolled my eyes at him as I listened.

"You know, that was a good idea, Jolie. You want to come over and look?"

"Now?"

"It's a good time. I shouldn't really let you see the files, because management doesn't know anything about your idea. Definitely don't bring Scoobie and George."

"I'll see you in a few minutes." I disconnected and looked at George, about to speak.

"You're *dating* him?"

I'd been about to tell George why I was going, but his presumptive tone annoyed me. "I've gone on dates before, you know."

"But you don't even know him."

"Yes, but he doesn't go out of his way to annoy me." I gave George a four-fingered wave and left him on the boardwalk outside Java Jolt.

I PULLED INTO the hospital parking lot not quite fifteen minutes later. I should have stopped by my house to feed Pebbles and Jazz first, but I was too excited to be delayed. I parked in the visitor area. There were still ten or twelve cars in that lot. Visiting hours didn't end until eight.

The elevator was slow and I punched the up button a couple of extra times. Scoobie would have offered to give me an injection of patience. Scoobie. *What should I do? Maybe he just likes the air conditioning better at my place.*

But I didn't think that was it. I got off the elevator and stopped after walking a few feet. All of the odd feelings I'd had the last few weeks gelled. *I love that man. You always have. This is different..."*

What I had always done was trust Scoobie. And he made me laugh. When my parents dumped me at Aunt Madge's for my junior year, he was my first friend. When the kids in the Ocean Alley High School in-crowd dumped me, he told me they didn't matter. And when I moved back to Ocean Alley after I dumped Robby, Scoobie was there again.

Never judging. Well, almost never. I smiled. I could hear him say, "You know it's the earth that moves around the sun, right? You aren't the center of the universe."

"Jolie?" Todd Everly's voice sounded tentative.

I came out of my reverie. "Sorry, I was just thinking about something."

He smiled. "Something good, I take it. Come on."

I realized he must have come to the elevator to look for me. "I'm sorry if I kept you waiting."

"Not at all. I figured I shouldn't show you the film without showing the police at the same time. I called the station and they're sending someone out."

"Sergeant Morehouse?"

"No idea. He is the one who's been around the most."

I followed him into his office. As he shut the door to the hall, he nodded at two cups of tea on a lamp table and took one for himself.

"I need a pick-me-up if I work late. You probably drink a lot of tea at your aunt's B&B."

"More than I did before I moved here, that's for sure." I looked at him and he saw my eagerness.

Todd smiled. Sit for a couple minutes. I want to get the replay in the right spot."

I started to follow him into his office, but his spare chair was piled with papers and his windbreaker, so I went back to the small outer office and sat. The tea was hot and smelled wonderful. "What's in this?"

"I keep a jar here. It's a spiced tea and I add some extra cinnamon with the sugar." His tone was distracted, so I decided to leave him alone.

As I cradled the mug of tea, I thought about my sudden feelings about Scoobie. Sudden? Not really. Well, maybe. Whether I'd known a long time and ignored them or whether my certainty had really been a long time coming, I didn't care. *How do I talk about this with him?* It was pleasant in Todd's outer office, and I decided that I should enjoy the feeling and put off big decisions.

I had drunk about half of the tea when I blinked a few times, trying to clear my vision. *I can't be that tired. Okay, maybe I am worn out*. I'd been going on adrenalin for more than two weeks. First the murder, then Lucas showing up—to say nothing of Kim - then the fundraiser. I had every right to go to bed early and...what? What would I do after I went to bed?

I tried to stand, and as I did the mostly empty cup of tea fell to the floor and spilled. Todd was looking at me from the doorway to his private office. "I'm having..."

"Trouble staying awake?" he asked. "Sit back down, Jolie. You must be really tired. You've had a lot going on."

He didn't need to ask me to sit. I'd already swayed and sat back down.

"Listen, if you don't feel good, I can call one of your friends. They know you're here, right?"

I shook my head. "You could...call...or Aunt Madge would, would whatchamacallit."

"Drive you?"

Suddenly my mouth was very dry and I felt my chin drop onto my chest.

I COULDN'T TELL where I was when I woke up. It was dark, and there were linens, sheets maybe, around me. I was lying on my side with my knees almost at my chest, and the shoulder I was lying on was stiff. Wherever I was, it was bumpy. And I needed a pillow.

I must have fallen asleep again, because the bumping had stopped. I was still lying on my side, but my legs were almost straight. A sound I wasn't used to reached my ears.

It was an unusual noise, kind of like rain hitting the pavement really hard. But not as rhythmic. I shivered. It seemed I was outdoors, but I couldn't say why. I didn't smell rain, and it was too dark to see anything.

The rhythm changed and I heard the sound of metal striking a stone or something metallic, and a man cursed. My confusion lifted a bit. It sounded like Todd Everly. *Am I dreaming?*

I tried to think clearly. The last thing I remembered was being in Todd's office. Why was I there? To see the security tapes! So why was I lying down? And why was it dark?

My eyes were closed. No wonder I couldn't see anything. I opened them. It was still dark, but I could see a fabric-colored kind of wall in front of me. Tweedy fabric.

Move, eyeballs.

As more things came into focus, I realized I was in a car. *My Toyota? Why am I the back seat of my own car?* I shifted, trying to sit up, but I was too woozy. *This can't be good.*

I moved my eyes more and saw that the back door of the car was open. That must be why I'd been able to stretch my legs. Light crunching noises reached me. It sounded like someone walking on dry leaves.

There was a gasp. "Jolie!"

"Todd?" My words were slurred. "Was there an accident?"

"Damn!" His voice was almost a sob. He opened the front driver's door and sat on the seat, but facing out of the car. "I thought you were already dead."

Excuse me?

"Already…? Why? What happened?"

His voice was hoarse. "You were going to figure it out."

The expectation of my demise was helping me wake up. "Figure out wha...oh. Who hit Lucas? You figured it out?"

I could barely hear him, so I managed to lean on my elbow and move my head closer to the space between the front seats.

"I didn't need help to figure it out."

"Can I have a drink of water?" Maybe if my mouth was not so dry I could think better. Or at least talk better.

Todd didn't respond for a few seconds. Then he said, "Sure. I saw you have some bottles in the trunk."

I tried to think. I had the idea about whoever called Lucas maybe being on the hospital's cameras at exactly that time. Todd thought that was a good idea and was going to go through some tapes.

Then Todd called and said he had found something. I met him at the elevator. Then what? And no matter what happened then, how did we get here?

Todd was outside the back door of my car and reached into the back seat with a bottle of water. "Don't drink too fast."

I couldn't see his face well, but he sounded sad or defeated or something. "Thanks." I stayed leaning on my elbow and reached for the bottle. He had taken off the cap, and I slowly raised the bottle to my lips and took a sip.

I could almost feel Todd staring at me, and met his gaze. He spoke just louder than a whisper. "I thought the stuff killed you."

"But we're not in the ER, are we?"

He squatted on the ground so he was at my level. "No. The tea was supposed to make you...sleep. I brought you out here after you drank it."

My thoughts were clunking into place. "You, you wanted me to drink the tea and die?"

He whispered. "The tapes are digital, and they're backed up. If you thought to look at people in the hospital who made calls when Lucas got his call, someone else might. But maybe not. Maybe just you. So..."

"Oh. And if I didn't tell anyone..."

"If you *couldn't* tell anyone, I'd be in the clear."

"How did we get here? And where are we? Why did you hurt Lucas? You don't even know him." I was feeling more awake now, and had realized that the rhythmic noise I had heard earlier was probably Todd digging a hole to put me in. This was not good.

Todd stared at me. He looked as if he might cry. "I turned off the camera at the delivery entrance and took you out in one of the big plastic suitcases we use to move security equipment."

That explains the bumping. "So, you hurt Lucas when he went to the hospital. That doesn't make sense."

"I just wanted to see if he recognized me. He saw me near there, just after, after..."

Then I got it. "You...killed Tanya Weiss? I don't believe it."

He shrugged and grunted at the same time. "It took me years to build my team. It's the best group I ever worked with, and she was going to contract out the entire security function. She said I could *bid the job*. That's what she called it. I know about my job. I don't know anything about bidding."

"Holy crap. So you really killed her?"

"I didn't mean to. I saw her in the hall. I'd just gotten an email from her. She said she was on her way to talk to me. About getting rid of me and my guys."

I didn't have a clue what to say. And I was way too woozy to run away.

"She was...she didn't care at all. I told her we worked our butts off. No contractor would do that. It was like she was telling the hospital to fire us, and we didn't deserve it."

He nodded, to himself, I guessed.

"When I stopped her in the hall, she could tell how mad I was. Tanya said she had to go into the ladies' room. I couldn't let...I followed her in. I don't even know why. It wasn't to kill her. But she did this wave thing."

He waved one hand, in a gesture I figured Tanya Weiss had meant to be dismissive.

He whispered. "She said there were lots of jobs for rent-a-cops. I don't...I don't even remember taking my flashlight off my belt." His voice trailed off, and then got stronger. "You see, that hospital...I've put so much into beefing up security. And I'm either there or working out. If I didn't have my job..."

It was as if Todd was trying to convince himself that killing Tanya was understandable. I had begun thinking more clearly. Todd had told me he was out of the building, that he got back just as Tanya Weiss' body was being taken out of the bathroom. But that was a lie. He'd been there. He knew there was no camera near the ladies' room. And who would look for him on other cameras? And if they saw him, so what?

"But why call Lucas? He didn't see you that day."

"He saw me. He was walking fast and looked down the corridor toward x-ray right after he passed me. He *did* see me."

"It was sort of an accident," I said, softly, hoping he would realize a deliberate murder was a much bigger deal and decide he wanted to let me go. "And Lucas was only thinking of one thing that day."

"His sister. I know that now."

He stood and walked a few feet away from my car and then came back and squatted again. His expression was anguished. "Why did you have to think of the phone call to Lucas being on a tape?"

I looked at Todd and then leaned all the way back on the seat. We were in my car. *Why are we in my car?*

His voice rose. "You could have left it alone!"

His anger was scaring me, and I was scared enough already. "What did you think you would gain by calling Lucas?"

Todd stood and paced a few feet away from the car and back again. "I knew he'd come if I said his sister was there. I was going to tell him I was mistaken and tell him he could look at some camera footage with me, to see if she had been in the ER waiting room, or something."

"That doesn't involve giving him a concussion."

"I told him he could get to her quicker coming in that side door. When I said I'd been wrong about her being there, he was almost frantic. I shrugged and started to walk away. Lucas shoved me. It almost pushed me to where the camera would get me. I had this small can of aerosol hair spray I carry, and I aimed it at his eyes. I don't even remember taking out my Taser."

This guy has amnesia about every time he used a weapon. Convenient.

I stared at Todd some more. He is not a large man, and with his brown curly hair he looks harmless. Obviously not. "Lucas said you sprayed something in his eyes, but he didn't say he got tasered."

He shrugged. "He might not have known. It was quick, his head kind of thudded when he fell. You don't have after-effects to a short dose. You're sore, like from overdoing a workout."

"So, he got up right away?"

"He cursed and started to get up, and I hit him hard, with my fist, on the side of his head." He flexed his right hand. "And then he was still and I gagged him and put him in that electrical closet."

"Well, for sure he'd know it was you who hit him!"

I couldn't see if he flushed, but his expression looked pained. "I had on a straight-haired wig, and a doctor's coat, and kind of tinted glasses. I wanted to see if he recognized me like that. If he did, Lucas would recognize me the way I usually look and he'd remember he saw me...by the restroom. I needed to know."

"Oh, that's a great disguise," I said. "You really thought he wouldn't figure it was you who hit him? And then you left him there to die?"

His tone was defensive. “It was good. And he wouldn’t have. I checked his vitals. Somebody would have found him pretty soon. Like you did.”

I was waking up more, and the more awake I was the more panicked I felt. *No one knows where I am!*

“Wait a minute. Didn’t Lucas see you that day Sergeant Morehouse brought him to the hospital to walk through what he saw the day Tanya Weiss was murdered?”

“No. When Sergeant Morehouse brought him over, I had one of my officers walk them around. But I couldn't avoid Lucas forever. I needed to see if he recognized me from the day of Tanya's...you know, death."

"So what? He didn't see you with her or in the ladies room, did he?"

"He saw me when I walked out of the ladies room."

"Ah." Now I got why Todd thought Lucas could be a threat to him. But he should have figured out that Lucas hadn’t noticed Todd or the restroom, or whether it was for men or women.

"So you see," Todd said, "I had to know."

None of his thinking made sense to me, but I’m not sure the thoughts of any amateur murderer would. At least on television, there seems to be some logic to what a killer does.

Then I was so angry I couldn’t talk. Because he killed Tanya Weiss and hurt Lucas, of course. But also because Todd was so stupid to have called Lucas from inside the hospital and near a security camera. If he hadn’t done that, he wouldn’t have felt threatened by my suggestion, and I wouldn’t be in the woods unable to get away. My anger passed, and I was exhausted. I lay back down. “You know what’s funny?”

“What? Nothing’s funny.”

“I decided not to think about the murder any more. Lucas and Kim were okay. I didn’t…I don’t like it that anyone got killed. But it just didn’t matter so much anymore. It never occurred to me that you…” I took a breath and stopped talking. “What did you put in that tea? I’m getting a really bad headache.”

Todd just looked at me. I started to laugh. Half laugh and half sob. “I guess it doesn’t matter. I can’t run away from you. And we probably aren’t where anyone can hear me if I yell.”

He stared at me. "I have a key to the operating suites. I was an EMT with a volunteer fire department for a while. I gave you a triple oral sedative dose in your tea, and then the stuff docs use to put patients to sleep with. But not enough." He sighed. "I didn't kill Tanya on purpose, and I didn't intend to hurt Lucas." His voice became more strained. "I can't kill you if I have to talk to you."

I began to shake. "I'm going to keep talking."

He grimaced and looked away from me. "We're six or seven miles west of Ocean Alley. In a strip of woods that backs into the Garden State Parkway." He stood and seemed to almost talk to himself. "I can't keep hurting people."

Todd looked at me. "I'll call an ambulance and walk out to the road to meet it."

CHAPTER TWENTY-FOUR

THE DOOR TO my hospital room opened and Sergeant Morehouse walked in.

I looked at him and then behind him. "Where's Scoobie?"

He grunted. "They called your aunt from the ER. She and Harry were painting at his old place, and their phones were downstairs. Ramona went over there. They're on their way."

"Where's Scoobie?"

"You're a damn parrot. George made Scoobie go with him to get drunk. Dana found 'em and told him you were going to be okay. But Scoobie didn't think he should leave your reporter friend. He said Dana should tell you, what was it? Oh, yeah. Yo Jolie."

"They don't drink!"

"Scoobie still doesn't. And the way George was pukin' outside the Sandpiper, I'm thinkin' he's done with it for a couple decades."

Morehouse sat on the foot of my bed.

"George lost his job," I said.

"I heard. I met that girl at the fundraiser. The Lucas guy's sister. Talked to Alicia about her. Kim's her name, right? She ain't wired too well. George maybe did the right thing."

"She's might get medicine again. And she won't be around people who think suicide is…the answer." I looked at Morehouse. "Where's Todd?"

"State Police were gonna take him to Trenton."

"How come you don't have him?"

"We aren't in Ocean Alley, in case you don't know. Paramedics took you to Jersey Shore Med Center in Neptune. It was closer and you were out of it. I coulda told 'em that was your normal."

"My norm… Oh. You drove up here."

Morehouse smiled. "I did. Can't have my favorite pest die when she's out of town."

"Gee, thanks."

Morehouse stood. "Madge has called me three times. She'll be here in a few minutes."

"It's all just…so hard to believe." I could feel tears coming, and I blinked to keep them in. "He said he did it because Tanya Weiss wanted to get rid of the security office and hire contractors."

"People lose their jobs all the time. They don't kill because of it. Not good to put on a resume."

"I liked Todd."

"Yeah. He was crying when they got to him. Said he *liked* you. Good thing he didn't *hate* you."

Aunt Madge and Harry arrived not long after Morehouse left. She stared at me for several seconds. "I'm tired of this, Jolie."

Harry looked surprised at her tone. "I think what Madge means is she hopes you feel better soon."

"Darling," she began.

I've never heard Aunt Madge call Harry that, and right now it didn't sound like a term of endearment.

She turned to Harry. "When have you heard me say something I don't mean?"

Aunt Madge can sometimes scare me with a look. Harry didn't seem cowed, but he did let her finish chewing me out.

"It's ridiculous," she continued. "Sergeant Morehouse said you had an idea about checking something on hospital cameras. Why didn't you tell the police?"

"Because he might not have checked, and he would have told me to butt out."

"Safer than butting in," she said.

"I don't like murderers going free."

"Neither do the police." She glared at me and I stuck my tongue out.

"I still have that photo of you running around town in your underpants when you were four."

My aunt, master manipulator.

THE HOSPITAL KEPT me overnight because my heart rate was so low. I was glad it wasn't the Ocean Alley Hospital. I'm really angry at them for hiring someone like Tanya Weiss. I don't think much of their choice for the head of their Board of Directors. Or head of Security.

I'd finished my breakfast tray and a nurse had just taken the IV out of my arm. Last night I was disoriented, so I hadn't paid much attention to the room. It was painted a cheerful shade of yellow, and the morning sun hit the wall across from my bed in a pattern of stripes because the window blinds were only partially open.

Breakfast hadn't been bad, and I was sitting up in bed finishing a cup of coffee that was pretty awful. Aunt Madge and Harry had called an hour ago and said they'd be up at ten to get me. I told them I could take a cab. Aunt Madge said the only way she talked my parents out of coming up from Florida was to say she would take me home and then have me call them. That was much better.

There was a light knock on my door.

"Come in."

The wood door opened with a soft whoosh. George stood looking at me and he wore an odd expression.

I frowned and looked behind him. "I can't look that bad. Where's Scoobie?"

"Anxious to see you, believe it or not. But he said you knew he had that big test, and you'd be okay with me coming to get you."

"Sure. If it's okay with Aunt Madge." I pointed to a plastic chair. "Morehouse told me you had a fun night."

"Damn. Half the town knows. And Madge said fine, as long as you don't tell your parents she didn't drive you home."

"I'm not twelve." George gave me a half amused look, and I added, "I hope Tiffany got a picture."

He glared at me, and then saw I was smiling. "Scoobie blocked the shot. He said I quoted some law about privacy. I don't think I know any."

"It's not like you observe them," I said.

"Yeah. Scoobie said something about being hoisted on my own petard."

"I think he got that from Aunt Madge. You okay?"

"I will be. I'm getting pissed. I think that's good." He paused. "You have any idea it was Everly?"

"Working on a story, are we?" When I saw George's dejected expression I grew more serious. "Nope. If he hadn't drugged me and driven me to the woods to bury me, I still wouldn't believe it."

"Scoobie's pretty upset about it."

"Me, too."

Neither of us said anything, and then George's expression grew more animated. "I've got an idea."

"About another newspaper job?"

"Nope. I don't really want to leave Ocean Alley. Even though everyone knows as soon as I mess up." He leaned toward the bed. "I looked up what it takes to be a private investigator in New Jersey."

"You mean, like a private detective?"

"Yeah. That's actually what it's called."

"Why do you want to do that?

"Same skills. I already know how to investigate, especially when people don't want me to."

I thought for a moment. I liked Sue Grafton's Kinsey Milhone books. I thought Kinsey had to train with private investigators before she got her own license. But that was California. "Are you qualified to be a detective?"

"I think I am, but the State of New Jersey probably won't. I have to work with an insurance or investigative firm for a year or so before I can apply." He grinned. "Or in law enforcement, but I doubt they'd have me."

A bunch of thoughts were going through my mind, which was tough, because the drug Todd Everly gave me yesterday evening still made me tired. "Wouldn't it be dangerous?"

"Mostly not. I might tick off a few more people than I did being a reporter, but I never mind doing that if it gets to the truth."

"I guess if that's what you want. I mean, of course. You look excited. That's great." I shifted in the bed. I'd had toast for breakfast and some crumbs had invaded the sheets.

"You wanna do it with me?"

For a minute I wasn't sure what *it* was. "What…you mean be a detective?" I laughed. "Everyone I know would disown me. Especially Scoobie."

Yes, Scoobie. I need to talk to Scoobie.

"I didn't exactly run it by him," George said. "You've always been pretty good at making up your own mind."

I looked at him and raised an eyebrow.

"I'm not asking you to date me. Just maybe work together."

"It's not something I do naturally."

"What, make up your own mind?"

"You're deliberately missing my point. I only look into…stuff if it affects me. Or Scoobie, or someone else I know."

"But especially Scoobie," he said, quietly.

I wasn't going to talk about Scoobie with George. It was too weird.

"I like working with Harry. Even if I have to deal with Lester. But I can see how you would want to be an investigator, or whatever."

"You think I'd be good at it?"

"As long as you don't mind irritating people. And you don't."

BY NOON I HAD BEEN home from the hospital for about an hour. Aunt Madge had come and gone. She had brought several of her breakfast muffins and left a huge bowl of chicken salad in the fridge. I thought about how she was in her eighties and I was in my thirties and I should really be waiting on her. It's just she never seems to need, or want, help. She's always too busy.

I was propped on my couch and Jazz had settled onto my stomach. As far as she was concerned, the world was right. Pebbles rustled a bit on the rug, and Jazz peered over to look at her. Apparently things with the skunk were as they should be, and Jazz stared at me some more.

"I'm not going anywhere. Not that you really care."

She yawned. She didn't care, except that she likes to sleep where it's warm, and that means near me. After about three more seconds of looking at me, she curled into a ball.

The newspaper was on the floor near Pebbles. A box on the front page said Todd Everly had been arrested for killing Tanya Weiss and kidnapping me, and it referred readers to the paper's web page. The news had come too late for a full article. I'd already had calls from people who read the web article, but I'd changed the message on my mobile phone to say I was fine and I'd catch up with callers tomorrow.

Lucas and Kim had gone to visit their aunts for a few days. Harry drove them into New York City to catch a train for Chicago. It was the first time I'd known where their mom's sisters lived. I think Harry helped Lucas and Kim arrange the trip, in large part so I didn't have two extra people in my small house until I felt better. Maybe they would stay with their extended family for a while instead of at the B&B. *Not my problem.*

I didn't think of the two of them as problems. I just needed time to think. Now that I was sure how I felt about Scoobie, I couldn't decide what to do. Should I tell him? What if he felt really different? Could we still be friends? Of course we could. But it would be…awkward.

Scoobie called my bungalow *our* house. I liked that. And he suggested that George could stay in his space at the rooming house. I smiled to myself. *Scoobie wanted to be sure George didn't stay with me.*

Not that George and I would date again. I liked him better for putting Kim above a story, and I liked having him as a friend. About the same as I liked having Ramona for a friend. You can never have enough friends. Especially if they help at Harvest for All fundraisers.

Someone came up the steps and onto my front porch and rapped on the door. I looked at Jazz. "You get it."

Before I could get up, a young man's voice called, "Jolie, it's Clark. I have flowers for you."

"Key's under the mat," I yelled. I don't usually leave it there, but I knew people might stop by, so Aunt Madge had put it there for me.

Clark opened the door and walked the short distance to the living room and stared at me. "You look the same."

"I'm okay. Let me smell. Then you can put them on the table." He walked to me and I inhaled the aroma of lilies and carnations. "Wonderful. Are they from Megan and Alicia?"

He put them on the table and turned to me with a quick smile. "How do you know they aren't from me?" He laughed at my expression. "I don't know who they're from. For some reason they were at the customer service desk at Mr. Markle's store, and he asked me to bring them to you."

I leaned on one elbow. "Hmm. Is there a card?"

"Yep. And Mr. Markle said I'm supposed to leave before you read it." Clark took a card from a clip attached to one of the stems. "I think he knows who it's from."

"No doubt," I said, dryly. Mr. Markle does not sell floral displays, but he does have a couple of buckets of bouquets of seasonal flowers. They aren't in vases, though, so someone must have taken one to the store. Mr. Markle would certainly let someone plop flowers in a vase, but I was surprised he'd let Clark deliver them.

After telling me he hoped I felt better, Clark let himself out. I fingered the envelope. It held something larger than the usual card that comes with flowers. I slit the envelope with a fingernail and pulled out a folded three-by-five card that had writing on both sides.

swimming
in deep
uncharted
water

on the coldest day of the year
in dreams so deep you could drown
melting the oldest of fear
with passion too hot to put down

is this heaven?
time will tell
memories/warnings:
the first time i fell

melting an ocean
of frozen tears
swelling emotions
so far...so near

start of a voyage
the end of our fate?
hearts out of storage
kept safe for a soul mate
Love,
Scoobie

I was sobbing when I finished, so I didn't hear the front door open. Scoobie was on the floor by the couch before I realized he was in the room. The best word to describe his expression would be frantic.

"It's wonderful!" I sobbed, and moved sideways so he could sit on the couch next to where I was lying. Jazz hissed as she jumped on the floor. Pebbles had already had the good sense to move.

Scoobie sat next to me and pulled me to him while I sobbed. It took almost a minute before I got calmer.

He tapped the back of my head with his finger. "I don't think I want to be around when you don't like one of my poems."

I sniffed and whispered. "I understood this one."

"Recognize any of it?" he asked.

I nodded into his shoulder, which was now wet. "The last part."

"Yeah. I showed you that when you first moved back."

I pulled a few inches from him and studied him. "You knew then?"

"Pretty much. You used to be a quicker study."

I gave a sniff that was part snort. He rolled his eyes and reached for a box of tissues on the floor by the couch. "It's not like there's a lot I don't know about you."

I blew my nose. "I think there's a lot I don't know about you." I tossed the tissue on the floor behind me.

He grinned and pulled me to him. Just as I shut my eyes to kiss him, Scoobie said, "Get your heart out of storage and come along for the ride."

* * * *

Vague Images is the seventh book of the Jolie Gentil cozy mystery series. You can enjoy other books in the Jolie Gentil Series.

Appraisal for Murder
Rekindling Motives
When the Carny Comes to Town
Any Port in a Storm
Trouble on the Doorstep
Behind the Walls

And the prequel:
Jolie and Scoobie High School Misadventures

Scoobie's poetry is actually that of real-life poet, James W. Larkin.

About the Author

Elaine L. Orr is the Amazon bestselling author of *Trouble on the Doorstep,* fifth in the Jolie Gentil series. She wrote plays and novellas for years and graduated to longer fiction. *Biding Time* was one of five finalists in the National Press Club's first fiction contest, in 1993. She is a regular attendee at conferences such as Muncie's Midwest Writers Workshop and Magna Cum Murder, and conducts presentations on electronic publishing and other writing-related topics. Her nonfiction includes material on caring for aging parents and carefully researched local and family history books. Some of her essays can be viewed on Yahoo Voices. Elaine grew up in Maryland and moved to the Midwest in 1994.

www.elaineorr.com
www.elaineorr.blogspot.com

Made in the USA
San Bernardino, CA
26 March 2016